A

RECKONING

OF

FIRE

A
RECKONING
OF
FIRE

JENNIFER OSUFSEN

LITTLE TYRANT press

A RECKONING OF FIRE by Jennifer Osufsen

Little Tyrant Press
Aurora, Minnesota 55705
www.littletyrantpress.com

Visit **www.jenniferosufsen.com** for more information about the author and her upcoming projects.

To my daughters,

Riley, Savannah, and Brooke,

I pray you are fiery, humble, and forgiving.

And to my sons,

Isaac and Jedidiah,

I pray you love as Jesus loves, strong and true.

Also by Jennifer Osufsen

Mercy Springs

Acknowledgements

Every fledgling story needs a reader impervious to mistakes, and I have a trusted few who are forgiving of careless typos and reworked plot details. Without their input and constant motivation to keep going, I would most likely never finish the dang thing.

Dawn Breen, you have pulled me from the depths of doubt and despair more times than I remember. For whatever the reason, you chose me as a friend; and I couldn't be more blessed. Christy Hilton and Mandy Leap, you have known me since fifth grade. Though we live thousands of miles apart, your friendships are precious to me. I treasure your opinions and our hysterical conversations. Paula Chapman, your sweet spirit and quiet confidence inspire me. I am forever thankful for your dauntless promotion of *Mercy Springs* in our community. Mack Hayes, you always had faith in me. Now get up and write *your* book, mister. I'm chomping at the bit. Rachel Shultz, your work with youth and horses is such an inspiration and a testament to your faithfulness. I am blessed to call you friend, and am thankful you chose to read along.

To Nikole Anderson, my friend and beta reader, who gobbled up the story and found all the error nuggets I missed when I pawed through it with my red pen. You have oodles of my gratitude! CJ Shackelton, dear friend and my other beta reader, your book fetish inspires me, and I'm grateful to be one of the authors included in your bountiful collection.

Many thanks to Corey Rawlinson, childhood friend and professional farrier, for your expert knowledge in all things horse feet.

My wonderful husband, Jesse, was my consultant in the blacksmithing arena. Your brain power amazes me, babe. You are my constant in a world of variables, and the last sixteen years have been better than I could have ever imagined.

To all the readers who fell in love with *Mercy Springs*, you are the impetus spurring me to write every word. You have faith in me, and I pray you love all the characters living in my head.

But God gets the ultimate glory. Without Him, I would have no story to write.

The Collapse

In 2040, a catastrophic economic disintegration, known as The Collapse, rocked the United States. For a decade the country floundered, eventually imploding. A few members of Congress remained; and taking advantage of a weakened society, seized control and redesigned the country as Unified Socialist America. Two years after the Reformation of the U.S.A., Texas seceded. The Second War of Secession followed, lasting a year and a half. In the end, the Republic of Texas was once again an independent nation.

After The Collapse, leery citizens reverted to a more primitive way of life. The economy shifted to a precious metals (gold, silver, copper, etc.) and barter system. While technology advanced, it was generally reserved for the wealthy and those in government, both in Socialist America and in Texas. Primitive modes of transportation and barter systems remained in place as a semblance of security for the people, should turmoil once again wreak havoc on the nations.

Unified Socialist America outlawed any one faith during the Reformation. The government decided that faith in one God violated the rights of all the people, persecuting those believing in other faiths. Hence, the people could worship all gods or none at all in designated centers of worship. The Republic of Texas, however, clung to the fundamental religious beliefs upon which the original United States of America was founded.

"Is not my word like fire," declares the Lord,
"and like a hammer that breaks a rock in pieces?"

Jeremiah 23:29 (NIV)

Prologue

If she listened closely, she could still hear Ginny's laughter echoing down the foot-worn wooden stairs. She lowered long-lashed eyelids and listened for high-pitched giggles bouncing off the peeling papered walls, could almost see the calloused bottoms of her little sister's bare feet as she raced outside to the tire swing hanging from the century oak in the side yard.

The dilapidated house smelled of mold and mouse urine. Cobwebs fluttered in the corners of the broken windows on the west side, made pretty by the light of the setting sun. Water stains marred the once pristine hardwood floors. She ran a finger across the mantle which used to hold family photos and mementos, her fingertip creating a shallow groove in the oily grime coating every flat surface in the abandoned home.

Joleigh stood in the middle of the living room, hands on her hips. She pivoted at the waist, taking in the husk of a house that was once her home. Gone were the soft furnishings her mother had cherished. In their place were scattered sticks and limbs, dry and moldering leaves, mouse droppings. Roaches skittered, and spiders scattered as fast as eight legs could carry them. Vandals' tags disgraced the walls and floors. Jagged remnants of glass jutted from peeling frames, stabbing the evening air.

Every cell in her body screamed at her to walk out the front door and never return. Fists balled at her sides and thighs tensed, ready for flight. She remained steadfast. She would see this through.

Her footsteps echoed, hollow in the stale air, as she skirted a bird's nest and entered the kitchen. Amazingly, the table remained. Faded yellow, scarred, filthy, but still there. It laid on its side, metal legs sticking out toward the back door. The curtain rod hung only from the left side, one lace curtain panel dangling precariously from the end, as if it refused to let go and fall to the ruined floor below.

Pretty sad day when she found herself identifying with a curtain.

Jo took a deep breath in, forced it out, and retreated to the main room. She got as far as the stairs before the gasping began.

The stairs.

She *had* to do this, get past it. Without looking up, she placed one boot on a riser, and then the next. Dust stirred with each step. On the second floor landing, she paused.

Not as much physical damage on the second floor, she observed. Like the house held its breath up here, rather than expelling the death rattle. It looked as if no one had ventured up here in the years it had been vacant. As if no one dared. She understood.

There were three bedrooms and a bathroom, all connected by a hallway. Three doors gaped open in expectation. But Jo's eye was drawn to the closed one. Pale blue paint gleamed untouched by time. A single white-painted flower adorned the door, midway from the top. The word "Ginny" was painted in bright pink in the center of the flower.

2

A tear escaped from the corner of her eye.

Ginny.

Instead of Ginny's phantom laughter, she heard her mother's antique milkglass vase shatter on the hardwood floor. The echoes of her stepfather's roar. The smack of his hand on her little sister's face. Jo closed her eyes and remembered running from her room to find Roy shaking Ginny, her sister's terrified eyes locked open as Roy bellowed at her. She had launched herself at him, frantically clawed at him, but he batted her away as he would a bothersome fly. She collided with the wall, stunned. Her stepfather railed and shook, slapped Ginny again, pointing to the broken glass at her feet, a wet clump of wild flowering onions in the midst of the vase remnants.

And then, he pushed her.

For years Ginny's eyes haunted Jo's dreams. The whites of her eyes surrounding the purest blue, as she tumbled backward down the stairs. Thudding down the steps, and a sickening thump. Then silence. Even Roy was quiet.

Jo stood at the landing and swallowed the bile rising in her throat, choked back the flood of tears threatening to erupt. She stared at Ginny's blue door, with her back to the stairs, refusing to see the memory of her sister's death. Hesitantly, she reached out a hand, withdrew it quickly. She sucked in her gut and straightened her shoulders. She *would* do this. For Ginny.

The cold brass doorknob warmed against the heat of her palm. She turned it, eased the bedroom door open.

A fine silver coat of dust preserved the room. The bed was made, pillows neat, tidy. Scrappy Bunny sat sprawled at the end, on top of the crocheted afghan. Jo grabbed the soft toy, held it to her heart.

She would keep this. Ginny, Jo, and their mother had made the animal one stormy afternoon out of clothes which no longer fit, before their father had died. Before her mother married Roy, and brought his Hell into their home.

With one hand she held Scrappy Bunny to her heart, and with the other, she dug in her pocket. The smooth round marble was cold, then warm. Its cat's eye center wiggled green and blue, the colors woven together.

She and Ginny had found the marble near old man Lewis' pond the day before Roy killed her sister. Jo laid the marble in the dust-free place that the stuffed animal had occupied moments before. She wiped tear-tracks from her cheeks.

"Happy Birthday, Ginny." Her voice echoed off the walls, tinny in her ears. "I miss you, sissy. And I won't rest until that devil pays for what he did to you."

Jo turned from the bed, but hesitated in the doorway. Her eyes fell on the marble left on the end of the bed, like an offering to a God she barely remembered. Regret filled her heart and she backtracked, snatching the marble from the bed and shoving it in her pocket. She couldn't leave it behind, and Ginny wasn't here to appreciate it. She whispered to the air, "I love you."

Her mother's voice ghosted through the air, borne on the winds of memory, and Jo found herself humming a lullaby down the stairs, the one her mother had sung to comfort them after Roy's rages had passed. She dragged her hand down the railing, heedless of the dust she stirred. Without pausing she gathered all the debris she could find, making a pile out of the litter cluttering the floor of the place she once knew as home.

Jo tucked Scrappy Bunny under her arm, and fished around in her pocket once again. Shadows crept along the walls, elongated in the dying light of sunset, tendrils of darkness clawing the center of the room where she stood.

She palmed the firestriker, took one last look around the room which once held a jumble of happy and horrible memories. With a flick of her finger, a flame sprang to life. She held the timid flame to the end of a brittle stick near the center of the tinder pile. With a *whoosh*, the fire ignited.

Jo strode from the house. Standing in knee-high weeds beneath the century oak, she watched the orange glow grow and breed inside the rotten shell of a house. Flames caressed the disintegrating window frames, engulfed the doors. Every tear shed, each slap, every bruise at the hands of that man fueled the inferno. Within minutes, fiery tongues licked the sky and smoke rolled, a sacrifice to a lost childhood.

Scrappy Bunny hung from her hand as the house went up in flames.

Let it burn.

Chapter 1

Jo snatched the red "SOLD" sign from the top of the bank's real estate placard disgracing the front window. Out of habit she turned the knob, tried to push into her office. Locked. Of course it was locked. Because the stupid bank had repossessed her livelihood. She held the narrow metal sign at arm's length and glared at it.

Her tense arm vibrated with the desire to throw it through the glass.

Instead, she turned on her rubber heel and marched steel-toed boots across the street, the offensive signboard slicing through the air at her side, *swish-wishing* as she pumped her arms. The nerve of Henry. He knew how close she was to having the money. Just a few more weeks. But no, he went and sold her shop. She growled as she slammed open the door of People's National Bank, the etched glass pane rattling in her wake.

Louella took one look at Jo's face and yelped out an "Eep!" before scurrying to the rear hall of offices. The teller alternated banging on Henry's door and shooting worried looks in Jo's direction. Louella peeked her head through a crack in the door, mumbled at Henry, glanced over her shoulder, and then high-tailed it toward the break room. Any other day, Jo would engage Louella in idle conversation. Nothing important, since the whole town would know about it in five minutes flat.

She waited at the waist-high teller's desk tapping her fingertips. If she had fingernails, the beat would be a furious staccato. Henry stepped deliberately from his office, smoothing his suit jacket over his wide pear-hips. His Adam's apple bobbed as he swallowed, but he met Jo's eyes and held her stare. She slammed the red placard onto the teller's desk with a cracking *snap!*

"Now, Jo …"

"Don't you 'Now, Jo' me, Henry Brackett. You knew I was raising the money. I've been on the road for weeks evening old scores, and hitting up every single person who owed me coin. And you went and sold my shop behind my back."

"How many times do we need to go over this? The bank had to repossess your business. We couldn't keep extending your line of credit. For Pete's sake, Jo, you're nearly a year behind on payments as it is. I think I've been more than generous." The banker ran a hand through what hair he had left on his head, upsetting his meticulous comb-over.

"But this is my *life*. It's in my blood. What else am I going to do?" She would not let her voice ease into the whiny tone she detested in other females. "This is all I know. Please, Henry, just a few more weeks. That's all I ask."

The older man sighed. "I went to bat for you as long as the board would allow. They're the ones who said to go ahead and sell it. Honestly, I am just as surprised as you it sold as quickly as it did. How was I to know it would sell before you returned?"

"Who?"

"Who what?"

"Who. Bought. My. Shop?"

He cleared his throat. "Uh, well, he's not from around here. Well, he wasn't. He moved into Shelley's boarding house last week. Guy from Austin, saw the listing and thought it would be an asset to his current business."

"So now we have an outsider city-boy running my shop? Good grief, Henry! What could he possibly know about it?"

"Listen, Jo, I really am sorry."

"Don't give me that crap. This was a family business. My daddy's place, and my uncle ran it after Dad died. Times got tough. Call city-boy up, tell him you have another offer and you need to hold off a few more weeks."

His sympathy seemed genuine, but Jo didn't have time for sympathy. Didn't want or need his pity. She knew what he was going to say before he said it.

"It's done. Papers are signed. He paid cash, Jo." He tried to place his hand atop hers, but she slid it out and balled her fist by her side.

Behind Henry, the teller eased her head out of the break room doorway.

Jo cleared her throat. "It's all right, Louella. I ain't gonna bite. Just mad, is all." The pleading look in her eyes was as close as she could come to begging. "Henry?"

He shook his head slowly, side to side, then shrugged his shoulders. "How much were you able to raise?"

Defeated, her shoulders slumped. "Enough to get me by for a couple months. Maybe."

Henry studied at his knotted hands. "There is another option, if you're not too proud to take it."

Her heart thumped in her chest. Another way to keep her place? "What?"

"The new, um, owner," he winced. "Well, sorry, Jo, he is. Anyway, he said he would keep you on as an employee, if you were agreeable to it."

"An employee!" The shriek echoed off the walls, and Louella backstepped, her eyes wide.

"Well, think about it. You got no other options at the moment, and it gives you a chance to keep doing what you love." Henry's face was flushed from his eyebrows down to his white starched shirt collar. She knew she shouldn't take it out on the man. Heck, he was old enough to be her father and then some.

An employee? Her knuckles turned white against the backdrop of the red SOLD placard staring back at her. Working for a soft-shoed city-boy as an employee, rather than calling the shots as the owner?

After ten deep breaths, she looked the banker in the eye. "I'm not gonna lie. I'll need some time to think on it."

"Don't take too long, girl. We close in three days, and it has to be signed in the agreement at closing." Henry held up his hands, surrender style. "It's what he wants, and he's the buyer. I've got no other choice, and it's looking like you don't either. So it boils down to whether or not you need a job."

She did. She had exaggerated the amount of funds she'd raised. She could manage expenses for a month, six weeks at most. About the only thing going for her was owning the cabin, her acreage and her horse free and clear.

"My tools?"

Henry smiled. "Those you keep. I made sure of it, since they were your daddy's. The forge stays, of course."

Well, it was something, at least.

"Give me an hour to think things through, and I'll let you know. I'll be at the diner if you need me."

He nodded, wiped the end of his nose with a threadbare yellowed hankie. "I just feel awful for you, but I did my best. I hope you believe me. Your dad was one of my best friends, honey. This just breaks my heart."

"You're not the only one walking away broken, Henry."

She left the red signboard on the teller's desk, and turned her back to him. Took a few deep breaths and squared her shoulders. She'd pick up the pieces, and put it all back together. Make it stronger.

Jo wanted to throw something, beat someone, break something. The ghost of a hammer haunted her palm and she ached to feel its heft, feel the jolt as it pinged and shaped hot metal. She channeled all the frustration and anger boiling inside into a small black box in her mind, shoved all the emotion inside, and slammed shut the top. Welded it closed, and jammed it into the dark recesses of her brain. She'd deal with it later.

Jo had a few things to work out, the least of which was becoming an employee to the clueless city-boy who had stolen her heart and soul for a handful of gold.

Chapter 2

Cullen reached the bank entrance at the same time a tall drink of blonde female barreled through. He held the door for her, doffing his hat and saying, "Ma'am," as she stormed through, growling and leaving dust devils in her wake. He stood, baffled, watching her stalk across the street and down the block. Most likely he would have admired her exit a good while longer, but Henry called out to him.

"You coming in, Mr. Miles?"

"Yep. How are you today, Mr. Brackett?"

"Call me Henry, please. What can we do for you today?"

Good question. Why was he here? Oh, yeah.

"I have the key to the office, but there's another on the door to the shop. The key I have doesn't fit both. Any chance you have another one on file?"

Henry snagged his lower lip between his teeth, frowned in concentration. The banker held a finger in the air, then disappeared down the hallway and into his office. Cullen heard drawers sliding and whisking closed. The teller peeked out of a door at the end of the hallway. Her eyebrows climbed into her cropped hairline, and she ducked back into the door from which she appeared. Louise? Lulu?

"Louella?" Henry yelled from his office. "Have you seen any other keys to the forge?"

Ah. Louella. She rapidly clopped across the hardwood floor in heels. The sound was all too similar to shod horses on pavement. She avoided looking in Cullen's direction and disappeared into Henry's office. The sound of more drawers opening and closing, opening and closing, and then Louella retreated to the door from whence she scuttled.

Henry's shoulders were slumped when he returned to the teller's booth. The older man shook his head, morose.

"I don't see any other keys in the file."

"Hey, that's okay. Can we ask the previous owner to turn it in?"

Thick, silvered eyebrows drew together in an inverted V, wrinkling the old banker's forehead.

"Well, now, Mr. Miles," he began.

"Call me Cullen."

"Cullen." He swallowed, his Adam's apple bobbing. "It might be a problem. You see, the previous owner can be a bit, um, difficult. Especially since the business was sold under duress."

"I'm sure we can work something out. If not, I guess I can call a locksmith."

"Closest one's in Bryan."

"Listen, this isn't just any lock. I haven't seen the like before. Very complicated. If I don't have a key for it, then it will take an expert to get in there. And I'd like to take a look around soon, Henry."

The banker nodded his graying head. "Doesn't surprise me in the least. Neal Camden was a master craftsman, an excellent blacksmith. He's the one who created the lock, I'm sure of it."

"Was?"

"Died a long time ago. His brother ran the place after his death, and then Jo."

Cullen ran a calloused hand over his face and sighed. "Look, I know it's close to quitting time for you folks, and I just want the key. Any chance this Joe is in town and I can just go ask the guy myself?"

Henry whistled low. "You're a brave one, I'll give ya that. Jo said she was heading over to the diner to consider your offer of employment."

"Wait. She? Joe's a girl?"

"Yes, sir. You passed her coming in. Jo is short for Joleigh. Jo Camden. And trust me, Mr. Miles ..."

"Cullen."

"Cullen. You may want to wait a day or so, let her simmer down a little. She's got quite the reputation for flying off the handle. And she's more than bitter about losing the family business."

The growler at the door. Super. Still, she was a woman. Very few females could withstand his charm once he worked his magic a little, flashed his grin.

"She's at the diner?"

Henry sighed as if Cullen had just announced he was going to walk across the Sahara without any water. "It's your funeral, buddy. Don't say I didn't warn you. Yeah, Jo's at the diner. If I were you, I'd enjoy your meal first. Might be the last one you eat."

He snorted around a half-smile and turned, gave a short farewell salute as he walked out into the late afternoon sun. The brim of the brown felt cowboy hat shielded his eyes. His elongated shadow stretched tall and skinny, extending from the tips of his worn leather boots, leading him down the cobbled sidewalk of downtown Coleville.

It was a small affair, downtown. People's National Bank was situated behind him, to the west. The buildings were newer, but constructed with an Old West feel. Just down Silver Street, which served as the main thoroughfare through town, squatted the stubby square building of the post office. Across from the post office was the general store. The first time he had stepped through the swinging front door of The Coleville Mercantile, Cullen had to remind himself he hadn't traveled back in time two hundred years. Dark-stained wooden shelves lined all four walls, stocked with canned and dry goods. The tops of hip-high whiskey barrels displayed various wares, from peanuts to children's toys. But the owner, Wilbur Reed, also carried modern items such as wrist communicators and paper thin electronic tablets. Wilbur even ran the store while wearing a crisp, starched white apron. The storekeeper waved to Cullen as he sauntered by. Cullen waved, and stepped out into the empty street leading over to Ruby's Plate, the local diner with a big reputation.

A gust of wind teased his hat, and he put a hand on top to keep it in place. Cullen quickly practiced his boyish grin under the shadow of his arm. This Jo wouldn't stand a chance. A smidgen of the Cullen Miles charm and she'd probably throw the key at him, and ask to make him dinner besides.

The golden bell at the top of the door jangled his entrance. The clock above the kitchen pass-through showed 4:00, too early for the evening crowd. Three booths were occupied along one wall, and a tall, leggy blonde perched on a polished wooden barstool at the long counter. She didn't look up when he came in. Instead, she stabbed at a piece of pecan pie as if she held a personal vendetta against it. Two other plates, empty except for crumbs, sat abandoned next to a full glass of what looked like Ruby's famous sweet tea.

Cullen rolled his neck, squared his shoulders, and wedged the grin in place. He hooked a thumb on his belt loop and strolled to the bar, snagging the stool beside Jo. About the time his rump hit the seat, Ruby came around the corner.

The whites of her eyes stood in direct contrast to the ebony of her skin, and those eyes of hers opened wide at the sight of Cullen sitting next to Jo. Her mouth gaped and closed repeatedly. But then she cleared her throat, and snapped the white cotton towel off her shoulder. She wiped the counter in front of him with one eyebrow raised, and said, "What can I get you, sugar?"

In the week he'd been in Coleville, he noticed Miss Ruby called everyone "sugar" and everyone called her Miss Ruby. Right now, she was shaking her head in amazement, and glancing fearfully between him and the woman at his side.

"How about some apple pie, Miss Ruby?"

"You sure you don't want a plate of crow, sugar?" She chuckled at her own joke, and the cook poked his head out of the pass-through and barked a laugh as well.

"And a glass of your sweet tea, please, if you don't mind," Cullen added. Ruby shook her head again, and started working on his order, all the while flicking glances between the two patrons at her counter.

Jo stabbed another bite of pie, the fork *tinking* against the porcelain plate. Cullen cleared his throat, but the woman continued to jab her fork into the pie and shove it in her mouth. He turned slightly to the left, refreshed his grin, and said, "Looks like you're a fan of Miss Ruby's pecan pie."

15

The fork paused in mid-stab. Jo turned her head, the blonde curtain of her hair shifting to the side so that he caught a glimpse of electric blue eyes staring at him. Then she returned to the pie, dismissing him. The frost wafting off the woman could chill his tea. He'd have no need for ice cubes.

"So, I'm new in town," he began, "and I don't recall having met you before." He held out his hand. "Cullen Miles."

His hand remained extended, and she continued to eat pie, paying him no attention whatsoever. This wasn't going quite as he had planned. He plopped the rejected hand in his lap.

"Seems like I should make your acquaintance, if you're Joleigh Camden."

Ah, now he had her attention. Her fork clattered against the counter and she turned a glacial stare on him. She didn't speak, but at least she wasn't massacring her dessert anymore.

"I bought the forge you were selling. I thought we'd meet earlier, but seems like you were out of town."

She continued to stare at him, this time with narrowed eyes. The muscles in her jaw were taut, ropy. He flashed The Grin, working his legendary magic.

"Um, yes, well. There's a key missing, the one for the smithy. I can't get in there to look at the place, assess the forge. I was hoping you'd help me out and give me the key."

Cullen noticed the absolute silence in the diner, and looked around. Men and women were frozen with utensils in mid-air, gawking at their conversation. The cook hung out of the order window, and Miss Ruby rubbed a continuous circle on one spot of the bar.

Jo broke the stillness by gently scooping the remaining bite of pecan pie onto her fork. She placed it into her mouth, chewed slowly, and swallowed. She took a swallow of tea from the glass in front of her, then turned her attention to Cullen. The deafening silence in the diner was beginning to unnerve him.

Without looking away from Cullen, Jo said, "Miss Ruby, the pie was incredible, as usual."

Her voice was sultry, like a bonfire on a frigid night under a starry sky. It grabbed his stomach and twisted.

She continued to hold his stare as she casually swallowed more tea.

Then she stood, the nearly full glass in hand, and tipped it over. The ice-cold sweet tea poured over Cullen's lap, shocking him as it splashed across him and onto the floor around him. A collective gasp echoed off the walls of the small diner, and not a few people chuckled. Cullen jumped to his feet, shoving the wooden stool into the one next to it, nearly toppling them. Ice cubes clattered to the floor. He gaped, mouth wide open, shocked at the cold wet soaking his jeans. Dumbfounded, he watched as Jo casually walked over to the door, and looked at the matron behind the counter, pointedly ignoring him.

"Put it on my tab, Miss Ruby."

And then she was gone, with only the jingle of a small golden bell to sound her exit.

Chapter 3

A thundering of hooves heralded her departure. In her wake, pale sand billowed into gritty mist hanging a foot above the rock-strewn earth. In the distance, lead-bottomed clouds stacked one atop the other. Lightning flickered within the confines of the towering storm. Jo focused on the horizon, rather than the curious stares of the few townsfolk who watched as she rumbled by. North she rode, into the storm. Overhead, blue sky still dominated.

As she reached the outskirts of town, and the weathered bridge spanning the creek which ran alongside the mill, she eased up on Kase's reins, allowing the horse to slow to a canter. The mare's hooves thumped hollowly on the sun-bleached hardwood, in time with the bumping pulse in Jo's neck.

The nerve of the city-slicker, traipsing into her town and asking for the key. She barked a laugh, scattering a flock of doves from the hill on the other side of the bridge. She'd give good coin to see the man try to figure out the forge lock. It had taken her years.

The funniest part of the whole thing was the lock had no key, per se. It was a blacksmith's puzzle. Her father had placed a key slot on the puzzle as a ploy, an iron red herring to discourage thieves in the days following the fight for independence. Lawlessness prevailed, even in those days. She still had the key he used to hang on a nail in the doorframe; it was nestled on the black felt bottom of her keepsake box.

Kase, her dun quarterhorse, picked her way amid the rocky path running parallel to the paved highway. The Old Spanish Road, or the Old San Antonio Road, was a slash on the map, a smooth black swath sweeping from northeast to southwest along the lower edge of Robertson County. Folks around here called it the OSR, and kicked the formalities out the door. The dot on the map called Coleville hunched behind her, southwest, and Jo started to feel a tinge of regret at leaving its citizens in her dust. Ahead, the horse path and the OSR split off from the trail leading to her cottage on Copperas Creek, about a mile due north from Coleville.

Half a dozen yards from the fork, Kase reared onto her hind legs, forelegs batting in the air. The horse bellowed; and like a compressed spring held between two fingers suddenly released, she bolted. Jo thought she heard the distinctive shaker of a rattlesnake, but she was too preoccupied with keeping herself in the saddle to look for the offender. Kase flung all eleven-hundred pounds along the path leading home. Jo hunkered over the saddle horn, the low limbs clawing and snatching at her hair as they sped beneath them. When they reached the clearing, she tugged on the leather reins sharply.

"Whoa, girl, whoa. Easy!"

What seemed like a race lasting minutes had, in reality, been only a handful of seconds. Kase slowed to a walk, her sides heaving and nostrils blowing heavily. Jo swung to the ground with the reins gripped in her calloused hand. Sweat glistened on the dun's pale coat, and adrenaline shivers rippled along the beast's withers and hips. She looped the reins over and around a nearby post oak branch.

She coasted a palm along the smooth horsehair that wasn't yellow or tan, but a shade in between. Jo shushed her with low, easing noises, then began humming as she ran a hand along each of the mare's legs. Paying close attention to the fetlocks and ankles, she looked for fang punctures and swelling. When she got around to the last leg inspection, she blew out a relieved breath. And then growled when she turned up the foot and discovered Kase had thrown a shoe.

The clearing on her right was half a mile from her cottage. Jo sighed and pulled her blonde locks on top of her head, holding it in place so that her arms formed arches in the air. A breeze kissed her neck lightly, but it didn't linger. The air grew calm once again, the grasses in the field standing tall as if rising from a graceful bow at the end of a waltz. Scattered bluebonnets blazed electric blue, but most were losing their brilliant color, easing into the slow fade leading to weed anonymity. Fiery Indian paintbrushes dotted the clearing, and a smattering of yellow buttercups remained close to the grassy ground. A half-moon ring of pecan, oak, and mesquite bordered the opposite side, creating a little pocket of Heaven which few ever saw.

Jo loosed the reins, slapped them against her palm. The horse had quieted, and nuzzled at her arm. She turned and petted the narrow face of her long-time friend, planted a kiss on the white blaze.

"Looks like we'll be hoofin' it back. Eh? Get it?"

The horse snuffled and flicked her head up and down. Jo snorted.

"Yeah, let's get home."

The half-mile trudge to the cabin gave her a chance to ponder her circumstances, such as they were. They took it easy, picking their way around sharp stones and fallen limbs. Jo launched quite a number of rocks into the scrubby woods shadowing the trail, each one a release of pent-up anxiety. By the time she topped the rise on the south side of her property line, the nebulous form of a plan took shape.

First off, she would swallow her pride and take the job. The funds gathered over the last few weeks in her desperate attempt to save the smithy would have to be redirected to the immediate costs of living. An idea coalesced in the recesses of her mind, like a fog rising over a pond in the cool autumn air. But to move from idea to action, she needed an income. Which meant eating a little crow. Tomorrow was soon enough.

She fingered the leather thong around her neck, pulled out the crude polished stone dangling from a primitive setting. The aquamarine shone brilliantly in the evening sun, azure fire gleaming against her hand. When she was nine years old, just after her daddy died, she had been wearing it one day in town. A grizzly old woman with hair black as night and wrinkles by the thousands stopped and reached out her hand, snagging the stone around Jo's neck. She had frozen, a lollipop glued to the roof of her mouth. The stranger had gazed at the stone, and peered into her young eyes with a squint.

"You Neal Camden's girl?"

Jo had simply nodded, and searched for her mother. But the old woman continued, the gem clutched in her rough hand.

"You have a difficult journey ahead of you, child. Do not part with this stone. It will one day lead to truth."

Then the leathery woman released the necklace, and tottered past Jo. She never saw the old lady again.

It was tempting to sell the gem, put the funds to a more tangible use. She eyed the blue stone, its cool heaviness warming in her hand.

No, she couldn't sell it. Her father had given it to her on her ninth birthday, only a month before he died.

Her throat tightened, eyes watered. Jo swallowed the lump, straightened her shoulders, and dropped the pendant down her shirt once more. She refused to cry. Not today.

Her whitewashed cottage was situated a stone's throw south of Copperas Creek. The horse frisked, nearly stepping on Jo's ankles. She looped the reins around the horn of the saddle, and smacked Kase on the rump. Needing no further encouragement, the horse trotted off to the open pen, straight to the saltlick.

It took half an hour to put the tack away and brush down the horse. She left Kase cropping grass in the fenced pasture. That chore done, she hummed her way to the house, ready for a cold glass of tea. She regretted wasting hers at the diner. Ruby made a mean glass of sweet tea.

With a smile on her face remembering the city-boy's startled eyes, she turned the knob and pushed open the front door. She nearly fainted at the sight.

Her home was wrecked. Framed photos were slung around the room, the glass shattered and cracked. Books littered the floor, pulled from the built-in shelves she had crafted by hand. Stuffing puffed through slices in the upholstery of her couch. Her favorite reading chair was shredded, its seat cushion tossed clear into the adjacent small dining area. Every item she owned had been tossed. She moved from room to room, and found the same in each one. Cabinets spilled their contents, papers littered the floors, and empty nail heads stared where art had once hung. Linens and blankets were strewn across the hardwood floors, pulled from the beds and tossed about. Not a single room was spared.

It was as though a giant pair of hands had reached down from above and shook the house, as if it were a snow globe in the hands of a child.

Jo collapsed on the edge of her bed, bewildered. Who would do such a thing? Everyone in town knew she was broke. No one she knew would have ransacked her home looking for money, for valuables. The tears that threatened before now spilled down her cheeks, the stress and the tension of the day leaking in salty water droplets which trailed down her dusty cheeks. Out of habit, she touched the lump under her shirt, the aquamarine hanging from her neck. So much for protection.

Wait! Her keepsake box! She fell to the floor, searching for disruption under her bed. Jo wiggled the loose floorboard near the head of the bed, and exhaled in relief when she extracted the polished hickory box from its hiding place. Could this have been what the looter sought?

She lifted the top. It eased open without a squeak, the hinges oiled and rust-free. Inside was a collection of seemingly useless objects. The shiny key from her dad's forge, a handful of gold and silver coins. Her pockets contained the remainder of her life savings, and would go in the box soon enough. Next to the key, a cat's eye marble. Ginny's marble. An old dollar bill from when Texas was a state. Three gemstones that had belonged to her mother; a ruby the size of her pinky nail, a smaller sapphire, and another aquamarine.

She reached for the marble, but hesitated, her hand hovering over the box. Jo closed the lid, and replaced the container beneath her bed.

Then she tapped the face of her wrist communicator, and instructed it to call the sheriff's office. A gruff voice answered.

"Sheriff's office."

"Duke, it's Jo. I need a guy out here. Someone tossed my house."

"I'm on my way."

Chapter 4

Jo shunned the violation of her home, choosing to sit on the front porch and contemplate the dragonflies flitting from one verdant stalk of grass to the next. Their restlessness mirrored her own. The dying sun glowed a vivid crimson on the horizon, setting fire to the sky and bleeding on the encroaching storm. A hasty breeze carried the scent of pasture.

Fury bubbled inside her chest. It felt like the water in a cast iron pot, heating on the stove. Her visit to the bank incensed her. But this? Someone breaking into her home, pillaging her possessions, flinging them about as though they were rubbish? This pushed her beyond boiling. Rage overflowed the rim of her mental black kettle, the scalding water sizzling and crackling as it hit the flames. She heard Duke and the other deputy, Logan, conversing quietly inside; knew they were going from room to room, recording the damage with their holocams. And suddenly, she needed to move.

Twenty minutes later, Duke wandered into the stable. Sweat drenched her hair, and soaked her shirt in patches. She propped the shovel against the rough-hewn boards of the stall and wiped her face with a forearm. She faced the deputy.

"Y'all about done in there?"

Duke nodded his head, taking in the shade of the stable with a long side-to-side glance. "Logan's on his way back to town. Can you come in tomorrow to finish up the report?"

Thunder rumbled across the sky, a grumbled whisper of the storm to come.

"Yeah, I need to come to town anyway. Got some unfinished business."

The deputy rasped a calloused hand over his chin, like two pieces of sandpaper filing against one another. When he spoke, it sounded as though he was chewing rocks. Two blue sapphires gleamed amidst his sun-leathered face, with deep grooves fanning around his eyes. Duke Massey took no flak from anyone, and he used the hard exterior to his advantage. If he hadn't bounced her on his knee and smuggled caramels to her as a child, she would probably fall in line with the rest of the townsfolk who steered clear of him. Instead, when he held his arms open to her, she fell against his chest. Duke held her tight, his heartbeat a mighty thump, grounding her in the here and now. Jo sniffled and pulled back, but not before giving him an appreciative squeeze back.

She took a hanky from her pocket and wiped her nose. "So what happens now?"

"We dusted for prints, but the only thing we found was a smudged partial. You can pray it's enough to flag a suspect."

Jo snorted. "I ain't much for praying these days."

"I know it."

"What else? I can tell you're keeping something back."

The grizzled man sighed. "I want you to stay in town for a while, Jo."

She narrowed her eyes, studied the shift to his shoulders and stance. "Show me."

Duke pulled out the holocam, held it open on his palm. He tapped the illuminated screen twice, swiped his finger along the edge. A 3-D image of the back door in her kitchen floated above the wafer-thin base, crisp in its detail but somewhat transparent. At just about the level where her head would reach, a note was pinned to the left side of the doorframe. Where once her blood raged white-hot, now it slid ice cold through her veins.

Securing the note to the flower papered wall was an eight-inch long chef's knife. It may as well have been plunged into her gut. Her stomach clutched, threatening to empty itself when she read the words scrawled across the paper.

WHERE IS IT?

Overhead, the sky rumbled in protest. Jo tried to swallow, but her mouth was a desert. Who had done this? Duke echoed her thoughts.

"Got any ideas?"

An idea sprouted, a theory tentatively grasping for the surface which she rapidly smothered. It couldn't be, not after all these years. The deputy squinted at her, but remained silent. She would not lie to him, but neither could she admit her suspicions.

"Some. For now, I don't think I'm in any danger. That's my knife acting as a push-pin, though. Just so you know." Jo ran a hand through her damp and gritty hair. "Is it all right if I start putting things back in order in there?" She jerked a thumb in the direction of the house.

He growled under his breath, an echo to the low grumble from the sky, deep and gravelly. "Should've known you'd be hardheaded about leaving."

"No one runs me out of my home, Duke. You know I can handle myself." Jo plastered a lopsided grin on her face and flexed her biceps playfully, at which Duke barked a laugh.

"I'll see ya in, girl," he said, waving her out of the stable.

The two marched side by side, kicking up dust in the path worn by many footfalls. A low, steel gray ceiling hung overhead; on the northern horizon, a solid pewter sheet of rain cascaded from the heavens.

"All right, I'm home," she grinned from the porch. "Go on, scoot. I promise to call if anything shady happens."

Duke twitched his mouth to the side, spat in the grass at his feet. "Farrier's on his way out. Hopefully he gets here before the bottom drops."

Jo narrowed her eyes at him, and the older lawman threw his hands in the air. "Don't look at me like that, girl. That dun of yours tore up the track from the Y-split to the clearing, and then your tracks were leading only three shod ones of hers. Doesn't take a genius. He should be out any minute."

"You didn't have to do that, but thanks," she conceded. "Now get on back before you're soaked." Jo shooed him away with a forced smile. She watched the backside of his gelding sway as it clopped down the lane, its black tail a'swishing the ever-present flying insects found in these woods. Duke rocked along to the rhythm. As he rounded the bend away from her house, he lifted his hat in salute, then replaced it on his graying head. He didn't look back. She shook her head, laughing under her breath, and turned to face the front door.

It gaped open, a yawning maw into the destruction of her once well-organized sanctuary. Slowly, she picked her way through the living room, stepping around strewn books and broken glass, weaving across the little dining area and into the kitchen. She found herself standing in front of an open cabinet door, a smoky lowball in one hand and the half-empty bottle of bourbon in the other. Her hands shook, and the short glass thumped the countertop. Jo stared at her hands, unblinking, until the tremors passed. Then she shoved the amber bottle onto the top shelf and slammed the door before she changed her mind.

The bottle was a reminder, a visual warning of the black depths in which she once swam; the liquid escape from the stress of the trial and the memories haunting her dreams. She closed her eyes, imagined the burned-barrel aftertaste searing her throat and vaporizing out her nostrils. Her resolve wavered. Jo craved the solace, and hated it all the same.

Her first smacked the countertop, and she spun out of the kitchen. She would shower the frustrations away tonight.

Ten steamy minutes later, she floated out of the bathroom ahead of a fog bank wearing nothing but a towel and her boots; the former because, even alone, she was modest to the point of prudeness; the latter to protect her feet from broken glass. Her hair straggled in wet, laciniate strands over her shoulders. The jerk who tossed her house had been thorough in the bathroom as well. Miraculously, one towel had remained perched vicariously on the edge of the vanity. The other towel spilled halfway out of the toilet, and onto the hardwood floor.

In the bedroom with the curtains drawn, she released the terry cloth bath sheet and quickly ran it back and forth over her soggy locks. No sooner had she dropped the towel over the footboard of the bed than a pounding came from the front of the house.

Jo immediately covered her nakedness with her hands, despite the fact that all the doors were locked, the curtains were closed, and no one was inside the house except her. She rolled her eyes to the ceiling, jerked her plush robe off its hook, and jabbed her hands through the sleeves. Meanwhile, she prepared the tongue-lashing she'd give Duke or Logan for interrupting her routine.

Through the house she clopped, like a freshly shod horse. Pointedly, Jo ignored the mess and wondered what it was the deputies had forgotten and why they couldn't just use a doggone communicator. With her mouth set in a grim line, she opened the front door.

City Boy darkened her porch. He stood with his hat across his chest, his mussed hair sticking out in all cardinal directions and then some. His grin was half-cocked, and a wedge of a dimple sat below his arrogant mouth. She noticed the scar along his left cheek, a white line drawn from the top of his tanned cheekbone to the temple winged with laugh-lines. She frowned at his smirk, and he rolled his eyes in return. Then he placed his hat atop his head, added a tilt to it for a little jaunt, and peered at her from beneath the brim. The half-cocked grin was replaced by a full-on smile as he eyed her up and down.

Hands on her hips, glaring, she opened her mouth to demand what he was doing on her property, just as he said, "I hear you're in need of a farrier, Miss Camden."

She wanted to punch that sneer off his smug city-boy face.

Chapter 5

"What happened to Jules?" Jules Newburn had been Coleville's only farrier for as long as she could remember.

"Uncle Jules retired. He's probably out on his boat in the Gulf of Mexico reeling in tuna and sea bass. Bought a little seaside cottage on Galveston Bay. Aunt Miriam threatened to break out her bikini."

The unwelcome guest on her doorstep laughed at his own joke, but Jo's mind buzzed. "*Uncle* Jules?"

Cullen bobbed his head once and grinned, the slyness oozing off his face.

"Jules never mentioned a nephew before," Jo added slowly. "Never mentioned a sibling for that matter."

"I'm not surprised. He's the black sheep of my mother's family." Shifting on his feet, he tucked his thumbs into the hip pockets of his faded denim jeans. "Not that I mind shooting the breeze with you, but the wind *is* picking up quite a bit out here. Mind if we move inside? I promise I don't bite."

Jo blinked, and noticed the wind bending the smaller trees at the edge of her cleared yard. Chubby raindrops pelted the dirt sporadically. She reached up to push her straggly wet mop out of her face and saw the fuzzy pink cuffs of her bathrobe. Oh, for goodness' sake! She was standing on her porch, talking to City Boy in her robe. Inwardly, she groaned. Jo extended an arm in mock hospitality, ushering Cullen inside.

"Mind the mess. Looks like I'm in the middle of forced reorganization."

Hurriedly, she retreated in the direction of her room. "Make yourself at home, but watch the broken glass." She looked over her shoulder to make sure he stayed in the living room. When she did, their eyes locked. Electricity fizzled around the edges of the glance. He stood in the midst of destruction, calm and sure, with his battered felt cowboy hat held in one hand near a thick thigh. Jo blinked. Why was she looking at his thighs? She growled and stomped over her scattered belongings, slamming her bedroom door behind her. Through the muffled barrier she could have sworn the man was laughing.

Hangers bounced and fell to the floor as she yanked shirt and jeans out of the diminutive closet. Exasperated, she sighed as she stooped to pick up the wooden hangers. What were two more pieces to tidy considering the state of the rest of her home? She grabbed underwear out of the tall chest of drawers nestled between the two doors of her bedroom. The dull thump-thump of City Boy's heels on the wood floors told her he was snooping. Jo hurriedly dropped her own boots to the floor and clambered atop the bed to dress. Cutting her feet on stray shards held little appeal.

As she shimmied into her jeans, his muffled voice seeped through the closed door.

"Deputy Massey told me about the home invasion when he called about your horse."

Jo froze with a sock hanging off the end of her foot.

"I'm real sorry, Miss Camden. Seems like the last thing you need right now."

That was the understatement of the year. But if this whole breaking and entering was about what she suspected, then it was only the beginning.

She hastily tugged on the remaining sock, then stomped her feet into her dusty boots.

"Duke also seemed to think you may be in a bit of danger," came the deep voice from the hallway.

Jo clenched her teeth. She grabbed the comb from the top of the dresser and stood in front of the mirror on the backside of the door. She pulled it through her damp tangles, then wove a hasty braid that hung heavily down her back. It left a wet patch on her t-shirt. Staring at her reflection, she grunted.

"Duke Massey talks too much," she growled at the door. And it sounded like he was trying to play matchmaker.

The glass crystal knob cooled her palm. She hesitated, then turned it. Hinges unused to being closed protested their movement. There he stood, Mr. Annoyingly Dark and Handsome. Golden-brown eyes the shade of fine aged whiskey sparkled in the dim light of the hallway. Jo twirled her eyes to the ceiling and shoved her way past the farrier.

"Don't you have a horse to shoe?"

Cullen chuckled. "Lead the way, ma'am."

Raindrops pelted a chaotic symphony against the porch's tin roof, thrumming in glee and exploding in a shower of droplets. They rushed to the rough-sided stable and were drenched by the time their boots splashed beneath the low lean-to overhang. Suddenly the wet patch on her back from the long braid seemed inconsequential. Every inch of her was soaked clean through.

An unfamiliar horse was tied to the skinny wooden railing. She assumed it belonged to City Boy. The gleam of well-oiled leather the color of cherry-wood beckoned, however, and she reluctantly reached out, running a wet finger along the intricate scrollwork carved into the saddle on the beast's back. Matching saddlebags draped elegantly. The initials "CM" sat among a flurry of detailed swirls and tiny, life-like flowers. Jo hummed her approval.

Thunder rolled lazily through the windswept trees, and the smell of damp dust permeated the air. The farrier's paint bobbed its head and pawed the ground. She did a quick bend to the side. He, a gelding.

"Shhhh," Jo calmed the horse.

"He's a tobiano." His voice coasted into her ear.

Her head spun to find his eyes directly over her shoulder. She narrowed her eyes in stern warning, and he backed up, hands in the air.

"Hey now, hold on ma'am. I said it before, but you didn't hear me. I only moved closer so you could. Honest. It's loud out here."

Grudgingly, she nodded. "He's beautiful."

Generous chestnut blobs bled into swirls of white across his hide. The white extended beneath the saddle, and showed prominently on his broad rump. Patchy white forelegs continued to scrape the ground as thunder groaned across the sky. She'd much rather spend time with the horse than his owner, but she squared her shoulders anyway and turned to face the interloper.

"Kase is in her stall." Jo pointed to the short dirt-floored passageway between the tack room and other side of the stable which housed three stalls. "First door to the right. I'll get a shoe."

"Brought some with me," he called from behind, but she was already opening the tack room door. The clank of metal told her he was rummaging in the saddle bags for his tools. A glance around the plank-walled room showed the person who ransacked her house neglected to search the tack room. Bridles and halters dangled serenely from their hooks, as did various lead ropes. Brushes and other implements hung in waiting. Two long metal rods extended from a bracket on the wall, spaced a couple inches apart. Horseshoe after horseshoe perched in a row. She ran a finger gently over the cool, rounded edge of a U-shaped shoe. Jo had made these. Would she have to buy them from City Boy from now on? Or would her future employer allow her to keep a few of the ones she made for him? Her blood boiled thinking about it. She snatched one off the rack and stormed out of the door, slamming it in her wake. Across the hall, Kase kicked the wall in objection.

Contrite, she hooked her chin over the high three-quarter door. "Sorry, Kase, baby. You didn't do anything wrong." The mare nickered forgiveness and nuzzled her outstretched hand. "I did."

Behind her, a bass voice cleared itself. Jo twitched, closed her eyes, clenched her jaw, and exhaled audibly.

"Mr. Miles, kindly stop sneaking up on me," she warned before facing him. She took her time nuzzling Kase, despite the gentle storm outside. Satisfied she made him wait long enough, she turned.

The yellow light on the far wall of the stable flickered like a lightning bug in summer, and she made a mental note to check the solar charger connections. In the pale cast of light, the farrier stood about three inches taller than her five-nine, with that half-cocked grin plastered on his face again. Calm ... she would stay as calm as a looking-glass pond.

"It's the front right hoof." There, cool as a cucumber.

He patted the embossed saddlebags over his shoulder. "Got everything I need right here, Miss Camden, so let's see what we've got."

Jo was familiar with each implement the man pulled out of his bags, but was completely caught off guard when the melodic sounds of string instruments filled the air. She lifted both eyebrows, and he shrugged, placing the thin tablet on a straw-covered battered wooden crate outside the stall. His hat joined it.

"Figured the storm might be making her antsy. I find music soothes the beasts, calms their nerves." His chiseled dimple flashed once again before he tucked his head.

City-Boy ran his hands along Kase's flank, then down the leg before smoothly positioning her foot between his chap-covered thighs. He clucked his tongue.

"This hoof looks pretty ragged, Miss Camden," he chided.

"Yeah, well, we put many a mile on those hooves the last three weeks trying to come up with enough gold to save my forge, *Mister* Miles. I'm not negligent. We got home today, as you may recall."

Blessedly, the man held his peace or he would have found out exactly how much it galled her to have him on her property.

Her mind wandered to the lilt and roll of the classical notes fluttering around the stall. While he cleaned the hoof and trimmed it, her thoughts meandered to the mess in her home; and to the image Duke showed her, the message pinned to the wall with her very imposing chef's knife. The rhythmic clip of the nippers barely registered as she categorically charted the process she would need in order to set her home to rights.

"Hadyn."

She looked at him quizzically. "What?"

"You were humming. It's Hadyn's String Quartets, Opus 33. Always reminds me of frisky foals, just after they've gotten their footing. How they romp around the pasture, and then settle down quietly next to mama after they've run their fill."

Jo stared at the baffling man. She settled for shaking her head. "Look, I need to get inside, see to cleaning up the mess. You okay out here?"

He paused, the rasp stilling in his hand briefly, before he began filing once more. "Sure. You should consider having the other three done."

"Just the one, please. Knock on the door before you leave, and I'll pay you."

"Yes, ma'am."

City Boy winked and flashed the dimple, while Hadyn's strings danced in the air. It was a good thing the rain still sheeted from the sky.

She needed to cool down.

Chapter 6

The professional in him refused to allow a horse to stand on one well-shod foot. In the end, Cullen appropriated three more shoes from Miss Priss' custom-made stash in the tack room and finished the job properly.

Overhead, buckets of rain pounded the stable roof. An occasional peal of thunder rippled across the sky. He thought it must be what sitting inside a steel drum would feel like. The horses remained placid, however. With the job done, he packed his gear and hung the saddlebags over the chest-high wall adjacent to her horse's quarters. He led his own horse into the neighboring stall. The easy-going paint bumped his thigh with a mostly brown face, snuffling his jealousy that Cullen had been with another horse.

"Now, Jasper. Don't you go getting all covetous on me now, old friend," he laughed. "I plan on spending a lot more time with both of these blonde females, human and equine. Here, maybe this will make it up to you."

He fished a crimson apple from the leather saddlebag and held it up to Jasper's face. "I mean it, buddy. Be on your best behavior. I have to go visit Miss Camden for a little while." The beast nibbled the apple from his open palm, the soft velvet of Jasper's nose tickling his hand. Cullen closed the stall door to the sound of contented crunching. He glanced at the saddle stand by the tack room, then leaned down to get a closer look at the carving on the supports. Beautiful work, a woodland scene of deer along a path between mesquite and oak trees, accented with scrollwork and leaves resembling long and twisting vines. It was no wonder she oohed and ahhed over the detailing on his saddle.

Cullen stood beneath the little barn's overhang. True darkness had fallen, not just storm-induced dimness. The path between her house and the stable was a winding muddy river, skirting around stunted trees and a few stumps. Rain cascaded from the heavens, and golden light beckoned from Jo's cabin. Her wavering silhouette glided from one frame to the next, walking and stooping. The softened shadow took away her hard lines, blurred the sharp edges of her resentment and anger. From here, he admired the sweet curve of her neck, the shape of a curved hip, without having a cold glass of Miss Ruby's iced sweet tea dumped in his lap for his attentions.

A glutton for punishment, his mother would say. Sighing, he replaced his hat, inhaled, and quickstepped into the deluge.

By the time he darkened her already murky front porch, the only part of him that remained dry was the brown-black tuft of hair sheltered by his thoroughly soaked felt hat. He swiped a dripping hand across his face, felt the day's end scruff. Cullen stood in a puddle of his own making, water rolling from his shoulders down to his mud-covered boots. Well, either he could undress on her porch and wring out his clothes, or he could knock on the door and hope for the best. He was pretty sure she wouldn't like seeing a naked near-stranger on her front porch. Raking as much water as he could from his clothing, he shook himself like a mutt and reached out to knock on the bright red door. His hand stalled, almost of its own accord, as the light sounds of the violin drifted around minute cracks in the door facing.

Intrigued, he placed his ear where the door met the trim. Vivaldi, had to be. "L'autunno", toward the end of the movement if he wasn't mistaken. This particular piece brought to mind an autumn trip in the Pennsylvania District, a horse-drawn carriage for two along a winding and hilly road while red, orange, and yellow leaves fell like rain. His smile cocked to the side as he settled in to listen once more.

And nearly fell into the living room as Miss Priss yanked open the front door. Thankfully his hands braced against the frame. Her scowl suggested she wouldn't want mud tracked into the house just now.

"People generally knock these days," she complained.

"Maybe I was just gathering intel."

"Maybe you were being nosy."

"Maybe I appreciate Vivaldi. Look, Miss Pr--," he paused. "Miss Camden. I think we got off on the wrong foot. There is no reason we can't be amicable to one another."

Jo lifted her chin, her eyes frosty-cold in the warm light. "Amicable. Huh. I think we left amicable on the table when you stole my forge out from under me."

"I did no such thing! There was a listing, I offered, it was accepted. I bought it under the assumption that a previous owner was selling of his own accord."

Cullen thought the woman ought to give growling lessons to wolves. She flung wide the door, and curtly instructed him to wait in the tiny foyer while she grabbed a towel.

41

"Drop your boots outside," she commanded, "and go easy on the towel. It's the last clean one I have, thanks to whatever jerk did this to my home. Don't worry about your feet. I swept up the glass." Her hands swept in a wide arc encompassing the quaint living area. "You might as well stay until the storm breaks."

"You don't have to do that, Miss Camden."

"I do what I want, Mister Miles, so just suck it up and sit a spell. I'll be in the kitchen salvaging what I can."

Secretly pleased, he wicked away as much water as he could with the already damp towel. While his reluctant host rattled away, he held muddied boots beneath the sheeting run-off from the porch roof, washing off the muck in the natural shower. Cullen was determined to gain ground with Joleigh Camden. He had to. The future of his new venture depended on it. Leaving his boots standing upside down on the porch, he made his way back inside. He ignored her suggestion, if it could be called that, to sit; and instead, he wandered into the kitchen. As he strolled through the domestic carnage, he stared in disbelief at the mayhem. Slashed upholstered chairs and a sofa spewed white stuffing from gaping maws. Oil paintings hung askew on the tan colored walls. He saw framed but glassless photographs on shelves, repositioned to what he assumed were their previous homes. The floors were indeed glass-free, albeit a tad dusty.

Though he barely knew her, Cullen felt his blood pressure rise in protest at the needless destruction of this woman's home.

Leaning against the doorframe leading to the kitchen, he watched as she washed the few remaining dishes left unbroken. Vivaldi streamed from a sound system in the far corner of the smooth, wax-polished countertop. He studied the shape of her arms, well-toned from her career as a blacksmith, biceps that bulged more than the average woman's, but not unattractively so. She had swapped t-shirts, he noticed, but the long blonde braid remained.

"First you eavesdrop at the door, and now you're staring at me as I wash dishes. Something I should know about you, Mr. Miles? Are you a stalker?"

He snorted. "I only stare at things worth staring at, Miss Camden."

Her hands stilled in the soapy water, and she rolled her neck. Gently, deliberately, she rinsed the teacup and placed it on the terry-cloth towel next to the sink. Then she grabbed the other towel to her right, and dried her hands. When she faced him, her eyes were like blue ice.

"Mister Miles, I neither desire nor care for your attentions."

Cullen eyed her frankly, slowly nodded. "We'll see."

"Look!" she yelled fiercely, towel flung over her shoulder, outstretched finger nailing him in place from across the room. "I have spent nearly every waking hour of the last three weeks riding across half the Republic, hitting up every debt owed to me so that I could keep my smithy. Then I come home to find a SOLD sign in the window of my office. Next, you interrupt my supper ..."

"Pie. Pecan pie."

She glared. "My *supper* of pecan pie, asking me to come unlock a door for you, the guy who bought my livelihood out from under me. Then I come home, find my place vandalized, a threat pinned to the wall with my rather large and sharp kitchen knife ..."

"Wait, what?! Someone threatened you?" Why did that make him so livid? He would have to explore that a bit, when not cornered by a screaming banshee.

"And for all I know it could have been you!" she finished with a stomp.

Cullen blinked. "Me?"

"Yes, you! I don't know you, haven't seen you before today. You could have come barking up my tree in the café, after your preliminary search here didn't yield any results!"

"Do you always use big words like 'preliminary' when you argue?"

One minute he was bantering with a banshee. The next, he was ducking as a freshly washed porcelain teacup hurtled at his head from across the room.

"Oh, come on now! Wait --!" He ducked again as she grabbed a plate from the drying towel.

But the crash never came. Slowly he unfolded himself from his head-covered crouch.

She was crying. Heaven help him, he couldn't handle crying females. *Dear Lord*, he found himself praying. *Make her stop.* But tears turned to sobs, and she fell to the floor, the plate clasped to her chest.

"Um, Miss Camden, I'm, um, really sorry. Uh, I'm not sure what I should – "

But his not so eloquent speech seemed less than comforting as she shook her head and sniffed. The tears streamed harder, falling like the rain outside, and she hiccupped uncontrollably. He spotted a white linen cloth napkin half-hanging off the little round dining table. Hastily, he snatched it between his thumb and forefinger, took two ginger steps, and hastily flung it onto her lap. He was back by the doorjamb in the blink of an eye.

"Miss Camden, I think you've had, uh, a very traumatic day. Maybe I should just go on ahead and scoot home. I think the rain is letting up. Here, I'll just … uh, check."

Edging his way around the far reaches of the miniscule kitchen, he sidestepped in a semicircle around her. He drew back the curtain, then gasped in surprise.

In the distance, low lying clouds practically clung to the horizon. Lightning fizzled and flickered, illuminating a dark sky menaced by a ferocious storm nearly on top of them. A flash of brilliant white struck again, this time showing a swirl to the clouds overhead. In a blink, chunks of ice were flung from the sky. Marble-sized hail beat a terrifying cacophony on the roof, just as Coleville's tornado siren wailed in the distance.

Eyes wide, he turned to Camden, and found her red-faced but no longer crying. She extended her hand and he grabbed it, then was pulled through the doorway, across the living room, and down the short hall to her bedroom. At the bottom of the open closet was a small trapdoor, and she flung it open.

"Down the hatch, City Boy."

Chapter 7

"City Boy?"

"There's a possible tornado out there, and you're questioning my choice of nickname for you? Really?"

Overhead, the wooden hatch was secured with a formidable sliding iron bolt. Jo lounged calmly on a poured concrete bench, her feet kicked out in front of her crossed at the ankles. A dim bare bulb glowed overhead, casting wan shadows in the recesses of the cramped storm cellar. Wall-mounted shelves held jars of preserved foods, bottles of water, and medical supplies. She looked everywhere other than at *him*.

"Good point."

Outside, the short-lived hail storm transitioned to winds howling in protest. The sound was eerie, a keening groan rising and falling like waves of the sea. Something thumped into the side of the house. Maybe a limb? The wail intensified.

"The horses! Cullen, what about the horses?" She was on her feet in an instant, and blinked surprise at the firm roughened hand covering her own. He peeled her fingers away from the iron bolt, then gripped her trembling hand in his own. His other hand drifted to her face, wiped away a lingering tear. Her cheeks flamed in response, and she jerked away. Once again, she collapsed onto the cold, hard seat. Elbows on knees, head in her hands, Jo studied the floor and attempted to school her features into something less damsel-in-distress. Had she really melted onto the kitchen floor in a crying girl mess? She groaned.

The toes of his socks appeared in her field of vision.

"Joleigh?" Hesitation was plain in his voice.

She sighed and looked up as he retreated half a step back. The miniature bunker didn't allow room for much more. He shifted, then sat alongside her.

"Jo. Call me Jo. Only my parents called me Joleigh, and they're gone. I figure you've seen me in my secret pink robe and crying on the kitchen floor. No need to stand on formality now."

He grunted. "Then call me Cullen. But I don't have a pink robe."

She barked a laugh, then sucked breath through her teeth as the stormed landed another wallop against the siding. Her head whipped to the side, as if she could stare through the poured cement walls to see outside. The wind shifted to a dull roar and she thought she heard rain pounding.

"Cullen, I –" But when she turned to him, his head was bowed over balled up fists.

They waited in cocooned silence; Jo with her eyes cast to the ceiling, her head resting against the cool wall, and Cullen with his head bowed. Moments passed with only the muted roar of the storm to keep them company. She jumped when he spoke.

"Do you pray?"

Without turning her head, she cut her eyes in his direction. "Not since I was a child. I used to pray a lot, but it never seemed to do any good."

"Now seems as good a time as any to start up again, if you don't mind me saying."

He was probably right, but the words eluded her.

Muffled thunder reverberated, creeping simultaneously through the trapdoor cracks and up through the floor.

"Do you think they're all right? The horses?" Try as she may, she couldn't keep the worry out of her tone.

"Not sure, but I prayed so. All we can do is trust and hope."

"I don't do well with waiting, or with hope. Or trusting, for that matter."

Cullen stood, his head nearly reaching the storm cellar's ceiling. With his ear angled toward a gap, he said, "I think it's safe to peek out."

Weary, Jo pulled herself to standing.

"Hey, chin up, buttercup."

"Easy for you to say. Your life isn't in shambles."

"I think I preferred crazy lady throwing antique dinnerware rather than this pity party," Cullen said under his breath.

Her fist flew of its own accord, and landed squarely on his upper right bicep.

"Hey!"

"You asked for it, bub. Ladies first."

He stepped to the side and gestured usher-style for Jo to come on over, but the ladder wasn't in its corner home. In fact, she thought as she searched, it wasn't in the shelter at all. She closed her eyes,

48

clenched her jaw, and remembered it was in the tack room. They had been in such a hurry to get inside the storm shelter that they had dropped like hammers on hot iron without a thought to getting out.

The day got better and better.

"Problem?"

"There was about a month ago, when my tack room ladder bit the dust. I solved that problem by taking the one from the storm shelter since I haven't used it in a decade."

"Figures," they said in unison.

Jo snorted at the humor of it all.

"Well, come on, hardhead. I'll give you a leg up, then you can find something for me to climb on."

Cullen stooped with cupped hands resting by his knee and a stupid grin on his face. The man was going to give her a migraine.

Slowly unclenching her jaw, she murmured, "Thanks," and then stiffened in mid-air when he dramatically grunted in protest.

"Just get on with it, City Boy. That is, if you're strong enough. Maybe *I* could give *you* a lift." She squealed as she catapulted through the trapdoor, and landing nearly in her bedroom. Quiet laughter floated from below.

The gall! She gritted her teeth, and a pain spike stabbed behind her right eye. A migraine, indeed.

"You all right out there?" he called. His voice quavered with restrained laughter.

Dusting her hands over her jeans, she straightened with as much dignity as she could pull together. She called over her shoulder, "And to think I was going to give you the key to the forge door."

As she walked away, she heard him complain, "What? Wait! Come on, Jo, let me out and we can talk about it."

Laughter bubbled, barely contained. She would let him fester a while. It'd serve him right. Despite her best intentions, the chuckle escaped, like effervescence in a glass of champagne.

She returned minutes later, a white ladder-back chair in hand. Leaning over the hole in her closet floor, she eyed the man glaring at her in the dim light.

"Glad to see you didn't get lost," he stated. "Or did you have to go build that?"

"Ha ha, funny man. You got it?"

"Yeah. I've always got it."

Jo rolled her eyes, but grinned nonetheless. "Turn off the light before you come up. And don't forget the chair."

"Yes, ma'am."

She pushed aside a bedroom window curtain. Outside, lightning flickered, illuminating leaves dancing to a slow, steady wind. No howling or roar, just the hum of a steady downpour.

Once he climbed out of the cellar, Cullen stretched out on the closet floor, his legs jutting into her bedroom. He dropped an arm into the darkness and pulled out the dining chair. Jo strode to the tiny foyer closet to retrieve raincoats, while Cullen deposited the chair in the kitchen. Without speaking, they pulled on the slickers. On the porch, they slid feet into waterlogged boots. Her hands shook, jittery at what they might find in the stable. His eyes shone with concern for his own horse as well.

Overhead, the skies cried. Limbs ranging in size from small to substantial littered the muddy yard. A section of metal roofing lay discarded, twisted and warped, halfway between the stable and the house. The heavens continued their lightshow, but the time between thunderous rumbles lengthened.

Jo flailed midway across the yard, slipping and skidding across the mucky path. A strong hand gripped her elbow, steadying her in the dark downpour. She had no idea what to feel about the warmth penetrating the thin rain slicker. Annoyance, exasperation, and gratefulness warred in her exhausted brain. Mumbled thanks barely audible above the rain would have to suffice. A squeeze on her elbow indicated Cullen heard her.

Enthusiastic neighing greeting them as they ducked into the stable. Relief coursed through her veins, relaxing twin knots at the base of her neck.

"Your handiwork?" Cullen asked, pointing at the dull gleam of the steel slide lock bolting the stall door. He pushed back the dark green hood of the oiled rain poncho.

"Yep. Hinges too."

"Just about the only things that held up."

He was right. The stall doors were battered things, with splintered and splitting wood jutting out on the lower third of both doors. Wonderful. Another expense in a world of financial hurt.

After the cooing, soothing, and checking of the horses was complete, they trudged back to the cottage. Cullen surprised her by removing his boots and plunking them by the front door. He sauntered to the shredded couch, plumped the mangled cushions, and as her eyebrows raised, casually made himself at home.

He patted the exploded pile of batting next to him in invitation.

"Now tell me all about this decorating style of yours, Miss Camden. I simply must have the name of your designer."

"It's ten at night, we just went through a tornado scare, and you're still joking?" Jo shook her head, but sank down anyway.

With a gentleness that belied his cocky nature, he looked her square in the eye. "If we can't joke about it, then you're going to start crying again. And I really, really don't want to see it." He grinned, and it softened the edge.

Sighing, she said, "I have no clue. No, that's not the whole truth. I have a suspicion. But it's so completely farfetched that I'm not sure whether to consider it or not."

"Shoot."

"You'll laugh."

"Try me."

"Buried treasure."

Cullen blinked. The dim light reflected in his whiskey eyes, and they sparkled with mirth. "You have to be kidding me."

"Legend has it, back in the late 1800s an outlaw robbed a gold miner who was on his way home from the California gold fields. The poor miner was set upon by thieves just outside of Round Rock, beaten and left for dead."

"It doesn't explain why someone would ransack your house more than a hundred miles away from Round Rock and two hundred years later."

Jo jabbed a finger at him. "Ha! See, there are also stories that one of the outlaw's gang members had a change of heart. The regretful thief made off with the treasure-laden wagon while he was on watch one night, or so the story goes. Weeks later, he found the miner. No one knows how. But because of the trouble the gold had caused, the poor man buried his treasure and didn't tell a soul where."

"Never in my life have I heard that story."

"It's a closely-held family secret."

That opened his eyes even further. "Are you telling me you're related to the unlucky gold miner?"

It was her turn to grin. "No one in the family, at least nowadays, puts any stock in the legend. Heck, if I had the treasure, I certainly wouldn't be agreeing to work for the guy who stole my business out from under me."

"Say that again."

"What? That you stole it? No matter how legit you think—"

He waved a hand. "No, no. The other part. Where you said you're agreeing to work for that guy."

"Look around, Cullen. I've got next to nothing left. My work is my life. And if I have to work for you to get my hands on my forge, I will."

His wide smile highlighted a crooked white incisor, and deepened the chin dimple. "That is the best news I've had all day."

"Well I'm glad you're enjoying yourself, boss."

He reached out a hand to her, but she shied back. She neither needed nor wanted his sympathy.

"Can you make it home in the dark?"

Disappointment painted his face, but it was gone in a blink. "Yeah, Jasper's saddle has a lighted breastplate."

"You can borrow the raincoat. I just … need some time to myself."

"I get it, Jo. I do."

A few minutes later, standing in the door, she watched the backside of Cullen Miles' horse pick its way along the muddy trail. As the darkness swallowed them and they disappeared into the trees, all she could think about was how much she didn't want to like the man.

And she was losing that particular battle.

Chapter 8

Friday, May 4, 2096

Coleville escaped mostly unscathed. A narrow swath of downed trees swept across a corner of neighboring Wheelock, according to the postmaster, Marshall Estes.

Jo fished her arm as far back into her post office box as possible to reach the last of the crammed stack of mail. "Marshall, you couldn't have just held all this in a crate or something?"

"How was I to know you'd be gone three weeks?"

She mumbled a response as the door tinkled in greeting.

"Well, well, well. Howdy, Jo! Ain't seen you around lately."

Inwardly, she groaned. Trying with all her might not to roll her eyes where the woman could see her, Jo turned to face the town's busybody. "Hello, Miss Darby. How's business?"

Behind skinny-framed glasses, the petite rumor house narrowed her eyes. Pursed lips tugged at the slicked-back bun pulled taut atop her tiny, nosy head.

"That's precisely the question I wanted to ask you, Miss Camden. What was that handsome newcomer doin' out at your place last night? Having a little tornado party of your own, then?"

She yearned to wipe that smirk off the meddlesome woman's face; but as she opened her mouth to put Darby Willis in her place, Marshall saved her the trouble.

"Darby, mind your own cotton-pickin' business. This ain't your beauty shop. Leave Jo alone."

"All right, all right, Marshall. Unruffle your feathers," Darby sniffed. "But I ain't the only one talking, ya know."

"Then you can tell all your friends and curious naysayers that Cullen Miles was out shoeing my horse when the weather hit," Jo supplied. "And they can ask Duke to corroborate."

Darby fanned herself with an envelope, fluttered and tittered like a mouse with its tail under the cat's paw. "Well, now, there's no reason to bring Duke into it, honey."

Smiling at the horror in Darby's eyes, she closed and locked the mailbox, and turned to wink at Marshall. She mouthed *Thank you*, and headed out the door. Let the woman think what she would.

She left Kase tied outside the post office, and walked across the narrow street to Ruby's. The robust woman eyed her up and down with a sly smile on her face, but her only comment was to ask, "The usual?"

Jo barked a laugh, and added, "Nothing happened, Miss Ruby."

"Mm-hmmm, I know that's right. I was scared to hear he was out there, be honest wi' you. I can still see the whites of that pretty boy's eyes when you dropped that glass of tea in his lap." Ruby bent over laughing, a joyful sound like a seal barking. The white towel stood out in stark contrast against her dark skin as she wiped the tears from her eyes. "Whew! You something else, Jo."

"I'm hungry, that's what."

"Why you ain't eatin' at your place? You never in here for breakfast."

"Well, I guess the rumor mill isn't as prolific as I thought."

Ruby's right eyebrow raised as she settled in for a good story. "Now don't hold out on me, girl." She pointed a thick finger to emphasize her point.

"Someone trashed my place. Ransacked everything, sliced open my furniture. A complete wreck. And no, I have no idea when it happened. It was like that when I got home yesterday. Couple days ago, probably. The refrigerator door was left open and everything in it spoiled."

"I'm gonna give Duke Massey a piece of my eloquent mind. He didn't say a thing over his coffee this mornin'." Ruby's towel circled in place on the bar top.

"I think the counter is clean, Miss Ruby," Jo pointed out.

"Hmm. What are you gonna do about working for that city feller?"

"Don't have much choice, and that's the bottom line. I need the money."

"You wouldn't be able to stand yourself without a fire at your back and a hammer in your pretty little hand anyway. What you gonna do? Take up knitting?" Ruby slapped the bar and cackled.

Jo laughed deep in her throat. "You know me too well, Miss Ruby."

"Since you were a baby in your mama's arms."

"I miss her. Daddy and Ginny too."

The bell on the door behind her tinkled welcome, and Ruby waved in greeting. Her chocolate colored eyes remained locked onto

Jo's. "I know you're thinking about that killer, so just stop it right now, Joleigh Agnes Camden."

Jo's shoulders hunched in reflex, and she peered out the corners of her eyes. Had anyone heard? "Shhh! Do *not* say the A word again!"

"What? You were named for a wonderful woman and one of my best friends, so hush your mouth, girl. Your grandmother, Agnes, brought a little piece of Heaven to this forsaken world."

"Okay, okay, stop waggin' your finger at me. And I wasn't thinking of that ... man ... either." She hoped to goodness lightning didn't strike the diner for the lie. "Now, where's my breakfast? I have to be at work in half an hour."

Oh, how that galled. An employee, rather than the owner. Accountable to someone other than herself. Well, maybe Mister Expand-My-Portfolio would see for himself how the iron and steel prices had tripled, thanks to the new American tariffs on exports to the Republic. A smithy went hand in hand with the farrier's trade, no question about it. But customers willing to pay triple price for quality work? Those weren't too plentiful these days.

She scarfed down golden hash browns and scrambled cheesy eggs, wolfed down three sinful strips of bacon, and chased those with three fluffy buttermilk pancakes. A small glass of orange juice, and a cold Dr Pepper topped off the feast. With a swipe of the napkin across her mouth, Jo scooted from the bar, pulling out one silver and a copper coin.

"That should take care of what I owe you the last few weeks."

Miss Ruby refunded them with a shove of her hefty hand. "Not today, sugar. You go on, now, and show that city slicker how a country girl works. You want a glass of cold sweet tea to go? You may need it." With a wink and a chuckle, she moseyed to the end of the counter to take an order.

At ten minutes shy of nine o'clock, she dismounted the dun mare and led her to the diminutive paddock nestled between the stone-walled forge and the line of mesquite and pecan trees. Oaks dotted here and there, and bright verdant leaves twitched in the young summer breeze.

Early May in Texas was fickle on good days, and downright temperamental on others. This cool, flirty breeze teased her into believing spring still clung to the land, but she was no fool. Summer lingered around the bend. Give it a week or two, and then little red lines on thermometers would steadily climb. Gossamer clouds sashayed across the wide sky, played coy with the glowing yellow ball floating overhead. If not for the debris scattered by last night's storm, no one would believe a minor twister had swept through the area. Except for the destruction that remained inside her home, Jo would have a hard time believing at this moment in time, when the sun warmed her back and the fresh breeze tickled her nose, that her life was in shambles. Or that she no longer owned the smithy, and would walk through the doors as an employee to a snobby city-boy.

A cloud shadow scooted across the ground, and Kase nickered, tossing her long face up and down. Behind Jo, an answering neigh resounded. She turned to find Cullen riding in on his gorgeous paint.

Speak of the devil and he will appear, or so the old saying went.

"Fancy meeting you here, Boss," she quipped.

"Did you bring the key, Sunshine?"

"Sunshine?"

"I like it better than Miss Priss." Cullen dismounted and led his animal past her, a wide smirk plastered across his haughty face.

Eyes wide, she spluttered, "Mi – *Miss Priss?*"

"Well?"

"Well, what?" Maybe if she got the bridle off Kase in a snap she could wrap the leather reins around that smart-aleck's neck and squeeze until his eyes popped out of his purple face. Miss Priss?

"Did you bring the key? To the forge. In order to gain entry?"

The gate clicked shut, and gravel crunched under his feet as he strutted past her, like a rooster in the hen house. Jo narrowed her eyes and tried to force laser beams into his retreating back. Since he didn't flinch she figured it wasn't a success. One day, she would perfect that. Without missing a stride, he looked over his shoulder and hollered.

"You coming or what? We're burning daylight!"

Strangulation or death-by-laser-beam were simply too elegant a death for the man. Something slow, meticulous. She chewed her bottom lip and followed him around the stonewalled forge to the front office, only to find the glass-paned door open wide and her new employer sitting behind *her* desk with his boots propped on the desktop.

"Are you growling?" he asked innocently. "That's not very ladylike, Jo."

Oh, she would show him ladylike. A sinister plot developed in her mind.

With rounded eyes, and dramatic lash flutters, she captured her lower lip between her teeth. She breathed deep, measured breaths, and at the right moment, hitched a gasp. Then she spun away from him in a huff, and lowered her head into her hands. Theatrical sobs sprung forth from the acting depths of her soul.

"I looked everywhere for the key, Mr. Miles," she hiccupped. "Really, I did." Sob, sob. Yeah, she was good. "This is all just too much for me." She let the crying escalate, but held back for good measure. Behind her, she heard heavy boots thud to the planked flooring.

"Now, Jo, come on now, honey," he pleaded. "Don't cry, please. We'll figure out something."

"I just can't!" she wailed. "You have no idea how hard this is for me. Just ... leave me alone!" She let her shoulders shake, and while her back was still to him, she reached up and yanked a hair out of her nose. Youch! That did it.

She spun to face him with tears in her eyes. "I have to get out of here!"

"Oh, man. Honey, I was just picking on you. Don't go. I'm sorry!" he yelled at her back.

With a hand smooshed against her mouth, she flew out the door and around the corner; threw herself up against the rock wall, and shook with muffled laughter. His audible groan floated into her ears, and she bent over double. A cackle escaped between her fingers.

"Jo? Miss Camden? Please," he called. "Come on back in here." His voice teased closer and she straightened in haste. His eyes locked on hers and narrowed.

Unable to contain her mirth, she exploded, slapping her knee and sliding against the rough wall until her bottom met damp ground.

She saw when realization hit.

"Why I ought to ... you were faking that?"

"You should … should see … your face!" she guffawed, hardly able to force words past the laughter. When he squared his broad shoulders and glared, she bellowed louder.

"That was just plain nasty! You ought to be ashamed of yourself."

"What?" she asked, wiping her eyes. "You told me to be more ladylike."

"I didn't mean it that way and you know it!" Glaring, he spit to the side. "Fine. You win. I'm going to the dang post office."

Five minutes later, the office door clattered open and Cullen stumbled in carrying a hefty wooden crate filled to overflowing with paper. She slumped in *her* desk chair, with *her* boots crossed on *her* desktop. To her left, the forge door gaped. He let gravity take the mail crate to the floor. She raised an eyebrow.

"Marshall won't appreciate you ruining his crates. He makes them by hand, you know."

"I didn't know, thank you very much." He jerked his dimpled chin at the opening in the wall. "Thought there wasn't a key."

"There isn't."

"How is it open, then?"

She lowered a lid in a slow wink. "Magic."

"You are insufferable."

"And you were being a jerk," she retorted. "Admit it."

Cullen retrieved a folding knife from his hip pocket, sliced open an envelope. "I will admit no such thing. Now show me how to open the door, Miss Camden."

"On one condition."

He tipped his head to the left. "Name it."

"You never, ever, call me Miss Priss again."

"Deal."

With a grin, Jo stood, but he held out a hand, halting her.

"And you never call me City Boy again. Got it?"

Ten seconds passed during a glaring match. "Deal." Jo spit on her hand and held it out. He returned the gesture, and they shook on it.

That should teach the man to never tell her to be ladylike again.

Chapter 9

Sparks flared with red-orange brilliance, exploding from the impact of the hammer and cascading to the dirt floor at her feet. She hefted it, adjusted her stance and grip. The hammer felt heavier than normal, as if gravity's pull were twice what it should be. Odd.

"You're doing it wrong, Joleigh."

Her father lounged in the shadowed corner, his rounded back against the stone wall, one boot over the other and arms crossed over his chest.

"I'm doing it like you taught me, Daddy."

She swung once more, but instead of sparks, the steel screamed. Bloodcurdling, hair-raising wails of pain erupted with each hammer blow.

"The iron is too hard," her father advised.

"It has to be hard, Daddy."

"Too much and it will snap."

She pulled the infant sword away from the anvil and shoved it into the fiery furnace, listened to the metal howl in pain. Blue tongues of flame licked the molten blade, first orange, then blazing red, and finally a brilliant white. Red eyes glowed from the depths of the furnace, and Jo was drawn inexorably toward them.

Falling, endless falling through a tunnel of fire, her skin the color of molten steel. She descended for ages before landing in a heap at the top of the wooden staircase of her childhood home. Roy stood shaking Ginny, her teeth knocking together, eyes wide, so wide. He picked up her younger sister, tossed her down the stairs, and then turned his gaze onto Jo.

Eyes of fire seared her soul. She tried to fling her hammer at his hand, but she couldn't lift it. With both hands she grasped the handle, grunted and hauled on it. He was coming for her. He was coming. His eyes glowed like twin suns, and the fire was hot enough to set off the alarm near the ceiling. Again and again, the alarm shrieked, falling in time with Roy's steps. Closer.

Closer.

He reached for the hammer and smiled.

She awoke from the dream drenched in sweat, shaking in the predawn light. On the nightstand, her wrist communicator beeped with an incoming call. Her mouth was desert dry. Red eyes glowed in memory and she shuddered. She tapped the face of the wristcom.

"Hello?"

"It's Duke."

Alert, she sat straight up. "What's going on?"

"I know it's early, girl, but you told me to call you if this should ever happen."

"Roy." Not a question. She was certain.

"Yeah. I'm sorry, Jo. The warden from the prison camp outside of Midland called, said he escaped sometime around midnight during shift change."

"Just a few hours ago, then?"

"Yep."

"Then it wasn't Roy who trashed my house."

"Not unless he discovered teleportation."

"What do I need to do now?"

She felt his sigh on the other end of the call. "I hate to say wait and see, but …"

"Yeah, I know."

"I'll keep ya posted."

"I know you will, Duke."

She yawned as she ended the call. Outside her window, the horizon breathed cerulean life into the slate sky. Stars winked and blinked lazily, white against the dark curtain of retreating night. Doves wooed one another, their eerie coo penetrating the glass window, and the mockingbirds played along in their early morning ritual.

Such a peaceful morning, when no peace remained in her heart.

Wide awake and agitated, she shuffled to the kitchen, opened the refrigerator door. It had taken Friday evening after work at the forge, and the entire weekend to set her home to rights. The fridge was stocked, and she snagged a cold Dr Pepper from the top shelf, twisted off the lid. A sigh of contentment escaped when the bubbles tickled her nose. Most people preferred their caffeine hot and from the bean. She liked hers cold and bubbly.

Her rear-end barely made a dent in the stiff new sofa cushion, and she longed for the sweet spot on her comfortable old couch. It, however, sat in a heap outside awaiting the recycling and disposal wagon to arrive later in the week. She supposed she could count her blessings that Wilbur at the Mercantile had a sofa in stock. When she was a kid, maybe seven or eight, her mama used to sit down with her and Ginny on the front porch. As the sun would sink into night, they would each say three things they were thankful for. It was easy to thank God for His blessings then, when everything was right. Before her father died of a heart attack.

Before her widowed mother married a monster to help provide for her children.

Jo breathed in the smell of new upholstery, sipped on her cold drink, and witnessed the birth of a new day. While the sky lightened from cobalt to sapphire, tickled by the pink-orange of the shy sun peeking over the horizon, she pictured her mother's shy smile. Ginny's grin had been the same. Cocked a hair to the right, not quite straight. Laura Camden – she refused to acknowledge the last name of that murderer – Laura laughed like tumbled gravel, low and full of mirth. Jo inherited her mama's laugh, and her daddy's smile, wide and proud. The day broke in the same manner, wide and proud, but she couldn't find a reason to smile.

Reality was a white cross beneath a century oak and the two headstones in the Baptist cemetery. Where was the joy in death?

Her mother's voice whispered, *"Rejoice in the Lord always, and again I say rejoice."*

Laura's voice could charm the songbirds, and she sang the hymn when she hung the laundry on the line, hummed the tune while washing dishes. A few weeks after her father passed away, nine-year old Jo had asked her mother how she could be joyful. Her mother had replied, "Because Jesus said so, dear. And He's the King. Your daddy loved the Lord, and one day I'll see him again. I find joy in that, honey bear. Now hand me that sheet."

No. When justice had been served, once and for all, she would find joy. She would be happy the day the Republic carried out the death sentence, and executed the man who murdered her sister and made Jo's life a tortuous existence for nearly two years.

The call from Duke only fed tinder to the slow-burning coals hidden deep within her soul, stoking the angry heat she thought she had banked after his arrest and conviction. Roy's escape from prison awakened uncertainty and fear, as well, but she blatantly shoved those two feelings to the dark corner of her mind and slammed the door. Action. She needed to do something. Anything.

An hour later, Kase was corralled and happily chewing near the feed trough, and Jo walked through the door to Camden Ironworks. Cullen hadn't mentioned changing the name of the smithy, and she was not about to bring up the subject. She brought up international news on the viewscreen, navigated to the site that monitored imports and exports tariff rates between the Republic and Socialist America.

Groaning, she scrubbed a hand over her face. Those numbers could not be right. Higher than Friday's reported rates. With a jab more forceful than necessary, she tapped the screen and severed the cable connection.

Steel and iron prices had tripled in the last year, and now America levied a nearly twenty-five percent increase on the export tax. For months, Jo watched helplessly as her savings covered the higher cost. Then after, bleakness as the bills piled up. The forge fire consumed notice after notice from the bank and other debtors. When the foreclosure announcement arrived more than a month ago, she had ridden off with a change of clothing and little more than a half-baked plan to collect every debt owed for hinges, horseshoes and decorative ironwork. As much as she believed in doing business the way her father and uncle had before her, the smithy was dying. The outstanding customer debt could no longer be ignored, nor could she continue to barter for services.

Though the dream had almost faded from her mind, she could still feel her father standing in a shadowy corner, telling her she was doing it all wrong. Her own memories of her father were shades and impressions. She learned the craft from her father's brother, Uncle Charlie, whose drawl was like warm honey and his convictions a blade -- hardened, quenched and sharpened.

She laid a hand on the cold forge and sighed, looked around the shop. Every tool in its place, awaiting her hands. With no orders and a pitiful stock of iron gathering dust in the corner, it took every ounce of courage and fortitude not to shatter into a million pieces.

Footsteps sounded behind her, measured and hollow thumps on the wood plank flooring of the office. She did not turn around.

"I've gone over the accounts, Jo," he said quietly.

Silence hovered, and floated on the dust motes dancing in the stale air.

He had a kind voice, she thought. Maybe she was looking at this takeover all wrong. The fledgling idea nestled in her brain nudged her, told her now was the time to speak up. She turned to him, straightened her shoulders.

"I have an idea, but it's unconventional."

"Risky, you mean," he clarified.

"Could be. But honestly, when you're at the bottom, the only place to go is up."

"All right. Lay it on me."

"Do you have a truck?"

He narrowed his eyes at her. "Yes, I do. It's parked behind Miss Ruby's place. The lot behind Shelley's inn wasn't big enough for the horse trailer and the truck, too. Why?"

"Scrap metal." She pressed on past his skeptic face, holding up a hand to forestall him. "After The Second War of Secession, when the Republic was new, how did this country survive? America had severed all ties, refused aid. We were forced to reclaim materials normally headed for the landfills. Including iron and steel."

"Every elementary student in Texas knows this," he pointed out.

"Exactly. But in the fifty years since the state was returned to a nation, we have since established trade with America. And instead of surviving on our own means, we depend on international trade for goods and resources."

"And you're suggesting we return to the days of old and scour the country looking for scrap metal to reclaim. Is that it?"

"Yes! When I was out collecting coin in the hopes of saving Camden Ironworks, I noticed heaps of discarded metal. Our country has become lazy. We can profit from that."

"Will it be worth the expense of traveling, of the additional reworking of the iron?"

"Look, the reality is that America is slapping us on the wrist again. These new import and export taxes, the tripling of steel prices. Haven't you watched the news? Did you think I was an irresponsible business owner who failed out of neglect or mismanagement?"

The look on his face said it was exactly what he thought. But what else flitted across his features? Embarrassment?

"I guess I didn't pay attention as well as I should have," he admitted. "I knew I was paying more for replacement tools and shoes. It's the reason when I saw the sale posting for your business I jumped at the opportunity. I thought if I could source my own materials, I would save money in the long run."

"You paid more for products because iron costs skyrocketed."

He rubbed his chin and leaned against the doorframe. "And you honestly think this scrap metal scavenger hunt will work?"

Jo rolled her head back, looked at the soot blackened ceiling. Then she sighed and said, "It's all we've got Cullen, and that's the honest truth."

For a few moments they stared at one another. She saw his jaw clench and relax, watched the dimple deepen as he chewed his bottom lip. Resignation and determination square his shoulders. He hitched his thumbs in his pockets.

"Let's do it."

Chapter 10

"Cool it, buddy. I've got some personal business to attend to before we can skedaddle out of here."

She had personal business, huh? On his time? Cullen ground his teeth, and heard the voices of both his mother and his dentist berating him. Obviously, they had never been around the likes of Jo Camden, or they would keep their imaginary mouths shut. Keeping the tenuous peace the two had established took priority, so he inhaled deeply and unclenched his jaw long enough to politely ask her intentions.

"What do you mean you have 'personal business'?"

Her narrowed sky-blue eyes conveyed his lack of success in the politeness arena.

"What I mean is," he clarified, "how can I help?" There, surely his concerned tone mollified the woman.

"How good are you at research?"

She still eyed him sideways; but Cullen chose to exhale quietly and pretend as though he didn't see the irritation smeared across her features.

Careful not to give too much away, he replied, "I have some skills. Came with the family tree, you could say."

She propped herself against the dusty worktable, her elbows supporting her weight. He tried to overlook her well-cut arms, but it was not every day a man shared a space with such a shapely woman. The guilt followed, and his mother's voice chided him. *"Women are not objects, Cullen David Miles."*

He cleared his throat and looked around the forge.

"You certainly kept the place neat."

"If only neatness could have paid the bills," she said in a low voice. Rubbing a hand over her face, she sighed. "Look, I only need a few hours to myself, to sort out some news Duke called me about this morning. Can you spare me for that long? You don't have to help me."

"You're a hard woman."

"I've had to be."

"I may not know as much as a blacksmith, but I do know one thing. Sometimes the most rigid steel will shatter with the right blow."

Surprise and alarm warred across Jo's face, from widened eyes to a clamped slash of a mouth.

"What? What did I say?"

"Nothing, sorry," she hurriedly waved. "Just a dream I had this morning. I've had a less than ideal life, Boss, but don't worry about me. I do fine."

"I can see that."

With a growl, she flung herself toward the doorway.

He grabbed her upper arm, saying, "Wait! I wasn't being snide, Jo. I meant that I could see you're resourceful."

And touchy, but he dared not open his yap.

"I'm resourceful, all right. And tired of all these surprise complications."

"You mean the break-in?"

Her only answer was a shrug. When she didn't elaborate, he cocked an eyebrow, encouraging her to explain.

"It's personal, Cullen. Two hours? You'll have a dedicated employee after, my word on it."

Twisting his lips to the side, he tasked a few brain cells to ponder her request. Or, at least, to make it appear so. If he had to wager, his coin would be on new curtains. Or dishes? Females were always fretting about home furnishings, and it would make sense in her case. Her home looked like a bomb site only a few days ago.

She cleared her throat.

"Um, yeah, sure. Go do what you've got to do. I'll be here, working on … the accounts." He would rather lay his head on her anvil and hammer it a few times. "I'll be waiting."

He enjoyed the view as she walked away, and then proceeded to kick himself for it even as he whistled a lighthearted melody. His mother's voice scolded him and he winced. Yeah, yeah, women aren't objects. Got it, Mom.

An hour into the books, Cullen considered the hammer and anvil approach again. The numbers were bleak. No income to speak of, a mountain of debt, and the only hope seemed to be rusting in heaps across the state. Why had he gotten a wild hair to buy the smithy? Well, he knew why, he simply wished it came with fewer complications.

To branch out on his own, fly far from the capitol-based family nest, and breathe without his father weighing and measuring him. Those were the primary goals. His brother served as a county representative, his sister a lawyer. Betsy Miles, his mother and the matriarch, wielded proper etiquette like a double-edged sword. No, he desired to be more than Secretary of State Sterling Miles' eldest son; to make a life with his hands *and* his mind. Which baffled Mrs. Betsy to no end, and made his father shake his head in disbelief.

The domed shadow of the Capitol Building cast a long shadow on one raised within its halls. Austin held security, a life of ease. Dinner parties every Saturday, and butlers to turn down a bed.

Austin smothered him in finery, suffocated him with duty.

Cullen needed grit, life; dirty, challenging work that blackened his fingernails and proved he was worth more than his father's power and wealth. He craved fresh air tinged with horse manure. And since Thursday, he desired time spent with a feisty blonde who could not stand the sight of him.

That would make his father shake his silvered head indeed.

Ten years ago, at the age of thirty, he announced to his parents he was leaving his partnership in an engineering firm to apprentice to a farrier on the outskirts of Austin. Secretary and Mrs. Miles had paused with forks in midair, poised over their filets mignon. Mother's silver knife clinked against the china as it fell from her hand. Father reclined against the tall back of the mahogany chair and cocked his head to the side, asked if this was some kind of joke. He made it clear he did not find it funny.

For two hours after, Cullen suffered a heated lecture from his father while his mother observed from the chaise, occasionally dabbing at her eyes with a silk handkerchief. Betsy could be quite dramatic when she deemed it necessary, he recalled with a twist of his mouth. Her only contribution to the discussion were disparaging remarks about her wayward brother, his uncle Jules.

Jules' retirement provided the perfect opportunity to establish roots in a community where it was not common knowledge Cullen was the son of the Secretary of State. But now, with depressing numbers taunting him from the accounting ledger, he idly wondered if his parents may have been right.

Disgusted, he pushed aside the leather-bound accounts register. It nudged a framed photograph, and he swiped a hand to catch it as it tipped over the desk's edge.

A white-headed toddler sat on what appeared to be her father's lap, grinning up at him with a gap-toothed smile. The little girl's arms nearly disappeared around the man's waist in a tight hug. In the photograph, the man seemed a few years younger than Cullen's current age. His crooked smile and vivid blue eyes shined, capturing the viewer's attention and oozing affection for the child sitting on his knee.

This.

This was the reason he branched away from his family's political and societal trunk. To find himself, to have a family which grew from the seeds of love and affection. To discover purpose other than money, power, and position.

To one day have a child who squeezed him tight around the middle so much it hurt, flooding his soul with immense joy.

In that moment of revelation, he understood Jo Camden.

Whatever it took to make her see him – the real him, not the bravado of a cocky rooster in a hen house – he would do.

Jo's idea of metal reclamation was solid, but one requiring research and planning. He needed his own computer system, rather than the antiquated viewscreen in the smithy office. Determined, he strode from the office, slamming shut the door behind him and eating up the sidewalk between the smithy and the boarding house with long, powerful strides.

He retrieved the lightweight equipment from his room, loading it into its black canvas carrying case. The bag thumped his leg as he returned down Sam Houston Avenue. A handful of residents carried out their business, running errands and shopping the modest stores. Cullen garnered a curious glance or two, probably because of his rapid gait, but they only registered briefly as he mentally planned and plotted. He needed maps, and the locations of city and county landfills. Recycling centers, too, he noted. Ideas swirled as he entered the office and booted up the system.

Let the woman take care of her personal business. He would have a database full of information when she returned, and they could get on with the business of pulling Camden Ironworks out of the muck.

An hour later, Jo blew in the office door with a gust of wind and frustration painted on her face. He froze with his hands in midair, suspended in their dance of swiping and pinning data. Her gaze swiveled from the air display to his face, and back again.

"Are you freaking kidding me?" she exploded.

He supposed he should be thankful for her tame outrage.

"What?"

"What?" she repeated. "I guess I should clarify. You have access to the SatNet, and you possess an airscreen system? And you didn't tell me?"

Sensing the vast emptiness below the tightrope he walked, he tactfully considered his response.

"You asked if I was good at research, and I said yes. But then you stormed off in a huff." Okay, maybe not the best reply, but it was all he had.

"You could have saved me at least an hour, Cullen. Duke's system shut down, and then I had to head to the library because you were sitting at my desk. But no luck there because the dang cable was cut between here and Wheelock. I had to beg, plead, and promise my firstborn to get Henry Brackett at the bank to let me access the SatNet for half an hour. And here you sit with a full system?"

Oh, how he admired her growl. Deep, gravelly. Just the right pitch.

"Look, I'm sorry. Honestly, I thought you were shopping for home stuff. You know, curtains and towels and stuff."

Jo's eyes shined white, the orbs rounded in surprise. "Do I look like the kind of woman who would take two hours of her new boss' time to shop for … for … lace and linen?"

He paused. "Well, now that you mention it, it does seem highly unlikely."

"ARH! Highly unlikely?! You mean as unlikely as a farrier owning a multi-thousand dollar piece of technology only found in the military and the government?"

He narrowed his eyes at her as he swiped and flicked one file in the air into another folder. The airscreen was impressive, with its glowing full-color imaging. Even more striking was her knowledge.

"Where have you seen this kind of equipment before, Jo?"

"In the Marine Corps of the Republic's headquarters office. Where I worked," she gritted through clenched teeth. "And how does a simple farrier come about having one? That's an interesting question as well."

"I could tell you, but then I'd have to kill you."

She threw her hands up in the air. "Cullen Miles, if you don't vacate that chair and let me on the SatNet, I *will* take you out."

"Only if you tell me what you need it for. Hey, don't look at me like that. This is expensive equipment."

She kicked the chair, rolling him into the narrow corner with a thud. With a flick of her wrist, and a flip of a few fingers, she elevated the airscreen to standing height and rotated it to better suit her position. Her hands danced in the air, almost like a data mining waltz. Screens flared to life, were scanned, discarded. Some were enlarged, swept into a virtual folder.

Cullen sat in shocked admiration.

"You want to know what I'm looking for?" Long fingers continued flicking and sweeping.

"You certainly have my attention."

She froze mid-swipe, pinning him with an electric-blue glint. The light from the screen illuminated her tanned face, colored a rainbow on her blonde hair.

She cocked a grin and stated, "I need to find a tracker."

Chapter 11

The eagerness to find a tracker barely edged out the thirst to kick Cullen Miles' blue-jeaned butt across the rocky ground of Robertson County. Between swipes, flicks and pins, Jo eyed him through the airscreen. He sat, reclined, boots crossed at the ankles, with a smug smile painted from ear to haughty ear.

"Did you need something?" she asked.

He barked a laugh. "Yeah, for you not to kill my machine."

"Don't worry," she snorted. "It's in very capable hands."

"So you mentioned. What did you do in the Corps?"

It was her turn for a smug smirk. "I could tell you, but then I'd have to kill you."

"Touché."

A few moments of silence passed. She scoured SatNet; he stared at her through floating glowing graphics. When she hollered, he jumped, nearly sliding out of the leather chair.

"Yes! Finally!"

She created the file, added in the list of top-rated trackers by percentage caught, then sent the file over to Duke. He would find it once his system rebooted. Why on earth the deputy's station was not on SatNet, she had no clue.

"You're a hard woman to figure out," Cullen asked from the dim corner.

She walked to the wall, switched on the overhead light, and turned to face her new employer. "You don't need to know my personal history for me to be a good employee."

The light reflected off his amber gold-flecked eyes. They held question, concern. Curiosity.

She caved. "Oh, hang on then."

Jo retrieved a stool from the forge's workbench, plunked it on the floor near the corner of the office desk.

"All right, curious cat. I'll answer two questions … for now. So ponder carefully."

"Why do you need a tracker?"

"That didn't take long."

"It's glaringly obvious I was going to ask it, so just answer already."

Where to start was a better question. She bit her lower lip, twitched her mouth to the side. Cullen grinned, and she demanded, "What?"

"You're cute when you bite your lip."

Snatching a pen from the cup, she flung it at him. "Shut up."

"Seriously cute."

"Bud, next time it'll be a set of tongs. Watch it."

He held his hands in the air. "Okay, okay. So … a tracker?"

"Duke – Deputy Massey – called before dawn to tell me a person of interest had escaped the prison out in Midland. I need a tracker to find the guy."

He shoved his chair back and stood. Hmmm. Amber eyes and broad shoulders, a chest that narrowed down to a trim waist. Oh, just hold on a cotton-pickin' minute. She had to stop that train of thought before it departed the station. The man was annoying, and her boss. Who cared how nice he looked in those jeans? Not her, no way. She caught herself humming. Startled by his sly grin, Jo cut off the hum in mid-tune.

"Shouldn't that be the sheriff's job?"

"Hmm?"

"Finding a tracker, Jo. Shouldn't the sheriff's office do the leg work in finding an escaped convict?"

"Duke knows how personal this is for me. We're working on it together. That's one question. What's the next one?"

He leaned toward her, his hands bracing his upper body on the hardwood desk. Beneath his wide, calloused hands, the wood gleamed bright, and her eyes traced his sun-darkened forearms to his shoulders. His gaze pinned her, and unwanted butterflies danced in her middle. She swallowed a knot the size of her fist, felt it land with an ominous thump.

"I'll save my other question for a later date, Jo."

Oh, boy. "I'd rather concentrate on saving my forge."

"My forge, you mean?" he clarified.

His matter-of-fact attitude dumped buckets of cold water on her daydreams. "Yeah, *your* forge." A stone expressed more emotion. "Our best bet lies in scrap metal. American tariffs increase daily, both on the steel and the import tax. We need to get creative, because we can't keep up with politicians."

He choked out a half-laugh and she shot a questioning look at him.

"Nothing," he responded. "Inside joke. What kind of metal are we looking to scavenge?" He paced the meager room, motioned for her to answer.

"Scavenge seems like such a harsh word. I prefer … reclaim. Yes, much better."

"Reclaim, whatever. Do you know what you'd be looking for in the heaps we'll find?"

"The short answer is, yes. The long answer? Depending on the job we need different kinds of steel and iron. Cutlery demands a higher carbon content than shoe irons."

He stopped pacing, halting a hair's breadth behind her. Reaching over her shoulder, he brought a file to life on the airscreen. His warm breath tickled the back of her neck, and she abruptly ducked beneath his outstretched arm to stand beside him. Did she imagine his sigh? Was it disappointment or relief?

And why was she asking herself these stupid questions? *His* forge, remember?

"This file shows the orders you have yet to fill, the ones outstanding before your debt collection spree. Now," he paused, "if we can verify your customers still need the goods, we will base our metal reclamation on those orders initially. While you were out I researched landfill and recycling locations."

"How did my file get on your system?"

"I transferred everything while you were out."

Narrowing her eyes, she pointed at him. "It was password protected."

83

"And for someone who admits to working with military computer systems, it was pathetically weak."

Heat suffused her cheeks, and irritation toed the anger line in her already frazzled brain. She lived in Coleville, population 437, for goodness' sake.

It galled that he was right.

"Well, Bossman, guess you need to call some customers."

He blinked. Blinked again, mouth gaped open.

"I figured you would handle the calls, Jo," he began. "I've got horses to shoe and hooves to inspect."

"I'm the blacksmith, not the receptionist."

"Now, wait just a minute …"

Her wrist communicator chimed and she beamed, turning away from her new employer. The small, circular screen indicated Duke was calling. She tapped the ear icon on the screen to direct the call to the nearly invisible earpiece.

"The list you sent me is crap."

"Good to hear your voice again, too," she laughed. "What do you mean, crap? They all possess high ratings in the private and government sector."

"Let me handle this one, all right? I know a guy."

Breathe in, breathe out, she commanded herself. She loved Duke like a salty old uncle, but she had the bit in her teeth and she was ready to ride.

"Are you grinding your teeth again?" His voice seemed amused. She unclenched her jaw and rolled her eyes, thankful he couldn't see it at the moment.

"Fine. Call your guy, find out the soonest he can be out here. But, I swear, Duke, if he —"

"Four hours."

"Four hours, what?"

"He will be in Coleville in four hours."

Deep breaths, Jo. In and out. "And he's good?"

"The best man hunter I know, God's honest truth. Worked with him some during his time in the army, helped him track down a couple of deserters. There's, um, a catch."

There it was. Too good to be true, she knew it. "What?"

"He's bringing his wife."

"That's it?"

Duke chuckled on the other end. "Yeah. I told him to meet us at the station at five."

Cullen stared at her from the other side of the blocky desk, not bothering to hide his curiosity. She rolled her eyes, and he chuckled.

"Oh, and tell your new boss to be there, too," Duke added.

She was going to kill the old man one day. "Any particular reason why?"

"He has connections." And with that bewildering statement, the deputy ended the call.

Rather than engage Cullen in deep and meaningful conversation, she aimed for the smithy. Long strides took her through the door and into the dim light of the cold forge. She threw open the shuttered windows set in wood-planked walls. Wan light slanted through dusty, grimy glass; motes lazily congregated in the weak sunbeams. Her father's voice echoed from the dream, telling her she was doing it all wrong. It was a rare thing, to dream of Daddy. She could count on one hand the times, and each one had been profound, striking her to the core.

She felt Cullen behind her, but didn't turn.

"My daddy was a blacksmith during the time of the Second Secession. These tools?" she asked, running a hand over a heavy hammer, a set of tongs. "He made them by hand, forged them from reclaimed iron found who knows where, soon after The Collapse. He said working with his hands brought him close to the Creator. When he was able to use his gift in the army on behalf of The Republic, he felt gratitude. Can you imagine?"

She blew the dust from the workbench, wiped a clean swathe with her hand. It came away black.

"He was practically a kid in the army, but he was one of the best blacksmiths they had. Neal Camden worked his way from private to a commissioned officer, eventually running the ironworks within ten years. After he left the service, he opened Camden Ironworks. When he died, the shop passed to his brother, Uncle Charlie. I learned the trade from him. Guess you could say this place is in my blood."

From the doorway, she heard shuffling feet. Turning, she caught a fleeting look of sympathy, gone in the blink of an amber eye.

"All I've seen are the horseshoes from the tack room, but they're fine work. I can attest to that. I know you'll continue to make them proud."

"But will they? I lost this place, Cullen. Fought tooth and nail to keep it, but it was gone like the heat from a quenched blade."

Slowly, he ambled toward her. With his thumbs tucked in his pockets, he managed to appear sullen and sultry at the same time. He stopped about a foot in front of her, tipped up her chin gently with the end of his forefinger.

"You'd make them proud, Joleigh."

Averting her eyes, she laughed to both lighten the mood and distract his attention. She sounded the retreat and eased out of his reach.

"And what about you?"

"Hmm?"

"Duke said you have connections. What did he mean by that?"

A cloud hazed over his eyes, and this time he looked away, picked up a set of tongs and tapped them against his other hand.

"Family, that's all."

Growling, she snatched the tool from his hand. "That's it? I practically give a speech, and you answer with three words?"

"You don't want to hear about me now, Jo. My personal life is of no concern now. Let's concentrate on finding your tracker. Which you still didn't say *why* you needed one."

"I don't recall being asked," she pointed out, smug.

"I'm saving my other question. I figured I'd find out soon enough."

She eyed him with her head cocked to the side, tipped up a half smile. "And so you will. At five o'clock tonight. Are you going to answer my question about your family?"

"Not yet. Trust me, you don't want to know."

Jo sniffed, then lightly punched him in the stomach. Her fist met a slab of muscle, and she stifled an astounded grunt.

"And *you* don't want to tick off this country girl."

She left him to turn off the lights, and lock up. If the boss wanted accounts, he could hop up onto on his high horse and go find them. Surely the man was able to charm the customers with his trademark grin and cocky swagger. It was his business now. She would let him sweat it out.

Jo was a blacksmith, not a receptionist.

Chapter 12

Four hours to kill.

She could ride home, piddle around the house. Or maybe walk over to the library and pick out a good suspense novel. Maybe a historical fiction? Peaches, the sassy bespectacled librarian, had told her about a Collapse-era novel with rave reviews when she detoured there earlier on the hunt for web access.

Jo stood at the wooden corral with a boot hiked up on the lowest rail, watching Kase idly nibble at the saltlick. A few flies buzzed around the dun mare's rump, but her tail diminished the nuisance with a few lazy flicks.

The early summer sun warmed the back of her neck, the heat penetrating her skin and soothing tired muscles. Her bare shoulders began to tingle as well, and she was glad she had thrown on a tank top instead of a t-shirt. A farmer's tan was inevitable, but today her upper arms soaked up the sun. Kase bobbed her long face as if to say it was too hot, and ambled over to the shade of the tall oak on the far side of the enclosure.

Four hours.

Aloud, she said to the mare, "I think I'll go for a walk."

Kase blew her approval with an equine raspberry and nodded her head, then returned to swishing away the flies.

Jo backtracked along the dusty alley nestled between the smithy and Ed Berry's laundry business, the Wash-n-Go. Folks told Eddie his idea was a lost cause this far away from the city, but doggone if he didn't prove everybody wrong. Not only had his fledgling venture survived, it flourished in the three years since he opened the sparkling glass doors.

She had to kick herself in the pride to not be envious of his success while her family's business was now in the hands of a city-boy outsider.

Turning left, she passed in front of the laundry and waved to Eddie. He dropped the pair of socks he was folding and waved back, a wide grin on his narrow face.

Coleville barely rated a tiny black dot on the Texas map. In fact, the one intersection in town required no stoplight because there were rarely two vehicles on the road at any given time. From space, the SatNet showed the plus sign shape of the two main thoroughfares, Silver Street and Sam Houston Avenue. A string of businesses lined both roads, their buildings squished against one another. Window awnings fluttered in the breeze, and hand-painted shingles swayed on their chains. A few of those chains were Jo's first jobs as an apprentice.

Which made her think of Camden Ironworks and its cold, neglected forge. She longed for the weight of the hammer in her hand, the blast of a stoked fire, and hiss of the quench. And even though she clung to the resolve to be no one's secretary, she found herself walking beneath the tinkling welcome bell of Jerry's Handy Hardware.

"Jo! Hang on a sec, girl, and I'll be right with you," Jerry exclaimed from behind the register. He measured out a brown bag of something clanky, screws or nails if she had to guess. It plopped down on the scale with a jangly thump. Two bags followed the first. Pete Johnson, the local carpenter, hummed a tune as he walked away from the counter, bags in one hand, and tipped his cap at Jo as he passed alongside her.

"See ya, Pete."

"Mm-hmm," came his typical reply.

Jerry slapped both hands on the wooden countertop. "Girl! I keep meaning to come over and talk a spell, but business picks up in waves. Sure am sorry to hear about the buy-out."

"Yeah, me too."

Her gaze passed over the neat rows of hardware, racks of tools, rolls of solar skins, windmill parts and accessories.

"Looks like you're low on garden tools, Jerry."

"That I am. After your shop was bought out, I tried to get a supplier out of Bryan. His price was quadruple what you quoted me six weeks ago!"

"Price of steel and import taxes are killing the smalltime blacksmiths, plain and simple."

He shook his salt and peppered head, a sad smile on his face. "I ain't gonna order international, and that's all there is to it."

Jo grinned at the shopkeeper. "I may have a solution, if you're interested."

"I'm listening." He leaned forward on his hands, a co-conspirator gleam in his eyes.

"If I can get your original order to you in two weeks, will you give the order to me?"

His eyebrows climbed high, striving to reach the retreating hairline. "You bet! But I didn't know you had another place lined up."

"You're looking at Camden Ironworks newest employee," she laughed. "Sad, but true. And Cullen and I have a new iron source. We need a few days to scout, but I can get that order to you in two weeks. We got a deal?"

Jerry shoved his hand out across the counter, and she grasped it firmly.

"You make your daddy proud, Jo."

Her cheeks were embarrassingly rosy when the bell tinkled her departure, but she hardly gave it much thought. She had landed an account. Bossman would grin, and that chin dimple of his would cave in on itself.

She shaded her eyes with a hand, and contemplated downtown Coleville. A sly grin drew up a corner of her mouth, and determination quickened her step.

She had work to do.

Three hours later, Jo corralled her mare. She stood, stretching in the late afternoon heat, working out muscles and listening to her joints pop and crack. Her booted feet hurt from walking and her butt was saddle sore, but she sauntered into the office with a broad smile on her pinked face. The room was dark, devoid of the new boss. She exhaled a relieved breath.

She quickly typed up the orders, logging them into the record system. More than a little disappointed that Cullen had taken his high-tech system with him to the inn, she plugged away on what felt like ancient equipment. It served its purpose, and she would make do. For now.

The numbers widened her grin. She knew she had made the right choice, visiting clients one-on-one. Eating crow sat heavy in her stomach at first, but as the orders flowed in she found that she could swallow her stiff pride if it meant getting the coins pouring in again.

But she still refused to think of herself as Cullen Miles' gopher.

Her wrist communicator glowed 4:45 as she filed the last commission, a decorative scrollwork gate for one of the larger houses in town. Shoving back from the desk, she stood and grabbed the photo of her and her dad. She laid a work-roughened finger alongside his face, trying to remember his voice, his smell. Those faded, over time. But today, after the dream this morning, he seemed more alive in her memory than ever before. Gently, she replaced the framed photograph.

"I'll make it right, Daddy. For you and for Uncle Charlie, for Mama and Ginny. I'll make it all right."

She switched off the light, locked the door. Foot traffic downtown had picked up closer to suppertime. Horses clip-clopped down the paved streets, and conversation buzzed in the air. Sunlight reflected off a jeweled necklace across the street, its owner harried and rushed as she was pulled forward by a boy about four years old, and tugging a toddler girl busying herself studying the stones on the ground. Phew! The thought of children at her age, this close to forty, boggled the mind and gave her hints of a panic attack. But the sunlight bouncing off the cut crystal around the child's neck reminded her of her own talisman, the aquamarine hanging on a leather thong around her neck.

Pulling it out from under her shirt, she fingered the smooth blue stone, its edges familiar and reassuring. Just as she was replacing the gem beneath her shirt once more, an old woman turned the corner. She walked slowly, her white hair hanging in a silvery sheet. The woman appeared ancient, and something about her tugged at Jo's mind. As if this had happened once before.

Her. The old woman, the one that grabbed her necklace as a child. She still heard the gravelly voice telling her she had a long journey ahead, that the stone would lead her to truth. Her mother had scooted her along at the time, but the encounter had shaken nine-year-old Jo to the core.

And now, almost thirty years later, the woman approached, her leathery lines surrounding sparkling eyes that seemed to know too much, to see more than she should.

Jo swallowed as the woman approached and stopped before her. The short-lived daydream of passing by unnoticed fled in a puff of imagination.

She was short, but not bent. More diminutive than in her child's mind.

"What you seek you will not find, until you find the one who loved you first," she said. As direct as always.

"How do you know me?" Jo asked.

"I speak for The One that knows us all, Joleigh Agnes Camden. Your journey begins today. Seek your first love."

Her feet felt as though they were encased in concrete, and she could do nothing but watch as the wrinkled lady continued down Silver Street. She never looked back.

Jo, on the other hand, shook herself out of her stupor. Her boots pounded the sidewalk harder than necessary, and she was gasping for breath as she opened the door to the sheriff's department.

"Duke, you're not going to believe what just happened," she began, before running headlong into a human slab of wall.

She looked up, then up some more, and found a ruggedly kind face smiling down at her.

Hesitantly, she edged a look around the giant's midsection, to find Duke laughing hysterically on the far side of the room. She narrowed her eyes at the audacity, and was just about to give him a piece of her mind, but Duke waved at her. It was all he could do, considering how hard he was guffawing. He wiped his eyes, rested his hands on his knees, then looked up and took a deep breath.

"Jo," Duke said, "I'd like you to meet your tracker."

She took two steps back to get the proper perspective before she gave herself a crick in the neck. He had to be the most enormous man she had seen in her life. Brilliant green eyes shone from a smiling face, and he stuck out his hand in greeting.

"Ben Tucker," he said. "Nice to meet you, Miss Camden."

The giant stepped aside, and a woman with a mess of red hair piled on top of her head grinned from behind him. She elbowed him in the side, and he grunted.

"And this is Cora, my wife."

"I'm very happy to meet you, Jo," his wife said. "I've been looking forward to a little vacation." She wasn't from around here with that accent.

The tracker's wife scooped up a chubby, red-headed baby girl. Plopping her on a hip, Cora said, "And this munchkin is Kate." The baby shoved a fat hand in her mouth and gnawed on it until drool flowed down her wrist, babbling all the while.

"Well," Jo remarked. "This ought to be an adventure."

Chapter 13

As Jo came to grips with the enormity of the tracker, the door behind her opened and clicked shut with a sigh. She knew without turning around the newcomer to the precinct office was Cullen. The audacious man needed to learn the concept of personal space. His warm breath coasted over her shoulder in peppermint waves.

"What'd I miss? And who's the colossus?"

Angling her face over her shoulder, she replied, "Ben Tucker. My new tracker."

"Our tracker. I'm going to see this through with you."

"Personal space, *Mister* Miles. If you please."

He grunted a laugh. "It's personal to me. You're my most valuable asset in a new business venture. It is in my best interest to make sure you are safe."

It was her turn to chuckle. "I meant, back up. You're fogging up my neck."

"Oh."

"But it's good to know you value your assets." When she heard the flirt in her voice, she cringed. Not good. Not good at all.

"Your wish is my command, oh warrior blacksmith," he said, brushing past her. His cotton sleeve grazed her bare, sun-pinked arm. A whiff of woodsy cologne skated by on the air.

Her eyes rolled heavenward, and Cullen stuck out his hand in greeting. To Ben's side, his wife grinned and skillfully raised a brow. Cora tilted her head back and to the side in a come-hither motion, and Jo was all too happy to get away from the testosterone cloud floating around the sheriff's station. Duke sidled over to the men, scratching the scruff on his face, then hooking a thumb into a pocket. The three put their heads together. The deep bass rumble sounded like a hive of bumblebees.

"Your boyfriend?" Cora asked when they reached the two desks on the other side of the room.

"What? No! He's my boss. At least, I let him think that."

"Oh, sorry. You two look so good together, and have this chemistry. I just assumed …"

Jo cast a glance at Cullen, who seemed dwarfed by the tracker. Chemistry, huh?

"Your husband is quite …"

"Large?" Cora laughed, juggling the baby on her hip. "Yes, he is most definitely massive."

"You two been married long?"

"A little over a year. Kate came along pretty quick, but we were both over the moon for her. I'm a midwife. Having no children was a bit like always being the bridesmaid and never the bride. Although I now view labor and delivery more intimately."

Cora glowed, had an almost surreal presence of joy, and it lightened Jo's mood.

"Being a mother seems to suit you well."

The woman's grin split her face. "Thank you! It's the hardest thing I've done, and that is saying something."

Ben's voice boomed from behind. "What scheme are you two women-folk cooking up over there?"

"Don't you wish you knew, honey?" Cora teased, winking at Jo. Joyful, definitely. She wished she knew the midwife's secret to happiness.

Duke's footsteps echoed off the dark hardwood floor as he strode to his desk. He grabbed a thin tablet from the desktop, and passed it to Ben.

"I pulled up Roy Milligan's file," he began. "It's a place to start. But Jo, you should fill Ben in on the personal history you have with the lowlife."

She studied the wall of people ringing her, shoulder to shoulder. To put her history, her trust, into the hands of strangers? The only exception was the gnarled deputy.

Duke, more family than friend, grizzled and steadfast. Her rock for countless years.

But what of the others? There was Cullen, in her life for four annoyingly frustrating days, who vacillated between flirtation and unwarranted possessiveness and bossiness in the blink of his long-lashed amber eyes. He avoided her probes into his personal life, as if he were protecting her from that side of him. What did he have to hide?

And now, the Tuckers. Jo glanced at her wristcom. Ten minutes. She had known Ben and Cora for ten minutes. Yet Duke asked her to open the door to the thorny labyrinth of her personal history with Roy Milligan.

The graying deputy walked over to her, gripped her shoulder with an arthritis-tormented hand. Looking her in the eye, he said, "I trust them, girl. All of them." With a last, gentle squeeze, he turned and stood beside her. She drew courage from his proximity.

With a deep inhale, she began her story.

"I was eleven years old when Roy Milligan killed my sister."

The hiss of cooled air exiting the wall registers dominated the sound in the room. All eyes settled on her in a mixture of reactions. Pity from Cora, sadness from Ben. Cullen seemed ... furious. She turned to Duke, and he gave her an encouraging nod.

"My mother married Roy Milligan when I was ten, just a year after my father died of a sudden heart attack."

She recalled Mama sitting her and Ginny down on the front porch, telling them she was marrying a nice man and he would be their stepfather. Jo cried, because she still missed her father. Ginny, on the other hand, had very little memory of their dad, and seemed happy. Mama said the man's name was Roy, and he would help provide for them, make life a little easier.

"Ginny was seven. She had been picking wild onions in the meadow near the house."

Jo could still smell the sweet aroma in the air.

"Mama had this white milkglass vase her mother had passed to her. I was upstairs reading in my room when Ginny came running up the stairs, her bare feet slapping the hardwood stairs. I heard the commotion, and tried to get to her before she woke up Roy. He had been sleeping off a binge from the night before."

She had tip-toed past him half an hour before to grab an apple from the kitchen. His foul-smelling breath filled the room, his open-mouth snores sawing through the silence of their home.

"But when I got out to the landing, Roy had stumbled up after her, yelling and shaking her."

Ginny's eyes were as round as saucers, tears dripping soundlessly as her stepfather shook her.

"She had put the wildflowers in mama's white vase. I think she was going to put them by mama's bed as a gift. I don't know. I'll never know."

Jo threw herself against Roy, tried to distract him from Ginny. He slapped her away, slamming her backwards, and with a hand still bunched in her little sister's dress, Roy shoved her head back into the wall several times. She must have blacked out for a few seconds.

"He shook her and shook her until she dropped the white vase. It shattered on the floor, spilling water and tiny white flowers all over Roy's feet. With a last push, he knocked Ginny down the stairs."

Her baby sister's scream still echoed in the depths of her memory, lived in a scarred and barely scabbed over wound in her brain. It was buried with the thumping sound of Ginny's body and head hitting the wooden stairs and handrail.

"I stared at the white shards by Roy's feet. I can remember the pattern the spilled water made, even to this day. I couldn't move." She swallowed, her throat dry and painful. "I just ... couldn't move. Couldn't speak. Couldn't scream."

His eyes floated in front of her own. In her memory, they are red, glaring like fire.

"He got in my face, told me if I ever told anyone what happened, he would kill me too. But he said he would make me watch him kill my mother first."

Screams from the bottom of the stairs. Her mother's wails high in the air, floating up the steps. And yet, Jo said nothing.

"Somehow I made it to the first floor. I don't know how. I heard Roy tell my mother Ginny fell down the stairs, that he tried to catch her but he missed."

Ginny's crumpled body laid cradled in her mother's arms, tears streaming down her mother's blotchy face. Roy had his arm around her mother, consoling her. He had narrowed his eyes at her and placed a finger against his lips, reminding her to be quiet.

"We buried Ginny under the century oak in the yard. Her death was ruled an accident with no one to provide a witness otherwise."

Duke appeared at her side with a glass of ice water, and she nodded her gratitude. He picked up where Jo stopped, and she loved him for it.

"Jo didn't speak for over a year," the deputy said. "Not a word. To anyone."

When had the others sat down? They all faced her, stunned expressions on their faces.

Her throat soothed by the cool liquid, Jo continued. "My mother died two years after Ginny from an aggressive cancer. My aunt and uncle raised me after that. Roy disappeared from our lives."

Ben shifted in his chair. "How soon after your mother married him did the abuse start?" he asked.

"Ben!" Cora exclaimed.

Jo cleared her throat. "It's okay. He's right. It was about a month after they married. I noticed bruises on my mother's arms. She started complaining about how klutzy she was, said she was running into things like doors. The day he killed Ginny wasn't the first time he had shaken and pushed us around. I knew how angry he would be if Ginny woke him up that day. It was why I tried to reach her first." Her voice broke at the end, and Duke enveloped her in a tight hug.

Cullen shoved back, his chair ricocheting off the wall. He paced the short distance between the desks and the front door. Finally, he halted, his jaw working around clenched teeth, his fists balled up at his sides. "And now he's escaped from prison? Why was he locked up?"

"Like I said, I went to live with my dad's brother and wife after mama died. One day I was talking with my aunt while we were making biscuits, and I let it slip. That Roy had pushed Ginny. Since he couldn't threaten my mother anymore, and I lived with my uncle – he was a big man, really big – I told them the story. They went to Duke, and I made an official statement. It didn't do much good at the time. No one knew where he was. But the warrant was issued for his arrest, nonetheless. Six months later, he was picked up for a bar fight in Austin."

"You testified against him?" Cullen asked, his eyebrows raised. "How old were you?"

"Fifteen."

Cora dabbed at a tear. Kate was asleep in her mother's arms, a thumb plugging her bow-shaped mouth. The midwife looked down at her child, then up to Jo's gaze. "It's no small feat to face the one who hurt you in a courtroom. Must have been hard for you."

"Not as hard as I thought it would be. I was angry, so very angry. I wanted him to suffer, and I still do. Death would be too easy for the man, as far as I'm concerned."

Duke added, "He was sentenced to life in prison. The man Milligan beat in the bar fight later died of his injuries. There were plenty of witnesses to the altercation. With the murder of Ginny Camden also brought to light, the jury convicted him in record time."

"A lot of good it does now that he's escaped." Jo failed to keep the bitterness from her tone.

Ben looked up from the tablet. His large hands dwarfed the handheld system. "Why was he in Midland? That's a medium-security work farm."

Duke snorted, disdain painted across his sun-roughened face. "He spent the first twenty years in Huntsville. He was released to Midland because of 'good behavior'. Plus, Huntsville needed the bed he occupied. He's been at the work farm the last three years."

Jo craned her neck as Ben stood. He pulled a palm-sized gizmo from his rear pocket, and held the two devices touching at the ends. Passing the larger one to Duke, he said, "I'll study his file tonight on my palm reader. Would it be okay if I came in tomorrow sometime to use your system? You would have access to more information, state records and whatnot, which I don't have clearance for."

Cullen spoke up. "Don't bother with Duke's system. It's a dinosaur." Duke barked a laugh and nodded. Her boss continued. "You're staying at the inn?"

Ben nodded and cocked his head to the side.

"Come over to 5B whenever you want, use my SatNet system," Cullen offered. "I have the clearance you need."

The gargantuan tracker rubbed his jawline. "I swear I know you from somewhere, Mr. Miles. Have you ever lived in Austin?"

Cullen waved him off. "Probably some weird coincidence. Like I said, come over when you need to." But he didn't answer the question, and Jo noticed how he avoided Ben's eyes.

The group began to mingle, and the baby awoke with a startled cry. Talk of supper caused her stomach to rumble, and she realized she hadn't eaten since breakfast. Hands were shaken, and boots headed to the door. Cullen avoided Ben, keeping his back to him and making small talk with Duke. He looked up and winked. She rolled her eyes in return, but she couldn't help the tiny grin that crept across her face. The man was a charmer.

But he was hiding something.

Chapter 14

Miss Ruby's chicken fried steak tasted as good in the common room of the boarding house as it did perched at her old fashioned countertop in the café. The flecked white gravy spilled over the crispy browned breading, nudging the mashed potatoes. He groaned aloud, savoring the fabulous dish. Green beans added color on the side. Most likely, the bacon grease they cooked in negated the health benefits of the vegetable.

Cullen didn't care. It was all he could do to keep the drool from leaking down his chin.

"I'm going to tell Dixie you're cheating on her, Benjamin," Cora teased from across the small, square table. To Cullen, Cora said, "Dixie owns the café in Cotton Springs."

"Don' oo dare," he managed around a mouthful. Swallowing, he issued an appraising look at Cullen. "How do you not weigh three hundred pounds? This is amazing."

"I've only been here a few days, so give it time." Cullen grinned, then shoved a forkful of mashed potato goodness into his mouth.

Cora balanced the plump baby on one knee, and alternated feeding herself and little Kate. The wee redhead seemed to enjoy the potatoes as well as the larger coppertop. "A few days?"

He gave her and Ben a rundown of the last few days, explaining how he arrived in Coleville and met his feisty new employee. In between bites, that is. A man had priorities. He paused in the story as Ben held up a fork.

"Let me get this straight," the tracker said. "Your first day in town, you get sweet tea dumped in your lap by the former owner of your new business. You arrive at said woman's house to find the aftermath of a break-in, then you shoe her horse, and take shelter during a tornado in her storm cellar?"

"Yep." He looked down at his plate and groaned when his fork scraped the empty space where the steak used to be. "She didn't get the call about Milligan's escape until early this morning. We're pretty sure he wasn't behind the break-in. But there was a threat pinned to the wall. Duke told me about it."

"Hang on." Ben pulled out his palm reader, scrolled through images until he found a photo. Holding it up to Cullen, he asked, "This the one?"

A sharp-looking kitchen knife, the kind chef's employed, jutted out from the wall, its blade a gleaming menace against a flowered wallpaper background. On the plain white square of paper were the words, *WHERE IS IT?*

"Any thoughts on the B&E?" A disappointed look flitted across Ben's face when he realized that his plate, too, was empty. Cora gently patted his hand with a smirk across her face.

"Buried treasure."

Cora's eyes widened, and Ben coughed, slapping a fist against his chest. "Say again," he managed when he gained his breath.

"Jo thinks it has something to do with buried treasure."

Cullen filled him in on the legend of the gold miner. Ben ran a hand across his face, sighing. "This case gets more interesting by the minute."

"You're telling me."

"What's your stake in all this, if you don't mind me asking? I know I recognize you from somewhere, and finding things is my business. You may as well spill it and be done with it."

Cullen got the distinct impression that his clever smile and confident smirk wouldn't work on the giant in front of him. Or on his wife, if he were being honest. With a twist of his mouth, he pushed back from the table, rocked his wooden dining chair on its hind legs.

"How familiar with politics are you?"

Ben snapped his fingers and pointed at Cullen. "Austin. I knew it. Hang on, hang on."

He let the man chew on the puzzle for a few moments. He watched Ben, and Cora watched Cullen. The two were a formidable pair. "Cullen *Miles?* Miles, as in Secretary of State Sterling Miles?"

"Good ole Daddy." He mock-toasted the tracker with his sweet tea.

Ben whistled through his teeth. "Your father is …"

"Hardheaded? Arrogant? Conceited?"

"I was going to say powerful. What are you doing out here in the sticks?"

Cullen's front chair legs thumped to the floor with a sudden clomp. "Exactly the reason, right there! Everyone expects me to be in Austin, clinging to my father's heels like my sister and brother do. Me? I want a life I create, not one that was handed to me at birth."

Cora spoke up while she mashed green beans into pulp with her fork. "Why hide it from Jo?"

"She has too much drama going on in her life at the moment to deal with the fact that it's my father in direct negotiations with the American Secretary of State concerning import and export tariffs. It's because of the tripled price of imported steel and the additional imposed taxes that she lost Camden Ironworks in the first place."

"In other words," Cora clarified, "you don't want to stir the hornet's nest?" She smiled and fed the baby a spoonful of green beans, which promptly exited the tiny girl's mouth and landed in her mother's lap. "I think we're done here. Gonna take this little one up and get her in bed. My advice, Cullen? No good can come of waiting. Tell her the truth, and see what you can do to work things out."

"You haven't seen Jo's temper," Cullen mumbled.

Across the table, Ben beamed a crooked smile. "I'm married to a redhead. Need I say more?"

When they left the deputy's office, Jo said she needed time to unwind and process the events of the last few days. How could he blame her? His head spun, and his involvement paled in comparison to hers. What did she do to relax? Read a book, or listen to classical music, maybe. Go for a ride and watch the sunset?

He caught himself as he wondered if she had a favorite poet. Sunset horse rides and poetry? Cullen swept a hand across the evening stubble on his face. The woman had crawled under his skin, plain and simple. And it itched. She had no business taking up space in his mind.

"Deep thoughts?" Ben inquired. He stood and stretched. "We'll find the guy. Don't worry."

"I'm more worried about getting that dang woman out of my head."

"Ha! Can't help you there, man. If it's any consolation, she seems like a good woman to have in residence. Based on first impressions, anyway." He glanced at his watch. "I should help Cora with the baby. I'll get in touch with you first thing in the morning, and we'll tackle this case. Tonight, I plan to delve into Milligan's case file, run any leads I find there. Maybe I could use your SatNet system after breakfast?" The man ran a hand across his midsection. "I swear I'm going to gain twenty pounds from this contract. Is Ruby's breakfast as good as her supper?"

"Better. Biscuits and gravy straight from Heaven."

The immense mountain of a man groaned around a smile. "Twenty pounds, mark my words." He tipped an imaginary hat as he turned to the stairwell. "Tomorrow morning, then. I just pray that Kate sleeps tonight. She's been a little stinker lately, thinking Cora's an all-night buffet."

Cullen laughed. "A whole other world of which I know nothing about."

"You're telling me! See ya."

Though he didn't have to, he gathered the plates and silverware. In the kitchen, Cullen scraped and rinsed the white stoneware dishes, loaded them into the dishwasher. In the handful of days he had stayed at the Silver Street Inn, he could count on one hand the number of times he saw the owner, Shelley Windsor. But somehow, despite being invisible most of the time, the house remained spotless, dust-free, and homey. The antebellum-style home boasted a modern kitchen, and it reminded him of his spacious childhood home in

Austin. But do the dishes himself? No, they had servants to handle the upkeep of the mansion.

Walking up the staircase, he ran a hand over the polished mahogany banister. Fine workmanship there; and according to the brochure tossed onto the desk in the sitting room, handmade by a master woodworker in the early 1900s from single trunk. Carved by a person who loved the craft, loved to use his hands; and didn't mind the curled wood shavings covering him from head to toe, or the late nights accomplishing his goal. Did the craftsman have a family? Giggling children running through the workshop, or a wife asking him for the fifth time if he's coming to supper?

Cullen craved these things. Two doors down, Kate protested her bedtime with broken cries and jagged wails muffled by insulated walls. A tiny smile turned up the corners of his mouth as he slid his key into the lock. He imagined opening the door to a home of his own, rather than the two-room suite rented by the week. The house would be modest, he thought, solidly built. A wide front porch with matching rocking chairs at one end, and a hanging swing at the other. His children would run to meet him as the key turned in the lock, screaming, "Daddy's home!" as he swept them up. He'd look up from sloppy kisses and hugs to see his wife grinning at him from across the room. Before, in these daydreams, his fantasized spouse had generic features, almost blurred. More impressions than details.

This time, the imagined wife wore Jo Camden's face.

He blinked, and found himself in the Silver Street Inn once more. How had the woman enchanted him so? Or was this God pointing him in the direction He wanted Cullen to wander? Over the course of Cullen's life, he learned the hard way to listen to the still, small voice of the Holy Spirit when it nudged him one way or another. This *thing* with Jo, whatever it was, had the same feel.

He understood the depths of her anger, after hearing the details of her childhood. The hurt, anguish, fury, disappointment, and despair Cullen saw in her made tragic sense.

A peek at the clock showed it was too early to climb in bed, and too late for much else other than reading or watching a movie. Neither held much appeal. He flashed back to his conversation in the office. At the time it entertained him to no end to see her worked up over the notion of being a gopher. Now he felt like a heel for adding annoyance to an already difficult day. He thought he knew a way to make it up to her. With the decision made, Cullen turned off the lights and made his way down the stairs and out of the door of the Silver Street Inn.

Antique lamps lit the street, pooling yellow puddles of light every dozen paces. The tall black lamps reached fifteen feet high, with two arched arms branching off to hold globed bulbs. Like the Inn, these dated back to the early 1900s, but they weren't native to Coleville. The town didn't exist until the next century. Peaches, the diminutive librarian, handed him a book about the history of the town soon after he arrived. Photos in the book held captions that told of the streetlights being salvaged and refurbished with solar and radiant heat conversion and storage. These particular lamps once graced the Riverwalk in San Antonio.

A cool breeze kissed the back of his neck, and his footsteps echoed off the bricks of business buildings lining the downtown thoroughfare. No clip-clop of horse hooves, no sound of tires skimming across asphalt. Crickets chirped in the evening, and an owl hooted overhead. A handful of people dotted sidewalks here and there. Where they walked, muted laughter and conversation drifted in their wake.

He could just make out the hanging shingle for Camden Ironworks ahead. All he needed was the leather-bound book where Jo kept her handwritten orders. Tonight he planned to transfer her archaic bookkeeping to his high-tech system. Tomorrow, he would visit each of the customers in person and ask for their continued patronage. His keys jangled in the still night air as he pulled them from his pocket.

A line of light showed between the window sill and the pulled shade. Jo must have forgotten to turn off a light. Well, he would address energy conservation another time. With one hand he inserted the key into the lock, and with the other took hold of the doorknob.

The door opened an inch under the pressure of his grip. Cullen narrowed his eyes. Surely she remembered to lock the door. He exhaled loudly through his nostrils, bit back the annoyance.

Inside the office, he found papers scattered across the floor. Jo's outdated viewscreen lay shattered atop the papers. Alarm bells rang in his head. He quickly tapped the emergency button on his wristcom, which activated his positioning system beacon.

"Sheriff's station. What is your emergency?"

"My office has been robbed."

Cullen turned in a circle, taking in the destruction. The violation.

"Address please?"

"It's Camden Ironworks. Cullen Miles. I need —"

Standing in the dark shadow behind the door was a man. He doubted he would have seen him if it hadn't been for the low glow of the shop light streaming through the office door.

"Hey!"

Before another word could escape his lips, the intruder raised something long, black, and menacing.

And then darkness descended with a sickening thunk.

Chapter 15

Shadows stalked the bobbing light from Kase's breastplate lantern. Leaves flickered and danced on their illuminated branches as they galloped along the path; but the darkness encroached, tendrils of gloom infiltrating the gaps and spaces where the glow halted. They threatened to weave their way into Jo's heart, black fingers of fear clutching at her chest as she rode headlong into Coleville.

Duke's alarming call came as she was settling onto the couch, a whodunnit in one hand and a cup of hot cocoa in the other. Her skin had crawled in response to the jagged edge to his voice. She had saddled Kase before her mind registered what her body was doing.

Jo ran the horse faster than necessary through the narrow winding trail extending from her house near Copperas Creek to the main road outside Coleville. The night air was astringent against her face. She slapped at mosquitoes and gnats, spat a few out, as her heels thumped the mare. Her heart beat in rhythm with the thunder of hooves.

Why Cullen? Anger bubbled and simmered low in her stomach. The anger she understood. He was innocent, had no history with the psycho who used to be her stepfather. But the fear that clenched her heart?

Was she afraid of losing a man she barely knew? The knowledge unsettled her nearly as much as knowing Roy was on the loose. Cullen Miles irritated her like a burr under a saddle. She didn't like him, couldn't stand that pretty-boy smirk of his. Sure, he had those amber eyes that sparkled when he needled her. All the more reason to not care a lick what happened to the fool.

The dirt path ahead transitioned to a gravel road, and soon she was over the bridge and onto Sam Houston Avenue. Shod hooves echoed hollowly, the sound bouncing to and fro against the now closed stores and shops. Ahead, Duke's patrol truck jutted diagonally across the road in front of the smithy, its headlights glowing. The red and blue strobes were blessedly dim. Ben Tucker stood half in the doorframe of the store, his head and shoulders leaning awkwardly outward, angled toward the street. He motioned to her as she drew near, and Jo flung herself out of the saddle before Kase had a chance to halt. Ben's jaw resembled knotted ropes, and he rubbed the back of his neck. Her stomach flip-flopped under her heart.

Who was she kidding? She was the fool.

"Is he …?"

"He's conscious." An arm the size of a tree trunk blocked her way into her office. His hesitation was transparent.

"But?"

"But unless you're okay with the sight of blood, I would wait a few minutes."

She balled her fists and leveled a look at the tracker. Jo didn't care how big he was. "Move. Now."

He raised a brow, but removed the offending arm.

One look at Cullen laid out on the floor, in a pool of blood, had her second-guessing her determination to reach him. Jo gulped, then closed her eyes. With her mind's voice, she pleaded with God. "I know it's been a long time, Lord, but help Cullen. Please."

She opened her eyes, and blinked to focus them. Cora looked up at Jo from her position at Cullen's head. The red-headed physician held a wad of bloody cotton gauze close to his left ear. Cora nodded with a frown to the open field bag beside her knee. A suture kit awaited, the light reflecting menacingly off the steel needles, forceps, and tiny scissors.

Schooling her thoughts into a cold hardness, she attempted to assess the scene through unemotional eyes. Because if she failed to do so, it would take Duke, Ben, and a platoon of Marines to hold her. But calm and cool, or all fired up, she would exact revenge for the man lying at her feet.

"Jo?" Cullen's voice rasped in the stillness of the night.

She fell to her knees at his side. "What happened?"

"Man. Behind door. Then nothing."

Duke sat in the leather chair behind her desk. "Cullen was reporting a break in with dispatch at the time of his attack."

Looking around the room, she noticed the scattered papers; on the desk, the wreckage of her decimated viewscreen system. Books heaped in careless piles on the floor. Desk drawers gaped ajar, their contents spilled or spilling out.

The vandal had hit her office, too.

"Did he get a good look at the guy?" Jo directed her question to Duke, because Cullen had closed his eyes once more.

She swore when Duke shook his head. Cullen groaned, and Cora immobilized his head when he tried to turn it left and right. The nervous fist in her gut tightened, and she swallowed back the rage once more.

Jo pinned the deputy with a stare. "Roy?"

He shrugged. "No clue. Fits more with the breaking and entering at your place, and we're not sure if or how Milligan fits into that event yet."

"You finished here?"

"Not hardly," he snorted. "I've done the holoscan, made the visual record. Still have to look for prints, though. Waiting on the good doc to stitch up Mr. Miles, and clear him to be moved from the crime scene. I'll be here an hour more, at least. Good news is that I pulled a few shoe prints. I'd chide you for needing to sweep, but in this case it helped." He pointed at her feet. "Care to bare your sole?"

Standing, she edged around Cullen; then she turned and lifted her leg at the knee, offering the boot sole in his direction. "Shoot."

"And his?"

"Same ones."

The holographic camera made quick work of the evidence. "Not official, mind you, but I can tell you right now that the prints I found don't match either of these. Tomorrow we'll ask Cullen if he has any other shoes we should rule out. Not going to even ask you, since that's the only pair of footwear you own."

"You say that like it's a bad thing," she remarked.

"Interpret it as you will."

"You'll let me know what you find?" Anxiety edged through at the end of the question, and his face seemed to soften in response.

"That's a dumb question, Jo. Of course, I will."

Cullen moaned, and she knelt by his side once more. She hesitated, but finally reached out and took his hand in hers. "Hey, snap out of it, Boss. The doc needs to stitch you up."

His eyes fluttered, then opened. "Jo?"

"Looks like you'll have another scar, City Boy."

Cullen closed his eyes, but the corner of his mouth drew up in half a smile. "We made a deal." He rolled his lips, moistening them. "No more name calling, Miss Priss."

Behind her, Duke laughed, then slapped himself on the chest, coughing. Jo narrowed her eyes at the deputy, daring him to say more.

"So we did. How about waking up so Cora can check you out?"

Duke ambled to the door adjoining the office to the smithy. "I'm going to get busy in here, Jo. Call me if you need me. And everyone? Make as little disturbance to the scene as possible." He disappeared into the half-light of the shop, his long, pale shadow trailing him.

As Cora began her examination, Jo took the seat already warmed by the lawman. She watched as Cullen followed the slight physician's fingers in the air, saw his pupils expand and contract. After touching his nose with both hands on the first attempt, Cora declared him concussion-free.

"But I don't see how," the doctor clarified.

"Hard head," Cullen replied. He tried to sit up, and managed to get halfway there when the color bled out of his face, only to be replaced by a green tinge. Cora quickly laid him back down.

"Maybe not so fast?" She pivoted to look at Jo. "Are all men stubborn?"

119

"I'm starting to believe it is a fact."

"Hmph. Well, Cullen, I'm going to give you something for the pain, and deaden the laceration area. Unfortunately, I only have my rudimentary field kit with me. I normally use a suture gel, but silk stitches will have to work tonight."

Eight elegant stitches, and a couple dozen uttered threats and manly grunts later, Cullen sat upright on his own with the red-headed doctor in his face.

"You *will* rest. This is not a request."

Ben poked his head in through the open front door. "Trust me, just do what she says, man. And her little white poppy pills are pretty nice, too."

Cora chucked a wad of unused gauze at her husband. "Shut your yap, mister."

He mock saluted, then returned to his post as sentry with a grin on his face.

"Like I was saying, rest. These stitches come out in a week. Make sure you keep the area dry for three days, and if it gets hot to the touch or starts seeping pus, you high-tail it to me. And you're off work tomorrow."

Cullen opened his mouth to protest, but Cora jabbed a forefinger in his direction. "You're not going to argue, are you?"

His jaw clacked shut. He swallowed, then mumbled, "No, ma'am."

"Hmph. Good decision."

From the doorway, Ben interjected, "Told ya!"

Cora arose, knuckled her back. "I think I'm done here." She handed Jo a small, amber glass vial with a cork stopper. "Give this to him once he's settled in his room."

"Me? But he's staying at … And I need to get home and … "

Though Cora looked up to Jo's height, the doctor gave the impression of looming over the blacksmith. The one raised eyebrow spoke a thousand reprimands.

"Yes, ma'am."

"Ben will get Cullen in bed, Jo," Cora clarified. "Just make sure he takes his pain medicine in an hour. The dose I gave him was only enough to take the edge off while I sewed him up."

A few minutes later, Jo watched Ben half-walk, half-tote Cullen in a modified fireman's carry down the sidewalk toward the hostel. The yellow glow of the streetlamps softened the hard lines of the duo. Sheltered in the door jamb, she felt the breeze in starts and fits; as if the town dozed, inhaling and exhaling while sweet dreams played in its slumber. When the men reached the intersection of Sam Houston Avenue and Silver Street, Cullen looked back.

His smile was a grim line across his face, but it took her breath away. Mentally, she cursed the flutter in her belly. Jo imagined a host of colorful butterflies swooping and swarming. Then, she envisioned flicking each of the quivering insects until they all either collapsed in lifeless mounds or flew off in annoyed exasperation.

See? Now she felt better.

"Jo! Get back here, girl!" She jumped when Duke's voice boomed from the smithy.

"I'm coming, old man! Hold your horses!"

Another trashed out space she would have to clean. She tried to ignore the violation in the short walk between office and shop, but the anger clawed its way up her throat despite her best efforts. Someone was going to pay for all this.

Duke stood in front of her workbench. A pegboard was mounted to the wall behind the tall surface. The black outlines of tools surrounded the implements themselves, a remnant of her father's days in the smithy. It was his little trick of keeping the place in order. The deputy jutted his chin in that direction. Every tool rested in its outlined place.

Except one.

"The one-inch ring tongs are missing."

He nodded. "Pretty sure that is what gave City Boy his new scar."

Jo snorted, saying, "Don't let him hear you call him that. We made a deal."

"So I heard."

"And the tongs aren't somewhere in the building?" she asked.

He shook his head. "I canvassed the entire place while you were mooning over your new employer."

"Hush your mouth. I most definitely do not moon."

"Hmph."

"Keep your ridiculous notions to yourself, old man."

"Don't you 'old man' me, young lady. Now, back to this nasty business. While knowing the weapon the intruder used and most likely still has in his possession is valuable knowledge, it's not the reason I called you in here."

The deputy stepped to the side. Her sharp intake of breath was the only sound.

A pristine white milkglass vase gleamed amidst the sooty blackness of the work surface.

Chapter 16

A flash of blinding white, a thousand times more brilliant than the sun at its zenith, exploded against the murky backdrop of memory. Jo saw not the interior of her beloved smithy, but a three-day growth of mangy beard through memory's unforgiving eye. Inky, soulless eyes devoid of emotion were set in a face ruddy and pockmarked by years of drug abuse. Oily, unkempt strings of hair brushing the tops of his shoulders; and the gaping hole where two upper bicuspids were knocked out in one fight or another.

She blinked, and Roy laid a grimy finger across his lips in warning.

Instead of seeing Ginny's broad grin, or the look of wonder on her face as she picked wildflowers in the meadow, she saw the visage of her murderer.

With another blink, the vision evaporated. The hate remained.

"Jo, honey," Duke pleaded. "You need to put the vase down. It's evidence."

Confused, she narrowed her eyes, then realized she clutched the vase hard enough to shatter it. Her arm was cocked, poised to throw. The deputy gingerly extended a liver-spotted hand. Jo placed the glassware in his care, then slid to the floor, a wooden post at her back.

She bowed her head over her knees, and took measured breaths. Duke remained silent.

After a few minutes, Jo croaked, "It has to be him. Roy. Who else could it be?"

His gray head bobbed in a slow nod, but his eyes told a different story. "Definitely ties Milligan to the break-in, but Jo … it doesn't *feel* right. I don't know. I'm getting old. Maybe I'm losing my touch."

"Hardly."

If she were truthful with herself, she had to admit the same thing, and she said so. "But who else knows about the vase?"

"You, me. Roy. The only other two that knew are long gone."

Sighing, the deputy rested his back against the workbench. Jo stood, paced the room. "I hate him, Duke. I really do."

"I know."

Jo paced another room-length, then stopped nearly nose-to-nose with the old grizzly bear of a man. With hands on her hips, she demanded, "Nothing else? You're not going to lecture me on forgiveness?"

"I can only preach the same sermon so many times. You know how I feel about it."

"Yeah, forgiveness will free me from hate. I remember. But the question is, what if I don't *want* to be free from the hate? What if it's all I have left?"

"Then you give Roy Milligan control over your life."

The growl erupted, ripping through her in a torrent of enmity, bitterness, and despair.

"Why?" she yelled at the ceiling. Then to Duke, "Why can't he just go away and leave me alone? Rot in his cell until the devil takes him, so I can move on with my life!"

Duke grabbed Jo by both arms, looked her in the eyes. "I don't know. What I do know is that I will not let you do this to yourself. Go home, get some shut eye. You'll feel better in the morning."

She sighed. "I can't. I'm on Cullen duty." Looking at her wristcom, she shook her head. "And I'm going to be late if I don't hustle."

The night air sank its teeth into her ruminations. A quarter-mile's walk to the bed and breakfast gave her plenty of time to both shiver, and contemplate her situation. Between making ends meet, building clientele, reclaiming scrap metal, and learning how to be an employee again, she hardly found the time to deal with normal life; much less an escaped convict bent on wrecking her home and life. And whatever Duke thought, Roy Milligan had something to do with both break-ins. She knew it.

Her boots echoed across the deserted street. She stopped beneath the glow of a lamp, its yellow beams creating a pool with her at the center. In the window of the seamstress' shop, her reflected face stared back with blackened orbs and shadowy lines. It was near this store that she met the wizened woman with the elusive warning. What was it, again?

Seek your first love. Was that truly just this morning?

Shaking herself, she continued along the sidewalk until her feet clomped up the steps to the Silver Street Inn.

A beautiful antique bureau adorned the foyer. Hand-turned legs, intricate carvings, a smooth chestnut gleam. And even more exquisite was the Dr Pepper bottle sitting on a coaster, condensation beading like diamonds. The note beside it had Shelley's loopy signature at the bottom.

You're going to need this.

Love,

Shelley

If the innkeeper were standing in front of her, Jo would have kissed her. Instead, she removed her dusty, worn-out boots and put them in the adjoining coat closet as a gesture of appreciation.

Upstairs, her feet sank into plush carpeting, and the groan of contentment escaped from her lips before she could stop it. After being in work boots all day, it was like walking on fluffy clouds of happiness. Outside the door to 5B, she wiggled her toes and rolled her shoulders. This had to be the longest day in history, and it wasn't over. 22:15 glowed on her wristcom.

Yep, going to be a longer one, yet.

With a quick rap on the door, she turned the knob, found it unlocked. She frowned at the lack of security.

"Of all the dumbest things," she muttered entering the room. She planned to give Ben a piece of her mind, but a glare from the red-headed doctor silenced her reprimand.

Cora signaled with a finger over her lips first, and pointed to the bedroom. Then she rested her hand on the stun pistol holstered at her hip. Jo raised an eyebrow in question. Cora's answer was a chin-jerk to the far side of the room where the kitchenette was situated.

"Didn't know you were licensed to carry."

"One day I'll have to tell you the story behind it. For now, let's just say that I am always prepared to defend myself," Cora answered.

"Deal. So what's going on with Cullen?"

"He's sleeping now." She turned her head in the direction of the bedroom door, which was cracked open about a foot. Glancing at her own wristcom, Cora said, "He'll need his second dose of medication in about twenty minutes. You up for an all-nighter?"

"Well, I was sort of hoping this was a sleeping post, but I'll do what it takes. I don't know why. That man chaps my hide."

Quietly, the physician laughed. "You two will make a great couple, once you get over yourselves."

"You sure you didn't get whacked on the head yourself?"

Cora grinned. "Every single morning I wake up next to my giant, I'm struck again with how much I love him. I guess you could equate the two."

"That was incredibly cheesy and adorable at the same time."

Jo leaned against the wood block countertop, crossed one foot over the other. She twisted the cap off the sweaty bottle, tossed it up and down in her palm. The bubbles burned happily on their way down her throat, and she sighed in contentment.

Cora tilted her head to the side and asked, "You ever think of having children?"

Brown fizzy bubbles spewed from her mouth, which didn't feel nearly as nice as when it went down half a second ago.

"What?!"

"Shhh! Cullen's sleeping," the doc reminded her around a smug grin.

Wiping her nose, Jo glared at Cora.

"Hey, don't get your feathers ruffled," the red-head laughed quietly. "You have nice hips for it."

"Hips?" Was this conversation really happening?

Nodding her topknot, the presumptuous midwife circled in front of her, eyed her up, down, and from the sides. "Mm-hmm. Nice, wide, baby-birthing hips. So, ever thought of settling down?"

"Who asks those kinds of questions?" Jo spluttered. "I've known you for what, half a day?"

The physician wrinkled her nose, shook her head. "Honestly, I didn't mean to offend. It's just what I do, you know? Babies and mothers, mostly. I only mentioned it because I think you would make a great mom."

Jo plunked her cold bottle on the countertop behind her, and faced the inquisition with arms crossed against her chest. "I repeat, you've only known me for half a day. And besides, you're wrong. I would be a horrible mother. Too much baggage on this train."

"You're what, early thirties? It's not too late."

"Thirty-eight, actually. But – listen, I'm not wife or mother material. I'm barely holding myself together as it is."

"Hmm. Know what I see?" Cora held up a finger. "Loyalty. You're here, tending a man you barely know because you're connected through the business, and his injury happened on your turf." She raised a second digit. "A caring nature; because, once again, you're taking care of a man you barely know."

Jo glared at the shorter woman. "And how do you know that I'm not going to poison him, knock him off to regain control of my shop?"

Cora snorted. "Unlikely, because three," she said, holding up a third finger, "you're honest. Those are all great qualities."

With a flick of her hand and an eye-roll, Jo dismissed the praise. "I'm just a hardheaded blacksmith who wants her life back. I have no intentions of marrying or birthing babies. Give me a hammer and light my forge, and I'm a happy lady."

A knock on the door blissfully halted the interrogation, and Jo jumped at the chance to escape. She was across the living room, turning the knob and swinging open the door, before she registered what she was doing. The human wall facing her could only be one person.

"Hey," Ben said, peeking his head around the threshold. "My bride still here?"

From behind, Cora answered. "Yep, but I'm on my way out."

"Good. The baby is getting all worked up. I don't have the equipment she wants."

"I swear, all I am is a milk buffet. Did you tell Shelley how much we appreciated her watching Kate a little while ago?"

Ben nodded, then jutted his chin to the bedroom door. "He's out?"

"Like a light," Cora confirmed. To Jo she said, "Here is the medistrip. Don't unwrap it until you're ready to apply it."

"In the bend of the elbow, or on the neck?"

The doctor snagged her lower lip between her teeth, thinking. "Let's go with neck. It'll hit the blood stream faster."

"Gotcha. Anything else?"

"When he wakes up, have him drink a lot of water. And think about our conversation."

Jo snorted. "I think our conversation was crazy. Y'all enjoy the rest of your night. Oh, hey, Ben?"

"Hmm?"

"Have you found anything in your research?"

"Not so far, but I think it would be a good idea to make the local rounds. Talk to residents, visit your place. You probably don't want to, but we'll need to dig through your brain to see if there were any other details you remember."

"Memory Lane, huh?" Ben nodded, and she sighed. "Okay. Knock when you're ready to head out."

After they closed the door quietly behind them, the room stilled and silence blanketed her mind. She padded across the soft carpet, pushed aside the linen curtain panel adorning the window.

Silver light danced across the tops of the squat oak and mesquite trees behind the inn. Overhead, the full moon stood sentry over the slumbering earth.

Jo placed her cheek against the cool glass pane, studied the night sky. Stars faded, humbled by the radiance of the luminous pearl hanging overhead. Not for the first time, she wondered if God still heard her cries, continued to care. Had He dismissed the earth and all creation, left them to their own destruction? Once upon a time, she had placed her trust in Him.

Once upon a time, she knew joy.

Chapter 17

"Penny for your thoughts?"

Jo spun from the window with a gasp, a hand across her heart. "Sweet Pete, you scared the heck out of me!"

"Sorry. I was thirsty."

At least he had the good sense to look sheepish. Seeing the bandage on his head caused her stomach to flop.

"Want anything?"

She shook her head, pointed to the kitchenette. "I've got a cold drink on the counter. Touch it, and you die." Jo smiled to take the sting out of the warning.

Cullen laughed. A wince and a frown followed immediately.

"The doc said you were out like a light."

With a shrug of his shoulders, and a grin on his face, he said, "I let her believe so."

"Ha! You were playing possum so she would leave you alone!"

"Guilty as charged." He opened the refrigerator, withdrew a water-filled glass carafe.

Jo watched from a few paces away, her rump resting on the back of the plush beige sofa, feet crossed in front of her. Noticing a hole in the toe of her sock, she casually re-crossed them and tucked under her big toe. She had no idea why. It wasn't like she possessed concern for the thoughts of the man filling a water glass ten feet from her.

"Why do we say that, anyway?"

"Say what?" Cullen stared at her over the lip of the clear glass.

"*Penny* for your thoughts," she clarified. "Pennies haven't been used in more than half a century."

He shrugged. "Who knows? Still wouldn't mind knowing what put that wistful look on your face."

With his head tipped back and his face skyward, he sipped the last few drops of water while ambling to the sink. The glass clinked against the porcelain coated steel. She was about to give him a whole slew of her thoughts; but he chose that moment to turn around and look at her with those amber eyes, and her mouth shut with a clack of teeth.

Then, Cullen's eyes rolled, the whites overtaking the amber, and he listed to the left. She flew across the space between them, and shoved her arms beneath his armpits just as his knees grazed the slate tile.

"Whoa! Hang on!"

But if he heard her cry, he showed no evidence. Cullen's dead weight drug her to the floor, and her body took the brunt as a makeshift cushion. Groaning, Jo rolled, easing her new boss to the floor. She kneeled beside him, checked his pulse. It fluttered beneath the third and fourth fingers. His chest rose and fell in a steady pattern.

Stubborn man faking sleep to appease the doctor, and now he was fainting like an antebellum debutante. She studied his face, tranquil in blacked out repose. Jo ran a curious finger along the silver scar jagging from his cheek through the winged laugh-lines at his temple, but yanked the offending hand toward her stomach. What was she thinking? She abhorred this conceited, business-stealing jerk.

Didn't she?

Doubt crept through the shadowy murk of resolve, chiseling away at the edges of aversion and enmity. Softened it somehow.

Jo never thought of herself as soft, and it rankled.

Enough of this. She smacked Cullen a hair above gently on the cheek opposite the wound. Once, twice, then a little harder, careful not to overdo it. His eyes fluttered open, dull pools of bourbon reflecting the light overhead.

"Did I pass out?"

"Fainted like a lovestruck female."

Cullen groaned. "Wonderful."

"Feel like getting up? It's past time for your meds anyway."

A grunt was the only answer.

"I'll take that as a yes. Come on, boss. Let's get to the sofa."

Standing, she held out a hand, planted her feet in place, and with knees bent, tugged like she was hauling in an anchor. She knew how much he weighed. He rose with a huff, faster than she planned. His face stopped a hair from her own.

Jo froze.

Cullen's breath met hers, mingled in the tense air. Electricity tingled beneath their interlocked palms. Panic set in as his features relaxed into a sultry smile. She knew that look, and she would have none of it.

Clearing her throat, she said, "You're not going to faint again, are you?"

The infuriating man didn't move a hair. And if she wasn't mistaken, he had pulled her in closer. "Not a chance," he breathed.

Her heart climbed into her throat, pulse pounding in a fight or flight rhythm. She quickly decided on both, retreating two steps and pinning him with a steady glare.

"Just what was that?"

Cullen blinked, a model of innocence. "What?"

"Don't give me *the look*," she growled. "You know, the one you tried on me the time I dumped tea in your arrogant lap." She jabbed a finger in the direction of the beige sofa. "Sit. Down."

With a cock of the head, and a slight grin, he did his best imitation of molasses and finally took a seat. He patted the cushion next to him with a questioning look.

"Not a chance, buster."

Jo kneeled a respectable distance from his seat, the medistrip lying on her outstretched hand. "This is what is going to happen. I'm going to apply this to your neck. You are going to hold still, and be a gentleman about this whole thing. After that, you are going to march yourself into the bedroom, climb in, and sleep soundly until morning when the doc comes to check on you. Got it?"

"I like it when you're bossy."

"Then you're going to abso-freaking-lutely love me by morning," she snapped. Her cheeks flared, hot and red when she realized what she said. Snarling, she peeled the backing from the medistrip, and pressed the meds where his jugular pulsed, slow and steady. Not even racing just a little, whereas hers galloped. She longed to scream like a child, yell about the unfairness of the whole situation, or complain to the universe and anyone else who would listen.

Once the longest ten seconds in history passed, Jo hastily snatched her hand away. Still experiencing the thump of his heart in her fingertips, she rubbed them against her jeans.

"It's not that distasteful," Cullen asked, with the first sign of insecurity ghosting across his features. "Is it?"

"No. Yes. Shoot, I don't know. Cullen, I can't be who you want me to be."

He leaned in again, catching her hand before she could stand. Sparks seemed to hover in the warmth of his palm. No, no, no, no.

"Jo. Please. I want us to be friends. That's all."

"Then I can't be the kind of friend you want. Now, release my hand."

Cullen sighed, disappointment turning down the corner of a mouth normally raised in amusement. It was disconcerting, and she regretted hurting him. Standing, she paced the room, her disloyal hands shoved into her pockets. Jo could almost feel the phantom sparks tracing their way along the lines on her hands. It itched. It annoyed.

And though it irked, it felt … nice.

She found herself by the window once more, drawn to the wan luminescence filtering from overhead to settle between the skeletal trunks of trees being tickled by the night wind.

"There's all this stuff," she said into the silence, fluttering a hand in the air. "Stuff in my head, needing to be worked out. Getting the shop running and producing an income, finding out who wrecked my house, putting Roy behind bars again. The only thing I'm sure of at this point is that I don't have time for relationships, of any sort."

Through the glass pane she watched a raccoon scuttle across the space between the tree line and the obscured shadowy recesses of the inn. Out of the dark, and into darkness. She had lived there, once. It felt like she walked the murky road once more; yet this time around, Jo would not succumb to the inky black bottom of the bottle.

Never again.

But the image of the half-empty whiskey bottle in the upper cupboard of her kitchen called to her, begged to be foremost in her mind. Reminded her of all the times she snuck out of the house as a teenager to drink with shady friends. It brought to life hazy memories of oblivion, of escape, during her time in the Marines. Temporary solace accompanied by a pounding head the next day, of paychecks shortened by her bottle-a-week habit. It was only a short ride to the cabin. She could finish the bottle and never buy another.

No!

She sent the crave howling with a firm mental kick. Jo wished for the thousandth time she had thrown it away, instead of keeping the half-empty container as a reminder to be strong in the face of temptation.

"Jo?" Cullen asked. When had he come to her side? "What can I do to help?"

"Nothing. There's nothing anyone can do. I'll handle it. I always do."

His calloused hand laid warm, rough heat on her bare arm. Though it sparked and sizzled, and her teeth could have ground wheat, she didn't move.

"Have you prayed, asked God what He would have you do?"

Exhaling deeply, she closed her eyes, pinched the bridge of her nose. "He's never come when I asked. Why would He now? I'm not a child anymore, Cullen. Long ago I stopped wishing God would hear me, since He ignored my pleas." She snorted. "He wants nothing to do with me, and that's that."

Her mother would have rolled over in her grave to see Jo rudely shrug off the man's touch and return to her casual observation of the night.

A glimmer of light, gone in a blink, twinkled from the understory of a gnarled mesquite. Her swift intake of breath hissed across her teeth. Every muscle in her body ached to flee the window, but she held her position.

Nonchalantly, she faced Cullen, forcing herself to relax her shoulders. His eyes grew into saucers when she seductively placed her arms onto his shoulders, and leaned in to whisper in his ear.

"Don't get any ideas, mister," she hissed. "Someone is watching."

He tensed beneath her embrace. "We're going to walk across this room slowly, and flip off the light. Understand?"

Cullen's breath on her neck sent unwanted chills down her spine. As if she didn't have enough to deal with.

"Perfectly."

"Watch it, mister."

The sashay to the other side of the room lasted eons. Once the light was extinguished, she said, "Go to the bedroom and close the curtains."

"I like the way you think," he murmured.

"I heard that," she whispered, rolling her eyes.

"Stop rolling your eyes at me."

"It's dark, Cullen. You can't see anything." The blasted man.

"Didn't have to see it. I could practically hear it."

"Shhh."

"Okay, okay. Spoil sport."

They crept across the plush floor on hands and knees, and eased up so they could see out the window, but remained unseen to the person outside. Tense moments passed, and then a glimmer. A tiny flame, flared to life, then transformed into an ember.

Cullen's face loomed way too close for comfort, but she didn't have much choice. "Got ourselves a smoker."

"Yep. That'll be good once Duke gets here. But I don't want to scare this guy off just yet. Could be a townie, out for a creepy midnight stroll."

"Hmmm."

"Yeah, I don't buy it either."

Minutes passed in uncomfortable silence. A cloud passed overhead, obscuring the moon. But the tiny orange ember flared as the smoker inhaled, moving closer to the rear of the building, floating in the gloom.

In the sky, the cloud continued its course; and in the light that flooded in its wake, their observer was unmasked.

Jo splayed a hand against the wall, sucked in a hasty breath. The hand constricted in on itself, forming a white-knuckled fist.

"Is that … ?"

"Roy Milligan."

Chapter 18

Morning light filtered through the gauzy window of Cullen's rented living room. Unblinking, he zoned out, mesmerized by dancing dust motes. He stood in the kitchenette, leaning against the countertop with a hot cup of coffee warming his hands.

So close. They had been so close. Duke, just finishing up with his evidence sweep of Jo's – his – shop, had hustled over to the rear of the inn. By the time the deputy arrived, the only things left by Jo's convict stepfather were a handful of smudged boot prints.

Cullen's head hurt. Not the normal dull pounding of a nagging headache, but at a level that obliterated the strongest migraine he ever experienced. The medistrip barely dinted it, like tossing a bucket of water on a roaring wildfire. All he wanted to do was sleep. Not that he got much shut-eye with Jo in the next room, stretched out on the couch. Blonde hair spilling over a throw pillow, her long legs tucked to fit. He groaned, and banished the image from his mind. Even that hurt.

But there he stood, staring at floating bits of dust, fantasizing about a woman he couldn't have. The forbidden fruit perched on the edge of the chair adjacent to the couch, twenty feet away, head down in conversation with the grizzly deputy seated on the sofa. She looked up at him, and Cullen smiled, saluting her with his steaming mug. Had she slept? Dark smudges grew below her eyes, purplish half-moons emphasizing an angry slant to her eyes. Her lips were a slash across her face. He had seen her mad, witnessed a quiet vulnerability at times, basked in a rare smile; but he wanted to throttle the man who put that dreadful expression on her face.

Bringing the mug to his lips, he closed his eyes, allowing the coffee steam to bathe his nose. A deep inhale preceded a scalding gulp. With a jaw-cracking yawn, he eventually opened his eyes, and found Jo observing from three feet away. The smile on her face was genuine, and he figured it was worth the humiliation.

"Tired, Sleeping Beauty?" she asked with a grin.

"More like Non-Sleeping Ruggedly Handsome."

"The snores said otherwise."

"But you agree that I'm ruggedly handsome?"

Jo snorted. "Now you're dreaming. Wake up, buttercup. We need to plan our attack."

From the couch behind her, Duke piped up. "If you kids are done picking on one another, we should get to business."

With her back to the older man, Jo rolled her eyes; they held a twinkle of affection and exasperation. She jerked her chin in the deputy's direction, and Cullen followed. Each footfall jarred the wound site. Step, thud, step, thump. He checked the time, noting the doc should be there any minute with another medistrip. Then he would get some relief from the overenthusiastic drum line beating out a rhythm in his aching head.

"What did you find?" Cullen asked the lawman.

"A whole lot of nothing, and a tiny bit of something. There were two sets of footprints out there." His eyes landed on Jo. "And you only saw one person?"

"It was Roy, I'm telling you. There is no way I would forget that monster."

"I believe ya, girl. The ones I suspect are Roy's overlay the others, like he was following someone. Now, I --"

A quick rap at the door announced a visitor. Duke motioned to Cullen to stay on the sofa – thank goodness – and ambled over to answer it.

"How's my patient this morning?" Cora carried little Kate on one hip, and her kit in the other. He prayed with all his heart that she packed some strong stuff in her bag. The baby squealed and drooled, and his head thumped a reply.

He grumbled.

"That well, huh?" She plopped the little one on the plush carpet and fished a teething ring out of her back pocket.

Just as Duke eased the door closed, a hefty hand wedged itself inside. The hand connected to the doc's enormous husband.

"Howdy."

Cullen growled again.

Jo grinned. "We really need to work on your manners, boss. What kind of etiquette do they teach city boys, anyway?"

"That if I don't have something nice to say, to not say it all," he retorted. "Doc, I beg you. Meds. Strong. Now."

"That's why I'm here. Just don't bite me."

Duke filled Ben in on the developments from the night before while Cora flashed an annoying light in his eyes, had him waving and pointing his arms all over, and touching his nose.

Sympathy filled Cora's face. "I think an injection will work best now, and a strip for later. That work for you?"

"Shoot."

Her laughter on any other day probably sounded like twinkling bells. Today, however, his mental percussion session decided to echo her with a few bass drum warm-ups. "Arm or neck?"

"What gets it there faster?"

"Neck."

"Go for it."

He angled his head to the side, exposing skin rough with the stubble of a few missed shaves. She applied the pneumatic injector against the soft hollow under his chin, pressed the release. A quick sting from the pulse of injected pain reliever, and then it was over.

"Let's check that —" she began, but Ben interrupted.

"Can I take you up on that SatNet offer?"

Cullen motioned to the bedroom. "I already approved you as a user. Let me know if you need anything."

"I'm not even going to ask how you accessed my federal file."

"Good idea."

Cora poked and prodded at the laceration on his forehead, but the analgesic was already working its magic. When the room tilted, spun, and righted itself, he asked, "What did you give me?"

"A little cocktail. Don't worry. You'll get past the woozy in about five minutes. There. New bandage, and it's not infected."

143

The baby had managed to low crawl her way to his feet, and was playing with his toes. His heart melted into a sloppy puddle. He looked up to find Jo watching Kate with a grin on her face; and when she raised her eyes to his, they locked. In that split second, Cullen knew he would fight for Jo. Battle any demon, wrestle any closet's skeleton, conquer any fear.

He held her eyes captive, knew she felt it too. But then confusion clouded her face, and she built the wall up once more. He could almost see each emotional brick she mortared, placed, and leveled.

Duke cleared his throat, gravel sliding down a mountainside, and the moment ended. Cullen nearly cringed at the relief in Jo's face.

"Like I was saying," the deputy began again. "As far as the second set of footprints, we need to eliminate footprints of everyone in the building. Then we can –"

Ben hooted from the bedroom, startling the baby and turning all eyes in his direction.

Duke threw his hands in the air. "I give up. Anyone else want to interrupt?"

"Bah-bah-ba-ba-ba," the baby interjected. Kate grinned and leaked a rivulet of drool from the corner of her mouth, then plugged it with a chubby fist.

"Figures," the older man barked with a smile, ruffling the toddler's hair. "Women."

"Hey," Jo and Cora exclaimed simultaneously.

"Y'all get in here and look at this!"

Cullen followed the group to the bedroom, crossing his fingers and hoping that none of them noticed the wobble from standing too quickly. They had fanned out behind Ben and the SatNet system.

Floating in midair, a bearded man's head and shoulders spun a slow 360 degrees. Grungy, oily hair fell out of the frame of the mug shot from the rear view of the man. Tiny, almond-shaped brown eyes straddled a nose broken one too many times; a grim slash of a mouth turned up on the right in a smirk. Or maybe he couldn't help it. A puckered scar ran from the right corner of his mouth two inches, pulling the corner of his lip toward his cheek.

Ben jabbed at the screen. "There."

Jo swiveled a bewildered squint between the tracker and the criminal hovering above the desk. "There who?"

"Jeremiah Franks."

Duke regarded the mug shot, and then shook his head. "Jo?"

"No clue."

Ben swiped the holographic photo to the side, pulled up a record with a flick and a sweep. He highlighted the last incarceration facility. Last, because there were about a dozen others. "Here. See? Midland Prison Farm."

"Well, him and a few hundred others," Jo remarked, shrugging. "What's special about this guy? Other than his rugged good looks."

Cullen snorted at the jab, and he caught her smirk.

"His status, is what. 'EI' means he no longer resides at the prison," Ben provided.

"Escaped Inmate?" Jo narrowed her eyes, reached over Ben's shoulder to expand the photo of the prisoner again.

Ben nodded. "Yep. Note the date? Three days before our boy lit out of the same prison."

"O-kay." Jo strung out the word with a question mark on the end. "I'm not tracking, sorry."

"You don't recognize him, then?"

"Why should I?"

With a few more carefully placed finger swipes, another name appeared on the screen.

"Bill Franks? Never heard of him either, Ben." Cullen heard the edge in Jo's voice and decided to step in.

"Let us in on the secret discovery, will ya Ben? Neither one of us got much sleep last night," Cullen said.

Ben's right eyebrow climbed to his forehead.

"Whoa, man. Not like that." At Jo's amused look, he added, "At *all*."

She frowned, and it took all the bearing he had not to laugh. He could get used to seeing her off balance a bit.

Ben rolled his eyes toward his wife, and shook his head. "Okay. Bill Franks is the next of kin contact for Jeremiah Franks. Bill is Jeremiah's father."

"Mm-hmm," Jo said. "And?"

"And Bill Franks is also the next of kin for one Roy Milligan."

"Impossible! He claimed to have no one living on his side of the family."

"Would you claim them?" Ben asked with a shrug. "Be that as it may, he does have kin. Bill Franks is Roy's uncle by marriage."

Cullen processed this bit of intelligence. "Does this next of kin have a verified address?"

The smile on Ben's face was feral, and he jutted his chin at Duke. "That he does. Ready to ride?"

Chapter 19

"No. Absolutely not." Doc Tucker jabbed an elegant finger at her newfound patient. The baby on her hip, who reached out to grab her mother's pointing digit, did nothing to detract from the authority echoing off the walls of the modest bedroom.

Seeing Cullen's eyes bugged out like golf balls nearly sent Jo into a fit of giggles. If she were prone to giggles. Which she was not.

"You were whacked in the head with a set of steel tongs last night. Therefore, you will not be riding anywhere today."

Cullen's head swiveled from her to Ben to Duke, and back to her. Jo felt somewhat bad for the guy, but shrugged her shoulders as if to say it was out of her hands.

"Not to mention, he swooned a little while ago," Jo pointed out. Her boss narrowed his eyes at her, and she surpressed another rising laugh.

Cora pinned her with a stare. "Swooned?"

"Fainted. Passed out. I caught him before he hit the floor."

"No. Riding. Do I make myself clear, Mr. Miles?"

"Last time I looked," Cullen began, "I was an adult man capable of making my own decisions."

"Hmph," Cora replied. "Not on my watch, buster."

Ben pushed away from the desk. "Hate to burst a whole lot of bubbles, but I wasn't talking to either of you. I need Duke with me. He's the law. You're the client. No offense," he added hastily when he saw the look on Jo's face. "There will be plenty for us to do around here, girl. But today, I have to keep it legal."

Jo seethed, her hands bunched at her sides and her jaw clinched. She could almost wipe that smug smile off Cullen's face with a fist, but the poor guy did just get smacked upside the head. She watched as he stepped around Cora, looking as though everything was as right as rain with this situation. Wait. Did he just wink at her? She narrowed her eyes, and opened her mouth to give the joker a piece of her mind; but a flick of his fingers at his side made her bite her tongue.

Cullen made a silly face for little Kate and ruffled her carrot-top hair, earning a chuckle from the baby. "I understand, Doc. No worries from me. Would it be okay if I did some desk work at the smithy? I'm way behind, and Jo probably needs some sleep."

What was he up to? His right brow raised, and he tilted his head toward her. Okay, she would play along, and wring his neck after everyone cleared out.

"Umm, yeah, sure. I didn't get much sleep anyway. Cullen snores."

Jo idly wondered if he rolled his eyes out of snore denial, or if he thought her agreement sounded lame. Probably both. The doc swung her head between the two of them, and adjusted the baby on her hip.

"I'm fine with desk work. I'd be surprised if you can concentrate on it, though. But I want Jo to walk you down there. You can call her

148

when you want to come back to the room. I'll leave two more medistrips with you, but wait four hours to take the next one." Cora patted Cullen on the arm. "I know from experience how much your head hurts. Take it easy, or you'll regret it."

Ben barked a laugh. "She'll make sure you regret it, trust me."

Those two were disgustingly cute together. Even the playful way Cora punched her husband in the arm was sweet. The two walked out of the bedroom, their arms linked. Duke, who had successfully blended in with the background, cleared his throat.

"Well, I better get over to Ben's. You two going to behave yourselves? I'm onto you, by the way. Ain't no use denying it. Stay out of trouble." The deputy leveled a look at her. "I don't want to answer a call with you as the victim."

Jo grabbed him in a bear hug. "*He's* up to something. I don't know what, yet. But I'll send you word."

After the door closed with a muffled thump, the two of them faced each other across the elegant room. She shoved her hands into her pockets. "Are we really going to the smithy?"

"Yes. At first."

"Spill it."

"Can't I surprise you now and then?"

"Nope. You're all out of surprises, mister. Used it up getting beaned with my tongs. You'll need to replace those, by the way."

"Me? You're the blacksmith. Make 'em yourself."

"Speaking of swinging my Thor hammer … I have something you'll want to see. At the office."

***

"How did I not remember it was such a mess?" Cullen groaned, scrubbed a hand over his face, wincing when his pinky finger brushed the bandage.

Twice in a handful of days, someone had violated her personal space. Well, technically the shop was Cullen's now; but it was nothing more than ink and a signature, as far as she was concerned. She looked forward to the day she could dump a small mountain of gold on the desk and buy back the smithy. Until then, she had to start somewhere. Unfortunately, her starting point was scattered all over the office floor.

Not to mention the crunchy pieces underfoot that once comprised her viewscreen system. She bent over, pinched a piece between her fingers, and took in the destruction.

"It was time to upgrade anyway," Jo said, disgust oozing out as she flung the debris across the room. "I found your money."

Cullen turned from the desk, where he was straightening papers. "Say again?"

"Yesterday morning, when we were discussing the unfilled orders."

"Was that only yesterday?"

"Though it feels like a month of Sundays, yeah. Anyway, you may recall that I ..."

" ... am not the receptionist. I remember." He threw his hands in the air, and papers coasted through the air, swaying on invisible air currents until finding rest among their comrades on the floor. "Any more declarations to make?"

"Actually, yes. I do. I made house calls. All but two of the clients would still like us to fill the orders." The side of her mouth pulled up in a grin at the look on his face. "I can see you're surprised. I'm a people person."

Snorting, he shook his head, and laced his hands behind his neck. "Sure, as long as you can beat them about the head with your hammer."

"I get along with everyone. As long as they keep their opinions to themselves, and generally agree with what I say."

"Mm-hmm. A real people pleaser. Okay, so you have clients. But circumstances –"

"Escaped murderers."

"*Dire* circumstances threaten to delay our scavenging."

"Reclaiming. Repurposing. Recycling. Take your pick."

"Woman!"

Jo threw back her head and cackled at the ceiling. When she finished, tears streamed from her eyes. "Oh. Okay, okay. I'm done." She swept a hand across her cheeks, her chest still vibrating from the effort of hilarity containment.

"So was that your plan? Your so-called 'desk work'?"

"Nope."

"Interesting," she said, pacing the room. Glass, paper, and bits of bio-plastic crunched and crackled beneath her weight. Things. Easily broken, easily destroyed. She shoved the anger and hurt, the violation, into the lockbox in her mind and slammed shut the lid. Not now. Leaning against the doorframe connecting the office to the shop, she met Cullen's eyes. "Are you going to make me guess?"

151

"I should. But," he said, grinning. "I'm not. We're going treasure hunting."

"Doc says you can't ride. And I'm the babysitter."

"Maybe if we ride slowly?"

"That depends."

"On?"

"On whether or not I'm going to have to catch your sorry butt if it falls off a horse." Eyes to the heavens, Jo counted to five. "All right, saddle up."

Thankfully, the inn was nowhere in the line of sight of the smithy. A confrontation with a certain fiery red-headed doctor was something she hoped to avoid at all costs. She seemed to know too much, and it downright made her skin all creepy-crawly. Saying she would be a good mother, hinting that she and Cullen would make a great couple. Casting a glance to her right, Jo made sure he still sat his saddle.

Overhead, gauzy cirrus clouds danced above puffy cumulus mounds. Three buzzards circled in the distance; a lazy, slow-motion tornado languidly descending toward the stunted trees. And thank goodness, the heat seemed to be taking a rest. Warm, sunny in fits and spurts, a steady breeze. The wind kicked up the smell of red clay and tall grass. Songbirds sang melody to the rhythm of clopping hooves.

Jo looped the reins around the pommel, dropped her hands to her sides. Gripping tight with her thighs, she eased her head back, until she stared at the playful May sky.

They rode along the path to her modest home near the creek. The meadow rested around the next bend. Neither had much to say, and both seemed to find comfort in the gorgeous early summer morning.

It was when Cullen veered from the path that she reined in with a soft, "Whoa, Kase."

His horse carried him a dozen paces past where she halted in confusion before he stopped and turned around.

She thumbed in the direction of home. "Thought you said we were going out to my place for this treasure hunt of yours."

"We are."

"Uh, path? Leads home? Let's go."

"Not your current home, Jo."

It was as if the heavens rained buckets of freezing rain from a clear, blue sky. She froze, every muscle tense.

"I only have one home," she forced through gritted teeth. "So help me, Cullen, I'll leave you here."

His horse brought him so close that their legs brushed against one another. "I know you don't want to do this. But if there is something out there, don't you think it's worth looking for?"

"There's nothing left." Jo tried desperately to keep the whine from her voice, but it came out more like a plea.

"Roy's doing this for a reason."

"Because he's insane, Cullen!"

"Maybe. But we owe it to Ginny to look at this from every angle."

"*We* don't owe my sister anything!" Anxiety clawed its way past her inner barriers. "There is nothing, absolutely nothing to find out there."

"Then we won't be there long," he reasoned. He reached out, clutched her hand in his rough and calloused one. She flinched and tried to pull back, but he only gripped tighter. "We can do this. Together, Jo."

He took the reins from her hands, and holding them, led her Judas horse forward despite her repeated commands to stop. Betrayed by her own horse, she held onto the saddle for dear life.

She closed her eyes, and prepared to visit the dead.

Chapter 20

The chimney remains rose from the ground, a broken and macabre headstone testifying that life once happened there. Uneven ground surrounded it, wildflowers and weeds together blooming in the steady sunlight. A home once rose from the surrounding clearing, her childhood home. A modest one, to be sure; but a place of happiness, excitement, and joy.

Love. Safety.

Jo ran a hand softly over the tops of the tall grass jutting up from where the living room once was. Wild onion, Indian paintbrushes, and bluebonnets with half their blooms bled out in waves from the mound of broken earth that once held a home.

Cullen stood to the side of the century oak, its broad, verdant leaves casting flickering shadows on his face. The tire swing swayed gently in the wind. A simple white cross marked Ginny's grave, near enough to the tire swing that it wouldn't be knocked over; but close enough for Jo to imagine the sheer bliss on her sister's face the last time she swung beneath the tree.

A dozen yards from Cullen, the horses cropped in the field. She motioned to him, and he started toward her. Her heart clenched when he stopped near the cross, removed his hat, and placed it on his chest. It nearly thudded to a standstill when he knelt, bowing his head.

Around her, life continued. Grasshoppers leapt in the field, flies bothered the horses, and tails swished in response. But within, time froze and imprinted itself on her memory. Craning her neck to the sky, Jo squeezed shut her eyes to keep the tears from falling. A chunk of mortar in the wall around her heart disintegrated. By the time she felt composed, Cullen stood beside her with a questioning look on his face.

She answered his silent query. "Yeah, I'm okay. Just … touched. You continue to surprise me, Cullen."

A hint of a grin played around his mouth, stretched to his eyes. "I guess I need to keep you on your toes."

Lightly tapping the bandage near his forehead, she replied, "You do that just fine, boss."

"So," Cullen said, rubbing his hands together. "Where's the buried treasure?"

Jo snorted. "You got me. Lived here most of my life, and searched high and low for weeks – months – after my dad told me the gold miner's story. I managed to find a few plastic jugs from the pre-Collapse era, a dozen or so bottle caps, and a harmonica. No gold, or anything else of value. If some ancestor of mine really was the guy who had his fortune stolen and then returned, he made sure no one would ever find it."

He looked like a bloodhound with scent in his nose, wandering around the overgrown ruins of the foundation. Running a hand over the soot-streaked stone fireplace, he angled his head around and raised a curious eyebrow. "Fire?"

"Yes."

"Were you living here when it went up?"

Jo shook her head, bit her lower lip. "No, I was already in my cabin near the creek. It was just a shell consumed by weeds, vines, and animals."

Cullen knelt near the hearth, brushed away dirt and detritus. "Lightning hit it?"

"Not exactly."

Narrowing his eyes, he said, "You?"

With a curt nod, she admitted, "Yeah, and I've never regretted it."

How could she describe the look on his face? A combination of amusement, sadness, and resignation all rolled into one. With a shrug of the shoulders, he continued prodding around the rough-hewn granite hearth. Methodically, he ran a finger over each stone, checking the mortared joints, trying to pry and wiggle them loose.

"Finding anything, Sherlock?"

"Your nicknames are getting more creative."

"You're welcome. So? Why the fascination with the fireplace?"

With a grunt and a heave, Cullen landed empty-handed on his rump with a thud. He winced, grabbed his head with both hands.

Ugh. Men. "Here, hang on." Jo's long stride took her to the horses swiftly, where she retrieved a stubby crowbar from her saddlebags. When she returned to the fireplace, she found Cullen brushing himself off, his back to her. With gold medal-worthy effort, she avoided admiring the way his jeans fit. Well, almost avoided.

She thrust the tool at him. "Try this."

His hands halted mid-sweep. Straightening, he said, "You seriously keep a *crowbar* in your saddlebags?"

Jo shrugged. "Who doesn't?"

With a snort, he took the offered implement and set to work on the stone.

"A long time ago," he began, "people often secured their valuables in places like fireplaces and hearths. Kind of like hiding keepsakes or money beneath a loose floorboard, or having hidden rooms."

Not that long ago, she thought, picturing her keepsake box in the shadowy recesses under the bedroom floor. She pondered the loose jewels resting alongside the other bits she had collected over the years. But no, her mother said they were removed from their gold settings so the metal could be melted down during a particularly hard time.

The grunting at the hearth continued as Cullen worked the leftmost stone. So much for him taking it easy and listening to the physician's advice. A grin pulled at the side of her mouth. He rested on his haunches, removed his hat, and dabbed the sweat away from his brow. The crowbar rested atop the hearth, abandoned, awaiting to be used again.

Jo sighed, resigned. "Here, let me do that. You're not supposed to exert yourself, remember?"

He glanced up at her, squinted, and then shielded his eyes from the sun behind her. "What's bothering you?"

"I don't want my butt chewed out by Doc, that's what."

"No, it's something else. You only twiddle that stone hanging around your throat when you're worried or sad."

Until he said it, she didn't realize the stone was between her fingers.

Rolling her eyes, she snatched the crowbar and nudged him aside. "Just thinking of my sister, is all."

Cullen nodded. "Thought that might be the case. Where did you get it?" He pointed at her necklace.

"Dad gave it to me just before he died. The only time I've taken it off was when the leather broke, and I replaced it." She gazed at the elongated stone for a brief moment more, then replaced it beneath her shirt. "An old crone once told me it would provide protection, whatever that means."

Jo chiseled at the mortar of the piece of rock Cullen had singled out, using the bent end of the pry bar. The cement sealant flaked off in brittle sheets, and then tried to separate the piece from the whole once more.

"Do you believe stones have supernatural powers?" Cullen asked. He was looking at her with amusement and genuine interest.

She shook her head. "No. Not really. It's only that ... well, the old woman knew who I was. And she told me I had a difficult journey ahead." Jo grunted out the last word, and the slab wiggled. Encouraged, she continued to maneuver the tool. "Actually, I ran into her the other day on my way to the sheriff's station, the day the Tuckers got into town." Growling, she forced all her weight on the high end of the crowbar. "Come on, you stupid rock! She said I needed to find my first love."

"The rock said something?"

With an *oof* she released her pressure, and swatted Cullen on the arm. "Of course not. The woman. She said if I wanted to find what I sought that I needed to seek out my first love. Whatever that means."

"Ah. Here, I'll take over," he said, holding out a hand.

"This is ridiculous, Cullen. There's no buried treasure here."

"Just a few minutes more, and then we'll look elsewhere."

"Ugh. Stubborn, hard-headed man. Fine, whatever."

Jo stood, brushed off the knees of her jeans. All around them, nature played in the warm sun. The shadow of a hawk skimmed the ground near her feet. Cullen grunted and let out a fierce yell before tumbling once again onto his backside.

"Yes!"

"You got it?"

"It's loose, yeah."

"Well, that's because I loosened it for you."

He barked a laugh. "Thanks. Now, let's see what's underneath."

Jo had her doubts that anything other than dirt and grubby, crawly things lived beneath the old sooty hearth. She squatted beside him as he used the flatter chisel end as a shovel. Undaunted, he dug.

And then there was a hollow *thump*.

"No way," she whispered, baffled.

Cullen rammed the end down once, twice more, and then scooped out the remaining soil with his hands. He brushed off the top of what appeared to be a simple rectangular metal box.

A few minutes later, the excavated container sat before them, warming in sunlight for the first time in who knew when.

"You do it," she directed Cullen. Her hands shook behind her back. "Go on, get it over with."

The hinge squealed in protest. Nestled inside was a package wrapped in oilcloth. No gold, nothing of value present. Besides, the

160

steel chest wasn't large enough to hold the treasure reportedly mined by her famous ancestor.

Cullen cast the question silently, and she shook her head. He took the hint, and unwrapped the brown oilcloth, withdrawing two items from inside. One appeared to be a simple, leather-bound journal. The other was a folded paper.

Jo decided, "I'll take the paper. You take the journal."

Upon closer examination, she found the paper not nearly as preserved as she had assumed. The corners crumbled, brittle dusty fragments sticking to her fingertips. With more finesse, she meticulously opened it.

It was a poem, but unlike any she had read. Not that she read a lot of poetry, honestly. More mystified than anything, she turned her attention to Cullen. He faced away from her, his head bent in reading. She put a hand on his shoulder, and his eyes found hers. His face had turned an unnatural shade of white.

"What?" The tremor in her voice gave away her instant fear. "What is it, Cullen? Tell me!"

He cleared his throat. "Your mother. This was your mother's journal." Cullen rubbed a hand over his mouth, closed his eyes. "I'm not sure you should look at this here. Not now."

This was how it felt to be hit in the stomach with a blazing cannonball. Her hands trembled as they exchanged the brittle paper for the journal. A coiling, flaming nexus pulsed just below her heart, radiating to her shaking fingers.

She turned to the last page, where he had been reading.

White hot rage erupted from behind her eyes, spread to her ringing ears. Her pulse spiked. Blood coursed throughout her body in preparation for fight or flight, making her lightheaded and dizzy. An unhuman howl sounded all around her. Belatedly, she realized the outcry came from her own lips.

In the middle of a wildflower garden, under a canopy of sun and billowy clouds, she vowed to kill Roy Milligan.

Chapter 21

The wind fingered the pages of the abandoned journal, a ghostly reader flipping through at breakneck speed. Cullen cast a shadow over it and the steel lockbox. But his attention was on the woman standing in the shade of an ancient oak.

She was doubled over, arms crossed protectively over her middle. Sobbing. He ached to hold her.

He didn't dare.

The journal. Words written in her mother's hand, condemning the man she had married, and sealing her fate. A crude acceptance rang from the elegant scrawl. It was a death sentence penned with exquisite form.

September 14, 2071

I fear this is my last entry. Roy is growing ever more suspicious. I found him last night rummaging through the bookcase looking for this journal. Jo, honey. How I wish I could see you grow. See you marry and have my grandchildren. I wish I had the courage to tell you the truth of my illness. But I fear the repercussions of such action. Should you ever find this diary, I pray that you forgive me. Roy is an evil creature. Once I am gone, you will have a good life free from that monster. You may never know how much I regret bringing him into our lives. Deep down, I know he took our Ginny. I could see it in your eyes. I can't bear the thought of you knowing he took me too. I do not have cancer, Jo. The test results I asked for in secret indicate arsenic poisoning. It's too far gone for me, honey. Your aunt and uncle will protect you. And though you may never read these words, I still plead for your forgiveness. Love you to the moon and back a million times, my darling.

When Cullen closed his eyes, he saw hers as they appeared while she read her mother's confession; violent blue supernovas set in a face white hot with rage. As if burned, she had flung the offending book to the ground, and stormed to the center of the placid field. Helpless, he stood guard while she bellowed at the sky, sending a flock of crows shrieking to the east. She grabbed stones, hurled them into the tree line. One projectile after another carried her wrath. Until the final one.

She held the last rock in her right hand. Her back was to him, so she couldn't see the times he had started forward and retreated. The times his hand reached out to her before hastily lowering itself to his side. Jo tried to throw the last stone, but the fight had drained from her. Arms loose, shoulders slumped, she stared at the nimble green weeds bending in the wind around her.

The stone fell to the ground.

She stumbled to Ginny's grave. And there she remained, now wracked by sobs. A keening wail escaped her lips.

He would deal with rebuke, but he was done watching her suffer alone.

In the span of three blinks, he held her. Wrapped arms muscled by his trade around the chiseled, tightened muscles of the woman he craved. She shivered like a leaf in autumn, let herself be held. Minutes passed. Her hair was silk under his rough hands.

Two, three sniffles, and she pulled back; stared at him with shining eyes. The tip of her nose was red, her lips swollen and splotchy.

"You're beautiful," he whispered into the silence.

Jo sniffed, rolled her eyes. "Whatever. I'm a mess." She tried to pull away, but Cullen tightened his grip. "Come on, let me go."

"No way."

She tensed, rigid in his arms. "I'm serious, Cullen."

"Stop fighting me."

"Fight is all I have left!"

With her head clutched tight to the hollow of his throat, he whispered, "You have me." Her blonde hair smelled of sunshine and jasmine.

And haltingly, the rigidity melted. He ran circles across her back, his hands snagging on her white cotton shirt. Her breath shivered across his chest, warm where the breeze was cool. Beneath the oak, light dappled and danced. Cullen knew she was going to pull back, half a second before she did. He let her.

For now.

She sniffed. "Did you read the other piece of paper? Ugh. I sound like a foghorn."

"A dang cute foghorn," he replied, tapping her on the red tip of her nose. "And no, I didn't. Shall we?" He hooked his arm and offered it to her as an escort, and she chuckled under her breath.

"Always Mr. Charm."

"I like it better than City Boy."

They sat side by side in the midday heat near the ruins of the homestead's fireplace. Cottony clouds danced across a cerulean sky, a slow waltz in the sultry sun. High above, it was as if God had wielded a massive paintbrush, slashing white cirrus streaks into the blue canopy. Under any other circumstances, it would be the perfect day for a picnic. His stomach growled in agreement.

A grin pulled up Jo's cheek, and she checked her wrist. "Lunch time, huh?"

"I seemed to have missed a couple of meals."

Wincing, she reached out a hand, gently angled his injured side toward her. "Headache?"

"It's fading. Doc's meds are good."

He studied her face, her eyes; she averted them in a flash, and stared at the crumbling parchment-like paper in her hands.

"Don't do that, Jo."

"What?" She continued her study.

"Blame yourself for this." Cullen pointed to the bandage.

"Still can't see his face?"

He shook his head. "It was all shadows and then black. I studied the images on SatNet. The memory's too fuzzy."

"Had to be him, though. I mean, who else could it be?"

Cullen shrugged. "So, what do you think of the poem? But it's not really a poem, is it?"

She needed to stop biting her lower lip like that. It drove him crazy.

"It's an off-the-wall one if it is. Listen," she began.

'The balcony holds the secret.
A head between two shoulders,
The mouth gapes wide.
What once was lost is now found inside.
Below, the colored snake slithers south to the star.'"

"More like a riddle," Cullen pondered.

"It's ancient. I mean, look at the penmanship."

His stomach rumbled again, with more force. Jo eyed him sideways and laughed. "Let's go. We'll study this over lunch."

The steel box warmed his hands. Jo ran her fingers over the leather-bound journal, hesitated. Opening the book, she sandwiched the crumbling riddle between the troublesome diary pages; she slid them both into the oilcloth sack. Cullen pried open the lid, offered it to Jo. She narrowed her eyes, and said, "What's that?"

Puzzled, he spun the open container to see inside. Gleaming dully from the corner, partially wedged under the deteriorating velvet bottom, was a key.

As long as his pinky finger, with a circular head, skinny shaft and a few jagged teeth at the tip, it resembled a stubby skeleton key. Engraved in the worn brass head were the letters *U.S.* in a bold serif print.

"And the mystery deepens," Jo said, her eyebrows raised. "Safe deposit key?"

"If I'm not mistaken, I'd say post office box. We'll ask Marshall in town, see what he thinks."

***

Forty-five minutes later, Cullen sat across the table from her wolfing down a piece of Miss Ruby's pecan pie. Jo passed him a napkin, pointed to the corner of his mouth. With a sheepish look, he dabbed away the gooey drip.

At arm's length was a good place for him to be. The man had inched his way under her skin. The white scar on his left cheek winked in and out as he chewed. A rust-colored stain bled through the bandage on the opposite temple. She fought the desire to touch his face.

What was wrong with her?

The smirky little voice living in the back corner of her brain told her she knew darn well what was happening. Well, she didn't have to listen. Too many things ranking above silly emotions at the moment.

Finding Roy Milligan.

Making him pay for Ginny, her mother. And now, for Cullen.

Oh, and the whole treasure hunt thing, and resuscitating the dying blacksmith shop.

"I can hear you thinking," he said around the last forkful of pie.

"I think you hear your own smacking, glutton."

A smile lit his eyes. "That too. That is some amazing pie. Like ambrosia."

"The burger and rings must have been heavenly as well. If you tasted them before you vacuumed them up."

"Hey," he said, pushing the small plate into the middle of the table. "It's nice to be able to eat something without it hanging around in my esophagus waiting to eject itself."

"Ick. Nice brain picture."

"You asked for it."

"So. What's first? Key or riddle?"

The wrapped journal sat heavily in her lap, and she appreciated the fact that he didn't list its exploration as an option.

"The key, I think. Marshall's just across the street."

He left a silver on the booth table. The early afternoon sun warmed the soles of her boots as they crossed the street. Lunch time foot traffic leaned toward the heavy side, as heavy as it got in a town this small. Three horse-drawn buggies idled along one side of Sam Houston Avenue, and one on the other. Louella Johnson, the teller, caught Jo's eye as she opened the heavy door to the bank. It wasn't imagination that made her believe the woman quickened her step after seeing Jo, which made her laugh inside.

"Stop scaring the public, Miss Camden," Cullen chided. She ribbed him with an elbow.

"The woman needs a backbone."

"Not everyone can be a superhero Marine blacksmith."

"But they could try," she pointed out with a grin.

The door tinkled its welcome, and the cool air of the post office caressed her face. Heavenly.

With a grunt and a heave, Marshall Estes hoisted a metal-framed canvas basket from a nearby desk to the higher countertop. "Jo. Mr. Miles. Didn't expect to see the two of you together, unless one of you were swinging from the business end of the gallows." He winked at Jo, took out a bundled stack of mail.

"Call me Cullen."

"Cullen, then. What are you two doing this fine day? I hear you had quite the adventure last night."

Jo shrugged at the questioning glance from her companion. "Small town."

"And the postmaster hears it all," Marshall said with a chuckle. "Darby was in an hour ago."

Rolling her eyes, Jo said, "Of course she was. That woman's tongue is lethal."

Cullen fished the mysterious key out of his pocket, clinked it on the smooth work surface. With his hand covering it, he said, "We were hoping you could help us solve a puzzle."

"I'm game. Whatcha got?"

Like a swindler with his shell game, Cullen lifted his cupped hand. Marshall's shaggy brows climbed to his salt and pepper hairline. "Where in tarnation did you get that?"

"Let's call it an inheritance for now," Jo said. "Ring any bells?"

"Sure, sure. It's an old post office box key. And I mean old, later 1800s."

"You seem pretty certain." Actually, he darn near drooled on it.

"I am. I collect old post boxes, as cliché as it may sound. As a matter of fact, Jo, your mama gave me one once as a Christmas gift. You were a little critter then. Hang on."

He scurried to his office in the rear corner of the facility. Turning to Cullen, she mouthed, "Can you believe this?"

Shaking his head, he leaned an elbow on the counter, took some weight off one side. "You okay?" She darted a glance at the bloodstained bandage.

"I'm good. And intrigued."

Marshall was grinning from ear to sun-darkened ear when he returned, a tidy little box tucked under his arm. "I've always wondered what was inside. Time period is right. Let's see if that key of yours opens the door."

"You've never tried to open it?"

With a look of horror, the postmaster said, "Oh no! I'd never destroy the integrity of the box. It's in mint condition."

Indeed, the embossed brass door of the little box shone with great care, its coppery gleam catching the light spilling in from the front window. The worn, tarnished key seemed garish in comparison. Cullen passed the key to her, sliding it across the countertop.

"The honor is yours, my dear," he said with a grin.

The key slid in smoothly, turned with a click.

"Well, I'll be," Marshall marveled.

Butterflies clambered in Jo's stomach, fluttered up into her chest. The tiny door swung open. Two items crouched inside: an age-yellowed envelope, the writing so faded with time as to be illegible; and a black velvet drawstring bag, no bigger than the palm of her hand.

"Go on," the postmaster urged. "I've been waiting for this moment for decades." The man was practically bouncing on his toes.

Jo withdrew the bag first, and spread apart the mouth of the tiny satchel, meticulously careful. She upended the bag into her waiting palm, inhaled sharply at what spilled out. Half a dozen rough, golden nuggets tumbled into her hand.

"It's real," Jo whispered. Beside her, Cullen nodded. She used her index finger to push around the precious nuggets. Two were pebble-sized, nearly spherical orbs. They resembled miniature, golden moons, with their pitted surfaces. The other four looked more like massive golden raisins, each about the size of the end of her thumb.

"What's in the envelope?" Marshall inquired. The postmaster's eyes glowed with the light of discovery, and he bobbed up and down on his toes behind the counter.

Remembering the fragile condition of the paper they found in the lockbox, Jo eased it out and slid a tentative fingernail under the back flap. It gave way, opening with a crackle. She peered inside.

"Nothing."

"An empty envelope," Marshall mused. "I wonder what it means."

Cullen shook his head a fraction of a turn, and she understood. No need to drag Marshall into the mystery any more than necessary. The last thing she needed was another person getting hurt on her behalf.

"Who knows? Maybe it was saved for the address," Jo answered lightly. "It's too bad the ink faded so much."

"Well, I tell you what," the postmaster beamed. "This is, by far, the most interesting box I have in my collection!"

Jo couldn't agree more.

Chapter 22

Cullen pushed through the glass-paned door of the sheriff's station half a second before Jo, hot on his heels. The afternoon blazed outside, and the clouds offered little relief. Even though the trip from the post office to the diminutive law enforcement station was a short stalk down the block, she felt sweat beading under her arms, on her chest. Early summer heat and nerves. She carried at her side a modest fortune, wrapped in antique velvet.

Jo expected a cool reprieve from the sun, but was instead buffeted by a warm gust of recirculated office air. Belatedly, she noticed the raised windows. The air conditioning must be on the fritz again.

Duke reclined in his chair, boots propped on the desk, fanning his leathered face with his hat. It halted in mid-swing when he saw the look on Jo's face.

"You really need to upgrade your air conditioner, old man," Jo chided while pulling up a chair.

"Tell me something I don't know."

"Okay," she complied, pulling out the velvet bag and upended its contents onto the cluttered surface. "I'm rich."

He grunted. "Apparently."

Cullen glanced around nervously, his attention swinging between the mound of glowing wealth and the front door.

"Relax, Cullen," Duke grumbled. "Logan's out back with Pete trying to repair that infernal machine."

His neck and shoulders may have lowered themselves minutely, but he still positioned himself between the door's line of sight and what lay on the desk being pushed around by Duke's worn fingers.

Jo was amused, relieved, and irritated. "You're blocking the fan, mister."

"Suck it up, ma'am."

Doggone that smile of his. She punched him lightly in the thigh, and turned her attention back to Duke. The old bear grinned like a cat in the cream. Jo narrowed her eyes at him, and he barked a laugh. His hands flew up in submission.

"So, looks like your financial situation has improved."

She rolled her eyes affectionately. "Yeah. There's more."

The journal came out next, and she gingerly withdrew the deteriorating parchment from its pages. The empty envelope followed.

"We haven't had much time to talk about it, but ..." Jo caught Cullen's eyes briefly. "This page? I think it's a map, concealed inside a riddle. There was a key inside the buried lockbox, as well as this page. And a journal. The key opened an antique post office box that my mother had given to Marshall Estes over twenty years ago. The gold and the envelope were in Marshall's box. With this little fortune, I'd say the two were connected."

"The long lost miner's gold?"

"Seems like. I think the riddle was mailed to someone in that faded old envelope. Someone in the family, way back. And," she added, glancing at Cullen, "I think Mom buried the riddle and separated it from the gold when I was young to keep it away from Roy. Am I crazy?"

The deputy raised his eyebrows. "Yeah, but that's a whole other issue. Hey! Ouch, you didn't have to smack me. But I think you may be onto something." He tipped his chin to the book in her hands. "And the journal?"

Swallowing a lump, Jo said, "Mom's."

He nodded slowly, stretched out his hand. She laid the careworn pages onto his palm.

"It's evidence," she began, "and I know you need to keep it. But I'd like to read it through." The lump had returned, and she fought it down. "You need to see the last entry."

Outside the opened windows, a horse clopped by. The whoosh of the fan inside filled the modest station with a low hum. Cullen tapped the toe of his boot. The silence roared and vibrated with tension.

A sigh rumbled gravelly across the desk. Duke pushed back, paced the worn floor. Slammed a hand flat against the top of his desk. Jo flinched at the *crack*.

"I always suspected," Duke snarled. "Laura was hardly ever sick. That aggressive cancer story never sounded like truth to me. Why? Why didn't she say anything?"

"We won't ever know for sure, but I think she was too far gone for it to have made a difference. I think it's even possible she did have cancer, but it was caused by the poison."

He rubbed his hands across his face, slumped down into his chair. "Yeah, I'll need to keep it for evidence. I'll be charging him with homicide when I slap the cuffs on him."

Cullen gripped her shoulder, a snug reminder of his support. She flicked a smile up at him, grim as it was. "Any word from Ben?" he asked the deputy.

"Yeah, just before you two moseyed in. The uncle lives this side of Bastrop. Dead end, there. It's a valid address, all right. But his daughter put him in a rehabilitation facility after a stroke last year. The daughter claims she hasn't seen her brother or Roy in years. Ben believes her. She let him look around the place. He's on the way back now."

"Any progress on the evidence from the crime scenes?" Jo felt her feet and hands getting fidgety. She needed action, to do something.

"Actually, yes. One of the sets of footprints from behind the inn matches a partial found at your cabin after the first break-in. There were just too many around the smithy to try to pull. Plus, the ground was dry, dusty. The only prints found in the blacksmith shop were yours and Cullen's." He hooked his thumbs through the whitened belt loops of his jeans. "I've got eyes out for him, Jo. But right now? He's a ghost."

"And you think his cousin is in on the whole operation?"

Duke nodded. "Everything is pointing in that direction."

Cullen spun her chair around, letting his hands brace him on the metal-framed arms. "We'll go back to my place--"

Jo whooped, shaking her head.

But he continued before she could get past the laughter in her chest. "And use the SatNet, do a little digging on our riddle. While we're at it, we can dig your mind out of the proverbial gutter." He leaned back, crossed his arms in front of him, and grinned.

"What do we do about that?" she asked, pointing to the gold nuggets on Duke's desk. She swiveled her head between the two men. "Ideas?"

Cullen rubbed his stubbly chin. "There's a safe at the inn, but after the last couple of break-ins I don't think it's a reliable choice."

"Agreed. What about a safe-deposit box? Are those two goons likely to rob a bank?"

Duke lifted a shoulder. "Who knows? How about I take the gold and the riddle, get a box, and give you the key later? Just in case one of them is watching the station?"

"I like it," Jo said, nodding. "And the diary?"

"I'll have Ruth copy it and send you the file. Hard copy needs to stay with me. If Roy were to find that, we'd lose the proof needed to prosecute him for Laura's death."

What she longed for was a chance to curl up in a cozy chair and snuggle down with her mother's journal, sneak a peek into the heart of the woman gone for so many years. Jo had so many unanswered questions. Instead, she sighed. "Okay."

"It's for the best, Jo," Duke said. "Come here."

He enveloped her in a sweaty hug, squeezed her tight. She hugged him in return, then said, "Yep, definitely need to fix the air conditioning."

Duke smacked her on the shoulder. "Get outta here, you two. Let me know what you figure out."

Sun fatigue, stress, or lack of sleep. Whatever the cause, Jo happily flopped like a beached fish onto the sofa in Cullen's rented living room, and sank into the deep cushions with an exhausted sigh. One arm rested across her forehead, the epitome of the fainting damsel. Across the room, in the kitchenette, Cullen chuckled. She raised the arm a hair, peeped at him with a half-lidded glance.

With his back leaned against the countertop, he pressed a clear glass of ice water against his forehead with one hand; the other gripped the bull-nosed edge of the oiled wood block, knuckles white.

"Hey," Jo said, sitting up. "You all right?"

"Headache. That's all."

"Cora left a medistrip in the bathroom. Want me to get it for you?"

"I think I'll grab a quick shower first, if it's okay with you. Let the water soothe it for a bit."

"Your place, man. I'm here for the moral support. And the Dr Pepper in the fridge."

Behind the beading glass, he rolled his eyes. "I see how it is."

"So glad we're on the same page. Finally. Go, scoot. Wash your cares away."

She caught herself watching his hips sway as he walked across the room, began to hum a little tune. He raised his eyebrows as he sauntered by.

"What?" she asked.

"You're humming."

"I'm just happy you're away from the kitchen so I can get my cold drink," she lied.

He stopped in the bedroom doorway. "Want me to log on to SatNet for you?"

A little work would distract her, keep her from thinking unladylike things. "Sure."

He gave her a thumbs-up, and vanished through the doorway. A few moments later, she caught the edge of the holo-display springing to life. "You're good to go."

The bathroom lock clicked home. As she settled down to work, a cold bottle of dark fizzy heaven standing at attention on the desk, she heard the shuffling of shucked clothes hitting the tile floor. She closed her eyes. Definitely not thinking of Cullen in the shower twenty feet away. Not thinking about it. Pure thoughts. Happy thoughts.

She was humming again.

Gah! Her brain betrayed her, and it seemed to take her heart hostage. Frustrated, she berated herself for wasting time, and used more force than necessary on the flexible keyboard at her fingertips. A few minutes more, and she chuckled at the muffled baritone wafting through the bathroom door. A shower singer, huh? Interesting.

Jo had committed the ancient riddle to memory, and began with key word searches. When nothing promising blipped after a dozen tries, she grunted and pulled up a map of the surrounding area. A vaporous idea began to coalesce from the formless meanderings of her mind. She was right on the cusp of it; she could feel it.

The map blinked off, and was replaced by the incoming call signal. Once, twice it pinged, requesting acceptance or redirect to voicemail. She didn't recognize the caller, but why would she?

Well, why not? It could be Ben calling with an update.

She tapped the Accept Call icon, swiped it to open the image viewer. With a wry smile, she announced, "Cullen Miles' office. How may I be of service?"

A woman in a sharp pinstriped navy blue suit sat in an opulent office. She smiled, a polite slash across an unlined face. "Standby for Secretary Miles, please."

Stunned, Jo nodded, not trusting herself to speak. *Secretary* Miles? The holding image looked suspiciously like a government seal. Her heart raced, and her palms felt clammy. It couldn't be.

But the official-looking seal vanished, and was replaced by a silver-haired man, his broad shoulders stretching wide inside his expensive suit. He exuded confidence and authority. His jawline was clenched into knotted ropes.

"I see he's hired a secretary. Well, then. Your name?"

Oh, it was going to be like that? She narrowed her eyes. "Miss Camden. What can I do for you, Mr. Secretary?"

"You can get my son in front of that screen. I have business to discuss with him."

In the adjacent bathroom, the shower shut off. She heard the curtain slide, imagined him grabbing a handy towel.

She'd strangle him with it.

"I'm sorry, Mr. Secretary, but he'll have to return your call. He's … indisposed at the moment."

"I will not have this continue. He refuses to return my calls, and it is of the utmost importance that I speak with him. Find him. Now."

"Very well. Standby."

Though it was most likely bad form, she placed the Secretary of State of the Republic of Texas on hold. He was lucky she didn't disconnect the call altogether.

Cullen would be coming clean in more ways than one this afternoon.

Chapter 23

Living, breathing fire. It roared, growled, and accepted her iron offering with a rustling gasp of the coals. Golden flames, nearly white, licked the cold steel with enthusiasm. Ginger and crimson danced, and whitish-blue tongues flickered hissing sparks. She pumped the bellows with her foot, feeding the dragon the oxygen it craved. The fire inhaled, snarled in delight.

Ever so slowly, the steel colored, heated and changing. In her mind's eye she imagined molecules shifting, switching, jiggling, and joggling for position in this new creation.

Nothing fancy, a garden spade. But with it, a person could till the earth, plant a seed. Then came weeding, watering, and caring. From the earth came life, and life-giving sustenance. While it wasn't an example of the more intricate scrollwork of a gate, or the fine craftsmanship of a working blade, this piece had a purpose to the one wielding it.

The steel shone the melded color of a blazing sunset. With her tongs, she pulled it from the mouth of the forge, placing it on an angle. Hammer rang against the iron end, like glowing red moldable clay. She needed to upset the steel, make it thicker and wider. Expertly, with little excess movement, she pounded the end until it was no longer malleable. Then she thrust it into the forge once more.

Jo lost herself in the motions. She channeled the anger, and fear; the frustrations, and what felt like betrayal, into the energy of smithing. Her shoulders ached, a fire all its own. Weeks away from the shop had left her weak, out of practice.

Heat the iron, pull and hammer. Next, onto the convex anvil to widen and curve, tapping out the gentle slope of the spade's point. The hammer clinked and tinked, echoing throughout the smithy. Her leather sleeved apron clung to her. Sweat not trickling, but steadily flowing.

Pump the bellows, feed the fire, pull and hammer. Over and over, until all that was left was the spade's tang, and soon that was shaped as well.

Jo examined the implement, held it at arm's length with the tongs first one way, then turning it the other. She inspected the thickness for uniformity, pulling it in a tad closer. Pleased, she shoved the spade head into the coals once more; but this time, just until it started to change to orange.

The die she chose was one of swirling vines and morning glories. Nothing too flashy, but just enough of an accent to brighten the day of the gardener wielding it. She withdrew the metal from the coals, placed it on the anvil lying on an angle. With a careful hand, she set the die and tapped it delicately into the left side of the softened metal.

She slid it home into the barrel of quenching oil, satisfied with the sound of hissing and popping. Waving it gently through the oil, she judged the time necessary to get it hand-warm. Time, and a whole lot of trial and error taught her when to withdraw it.

Behind her at the waist high workstation, the tempering oven was preheated to 439°. The last step would take the hardened, brittle steel and soften it a hair. It was also the longest step, requiring hours of attention and patience. She placed the implement into the oven, set a timer for two hours for the first cycle.

Leaning onto the worktop, she braced herself and bent over at the waist, elongating her back and lowering her head between her outstretched arms. A skinny triangle of sunshine grew from the creaking door to her feet, then eased back into darkness. She really didn't want to talk to Cullen right now.

"I should have told you, Jo."

She lowered her arms, touched hands to toes, and held it there.

"It's a sticky family mess."

Rolling up slowly, she turned her back to him and arched herself to the left, then to the right. Twisting at the waist, she worked out the kinks and spasms of the familiar muscle burn.

"With everything that has happened the last few days ... well, it was the last thing on my mind."

She pulled one arm across her body, bracing the elbow with the other hand; and then reversed the position.

"Will you just look at me?"

Jo breathed deeply, attempted to unclench her jaw. She rolled her head side to side, popping the cervical vertebrae in the process. Then she turned to face him.

He looked miserable in the dusty light of the shop. Her stomach knotted for a millisecond in sympathy, but anger swept it away.

"There's no need to trouble yourself, Cullen. You don't owe me a thing. I'm just the help."

Throwing his head back, he studied the ceiling. "Don't do this. You know how I feel about you."

"Oh, really? I've known you about a week. A week! How could you have any semblance of real feelings toward me?"

She should have known better than to crack open the door to her heart. The fracture hurt.

"Yeah, I come from a powerful and rich family. It's not something I go around talking about. Mainly because it's the reason I'm here instead of Austin, mooching off my parents."

He wanted a fight? Okay. "The man who called your room today – your father – is the reason our steel prices have increased, Cullen! He refuses to touch the increased tariffs, and has said he has no intention of opening talks with a country intent on bullying its neighbor. Because of his lack of diplomacy, taxes steadily increase. How could that *not* affect my business? Tell me that!"

"I know! Jo, you have to believe that I'm on your side. It's the reason I've been ignoring his calls."

"Convenient to say that now. Why aren't we knocking on his palatial door, demanding he reopen trade talks?"

"Because he's an overbearing politician who doesn't listen to anyone! Especially his black sheep son." Cullen barked a harsh laugh. "I honestly have no idea why he wants me around."

"I've asked myself the same question."

She regretted the come-back the second it left her lips. Sighing, held up a hand. "I'm sorry. That was wrong. I'm angry. And honestly, hurt."

"Can we start over? Minus the cold glass of tea in my lap? I'd really like to do without that, if possible."

He reminded her of a stray dog, approaching food in an outstretched hand. The way he eased toward her was hesitant, hopeful. Her stomach clenched once more and released a thousand butterflies. They swirled, dipped, and dived in her chest the closer he came.

Then he stood a foot away, looking down at her with a crooked grin. He had replaced the bandage on his temple with an almost clear one. Smile lines winged his eyes the coppery color of a summer creek bed. The butterflies clamored for attention in her throat.

Cullen reached out, swept away the sweat from her hairline with a gentle thumb. She was frozen, trapped. And not sure if she wanted to escape.

Behind her the coals shifted in the forge, sighed as the heat escaped. With his eyes on hers, he ran his other thumb along her jawline, sending shivers down her neck and into her spine. Her hands tingled at her sides, toes curled in her boots. His thumb finished its study, and moved to her lower lip, caressing it with a light brush. Like sparks cast from an open fire.

Cullen's hand shifted, cupped the back of her neck. Her traitor's heart raced, expectant. Wanting, denying, craving. Each butterfly seemed to have a different identity, all trying to escape through her sternum.

With his face inches from hers, he whispered, "Can we start over, Joleigh? No secrets?"

She nodded, unable to speak; barely capable of rational thought. He cast his eyes down to her lips, and she found them opening without her consent. His gaze flickered back to her eyes, and he leaned in.

"Have dinner with me?"

"Okay," she managed, hardly above a whisper.

She closed her eyes as he covered the space between them, her body inching toward his. The kiss she expected never arrived.

Instead, he kissed the middle of her forehead, his lips scorching her already hot skin.

"See you at seven?"

Her body trembled as he pulled away, a spring in full recoil. "Yeah, okay. Where?"

"I'll have Shelley cook us up something special."

Her tummy quivered, and her palms were clammy. She felt as though she had run a marathon. As he turned to go, Jo placed her hands across her stomach. She found her tongue when he reached the outer door.

"Cullen?"

He turned, smiled in the shadows. "Yeah?"

"I don't like tomatoes."

Chuckling, he said, "Got it."

And then he was gone.

Chapter 24

"*I don't like tomatoes,*" she growled into the silence. "That was really lame, Camden. Genius."

Jo plopped onto the stool, wired and jittery; aching for a kiss that didn't happen and irritated with herself for it. But somehow, this was sweeter. Slower.

What did he see in her? She peeled the sleeved apron off her drenched body, held it in front of her with both hands, letting it drag the floor. A sweaty mess, physically and emotionally. Webs of a tangled past had woven their way into the present, enveloping and consuming her life. And yet, Cullen pursued her, undaunted.

Enough. The man had literally taken a beating on her behalf; and she repaid his kindness with scorn, boorishness, and bad manners. Her mother, Laura, would have reprimanded her up one end and down the other for her behavior. It was time to adjust her attitude, because too much was at stake to be petty and callous.

The timer on the tempering oven still indicated nearly two hours for this first treatment. A second would follow after the metal cooled to room temperature. She stood, and hung the leather apron on its peg. In a cabinet under her worktop, she kept a variety of spare clothes. Judging by the smut, sweat, and grime covering her white t-shirt, a wardrobe change was in order. She grabbed the tee on top, attempted to shake out the wrinkles.

For the first time in the history of ever, she paused before changing in the middle of the shop. Normally, it was a no-brainer if she had the shop to herself; which had been the case since Uncle Charlie passed away five years ago.

Jo stalked through the shop into the office, checked the tiny bathroom. No bad buys, no charming employers.

The cool air of the office chilled her glistening skin. Shivering, she pulled on the clean maroon shirt, brushed off her jeans. Hanging her head upside down, she re-tied her hair into a sloppy bun, keeping it off her neck. The aquamarine pendant dangled freely in front of her face until she righted herself, tucking it into the front of her shirt.

Earlier, after storming away from Cullen's room at the Silver Street Inn, she had stomped through the office and pointedly ignored the clutter and chaos still ravaging the space. Oddly, fear quivered abandoned in the dark corner of her mind. Anger hogged center stage, demanded she pay attention. How dare Roy come here, wreck her home and her business? Well, Cullen's business, but one and the same to her. Roy would pay for the destruction, for hurting Cullen; and more importantly, he would suffer for murdering her mother. Fear remained absent from the equation. Banished.

She gathered loose papers, sorted them into stacks. Swept up debris, broken glass, and the remnants of her viewscreen system. Jo would be lying if she said she didn't have gear envy. Cullen's SatNet system made her salivate. When she reached the far side of the room, near the built-in bookshelf, her toe kicked a black walnut frame. Its glass lay shattered beneath it, the photo askew under the pieces.

Her father, frozen in time, his hammer caught in mid-strike against what she suspected was a knife blank, sparks flying around his glowing face. With a finger, she traced his arm. She hugged the photo tight to her chest. Jo carried the frame and photo, slid them into the bottom drawer of the desk. She kicked the drawer closed, but it stuck out about two inches. Grunting, she squatted in front of it, tried shoving it. No give. She rolled her eyes, and clambered under the desk to see what was keeping it from fully closing.

Something dark, rectangular. Lying supine on the now-cleaned floor, she scooted under the desk, and grabbed the obstruction. A book. She wriggled out, holding the book to the light once she was out. *Holy Bible* gleamed, embossed in gold on the front leather cover, with *Neal Camden* stamped in the same manner on the lower right corner. Her father's Bible.

Cross-legged on the floor, she thumbed through the faded, gilded-edge pages. She admired the underlines and circles, the notes scrawled in the margin. The back half of the binding gave way; a hunk of pages threatened to fall. How many days had she come upon her father, rocking on the front porch with this Bible in his lap.

"Come sit on my lap, sugar bear," Daddy said. "I'll tell you a love story you'll never forget."

"Are there princesses and knights?" she asked.

"There are kings, and then there is The King." He patted his leg. "Want to learn about true love?"

She squealed and clapped her hands. "Yes, sir! I hope they live happily ever after."

"Ah," he said, his face very serious. "To live happily ever after, you have to love The King with all your heart, with all your soul, and with all your strength."

"What's the King's name, Daddy?"

"His name is Jesus, sweetheart."

Jo sniffed, wiped a tear before it fell. What a day.

Through the door to the smithy she heard the ring of the heat treat oven's timer. She stood, laid the Bible on the desk, dusted off her backside. A niggling voice in her head told her to spend a little time reading God's Word. She would, when she had time. For now, the spade beckoned.

With glove-protected hands, Jo pulled the spade from the heat and laid it on the cooling rack. Once it was back to room temperature, it would return for another two-hour cycle of heat treating. Then she would move to polishing and grinding, and affixing the hardened walnut handle. In the days when the forge fire rarely died, she would have four or five projects running at once. Now, with the lack of steel and the abundance of mayhem, she felt lucky to get this one piece hammered out. Metal therapy to help her think.

She returned to the office to finish cleaning the mess Roy or whoever had left in their wake, and her eyes landed on the leather-bound Bible. Jo ran a finger over the cover, and sighed. She opened it to a random page, leaned over the desk to read standing up. Behind her, in the smithy, the door opened and clanged shut. She smiled at the thought of Cullen not being able to wait until supper in what, two hours?

"I'm in the office, Boss," she yelled without turning her head.

The book of Daniel was open before her. Closing her eyes, she twirled her finger in the air, and plunked it down on the page. She opened her eyes, and read the verse beneath her finger. Chapter nine, verse nine, she noted.

"The Lord our God is merciful and forgiving, even though we have rebelled against him," she said aloud. Hmmm. Rebellious described her perfectly.

His footsteps sounded behind her. "Hey, I found my dad's Bible wedged behind the desk drawer. Check it out."

The whisper of a blade sliding from a sheath was the only warning. Cold steel bit the skin under her chin. Her hands flew to the thick forearm coiled tightly around her shoulders, pinning her arms to her sides. His other hand pressed the knife against her neck.

"Move, scream, and it's over, Jo," Roy said.

She would know his voice anywhere.

"Do you understand me?"

She swallowed, felt the blade nip her. "Yes," she whispered.

Think, Camden. Think.

Every scenario played in her mind; plans considered and discarded in milliseconds. His scent, musk and dirt, flooded her nose. He smelled of sweat and filth, week old coffee mixed with tobacco, and rancid body odor.

"What do you want, Roy?"

"I'm not the same person I was when you were a kid."

"Somehow, I doubt that. You're holding a knife to my throat."

He sighed, his breath coasting through her hair. "Look, this is for my protection. Sorry."

His protection? "Still not buying it."

The arm encircling her tightened. "Where are they?"

"Who?"

"Not who. What. The jewels, the gold. Your mama had a couple baubles, said they were from jewelry she melted down. That may be true, but it ain't the whole truth. There's more of it."

Would she be able to get a heel onto his instep? More likely the motion would put that blade deep in her throat.

"No clue. Never heard of any treasure."

He growled, "Look. I'm trying to protect you. Give it up, or I won't be able to protect you from him."

"Who?"

"Never mind." He jostled her, adjusted his grip. "Tell me what I need to know, and then I'm gone. I'm telling you, I've changed. But … this is the only way to keep you from getting hurt."

Yeah, right. Sweat poured from her brow. "All I've got are the jewels Mama gave me. They're in a box under my bed, out at my place. Loose floor board. But, please, don't take anything else from it. Just the gems."

"He's not gonna like that. But it's something." He paused, breathed heavily down on her head. "Put your hands behind your back, now. Nice and slow. This knife is sharp, and I don't wanna nick ya."

"How about you just move it away, and I let you go?" Jo asked.

She felt rather than saw him swing his head side to side. "Can't do it. Hands, Jo."

She complied, because she honestly couldn't find a way out of this one. A cool strip wound around her wrists, tightened down. The tight webbing bit into the skin. With the way it cinched down one-handed, it was probably a carbon fiber police binding. The kind used in the place of hand cuffs in some places. Once it was in place, only a special tool could unlock it. The material was tough and durable, and strengthened by stretching.

"All right, nice and slow to the chair."

"Who's with you, Roy?"

No answer. She lowered herself into the swivel chair, her back to him.

"I saw you outside the inn the other night. The cops know you're here."

He swore under his breath, but kept the knife under her chin. "It's not the way it looks, I swear. I was watching *him*."

"Go search the old homestead. I'm sure you remember where it is." Jo hoped he felt the venom of her words.

"One day, I hope you'll forgive me for the things I've done. Now sit in the chair, and scoot under the desk." He paused while she slowly complied. "I'm sorry for this."

A moment's hesitation, and then a hairy elbow and forearm clamped around her throat, his weapon discarded and clanking on the floor. Jo writhed, fought as hard as she could. But her legs were trapped beneath the desk, and her hands were restrained behind her back. Lights flickered, like fireflies in summer. She fought, but the edges of her vision grew gray, tunneling to black oblivion.

Chapter 25

The grandfather clock in the foyer of the Silver Street Inn tolled twice, marking seven-thirty. For the fifth time, Cullen opened the door and surveyed the street for Jo. Where was the blasted woman? Probably punishing him for his presumption earlier. Stupid. All the while his hands cupped her face, his brained screamed warning. At the very last second, his intended trajectory altered course, and the kiss landed in the middle of her forehead. In the end, he thought it was better that way. Slower, like with a skittish wild dog.

And yet, there was an unscratchable itch between his shoulder blades that resented being ignored. Fine, this point went to her. Tapping his wristcom, he spoke her name aloud, listened as the call rang a few times. Tersely, Jo's recorded voice instructed him to leave a message.

"Cullen, here. It's 7:30, and Shelley's masterpiece is cooling. Give me a call, let me know when you think you'll get over."

Granted, he had only known her about a week. Saying it didn't seem like her amounted to a huge assumption about her character. He paced the floral hall runner, as nervous as a boy on his first date. Checked his wristcom again. Glanced at the grandfather clock. Then he decided.

Poking his head through the open doorway between the dining room and kitchen, he told Shelley, "I'm going to check on Jo. I have a bad feeling."

The little woman frowned, her normal laugh lines turned down in worry. "Want me to call Duke over?"

He shook his head. "This is me being paranoid."

Shelley nodded in the direction of his bandage, continuing to stir the alfredo sauce. "I'd say you have a right to be. Run on, I'll keep the food warm."

"You're an angel, Shell." He threw a wave over his head on the way out.

Down the block, left at the corner. Lamplights lining the downtown thoroughfare flickered to life as he stalked past. The heat from the day snuggled cozily into the coolness of evening. A bloodied sun hung expectantly above the horizon, hemorrhaging the last vestiges of the star's life into a clear, multihued sky.

In the distance, the wooden sign above the office door sashayed in the breeze. Coleville's charm beckoned him to make it a permanent home. There was a quaint bungalow two streets over listed with an agent out of Bryan. As soon as this business of the break-ins panned out, he'd give the lady a call, schedule a showing. Being closer to Jo only made the deal sweeter.

But if she were in her shop hammering on a piece of hot metal, instead of eating a nice meal with him, he might have a few choice morsels to say about it.

As he drew nearer to the shop, he began to rush. His feet carried him the last few steps, and then through the door that had been left ajar.

"Oh, God, help me! Jo!"

Her head slumped forward from her seated position, resting on its side. Please be alive, he chanted. He checked the carotid, found a slow, steady pulse. Cullen exhaled in a gust, shook her shoulders.

"Jo. Can you hear me?"

Nothing, no movement, no indication of consciousness.

He quickly pinged the emergency beacon on his wrist. A female voice answered, "Sheriff's office. What is your emergency?"

"Get Duke down to the smithy. Jo's unconscious." His eyebrows rose briefly at her sworn response. Colorful.

"He's on the way."

Cullen attempted to ease her from the chair to the floor, and that was when he noticed her hands, restrained at her back. He eased his arms between hers and lifted, scooting the chair to the wall. Grunting, he lowered her to the hardwood floor, laid Jo on her side. A quick examination showed a dark purple bruise splotching around her neck, as though something had tightened around it. Not something. Someone.

Roy or his accomplice.

He patted her cheeks, repeated her name. Duke flew through the door, breaking a stick and waving it under her nose.

Jo's eyes exploded open, blue irises standing in stark contrast to the whites. A handful of squiggly veins shone red amidst the white. She gasped and coughed hoarsely as her shoulders hunched forward in jerks.

A deep groan rumbled through her swollen throat.

"She's restrained, Duke," Cullen said, pointing to her laced wrists.

"Here," the deputy barked. He pulled a slim tool from a case on his belt, passed it to Cullen. "There's a catch on the ratchet. Put that in there and twist."

Her hands sprung free, and another rattling bark shook her shoulders. She moaned, lying face down on the unforgiving floor. Cullen rubbed circles on her back while Duke checked her over. The deputy called dispatch, told them to send an ambulance to Camden Ironworks.

"Don't ... need ... ambulance," she managed.

"There is no way you are getting out of this, girl, so don't even try it," Duke growled. "Who did this?"

"Roy."

She struggled to sit up. Cullen eased behind her, assisted as much as Jo would let him. Turning those gorgeous blue eyes on him, she whispered, "Water?"

A quick nod, and he trotted over to the compact bathroom. He rinsed out the cup he found near the sink, filled it with cool water from the tap. Jo muttered her thanks, sipping the liquid. She cringed and repeated, brushed her hair away from her face.

Her wrists still bore the restraint marks. The way she rolled her shoulders told him her arms were sore too.

Outside the picture window, shadows descended onto Sam Houston Avenue. A strip of stars in a darkening sky sat atop the business across the street.

"What time is it?" she whispered, a little stronger than before.

"Nearly eight."

"I missed supper."

Cullen angled his head closer to hear the quiet words. "I forgive you."

"I just want this to stop."

"I know."

Side by side they sat on the floor of Camden Ironworks, heads tilted and resting against one another, watching darkness fall on Coleville.

***

Jo endured the ambulance ride with a clenched jaw and a hefty amount of humiliation. How had she been so foolish? Cullen's attack, the break-ins, seeing Roy outside of the inn. Colored lights flashed on equipment panels to her right and left, red and green blinking beacons. Chirps sounded now and then. The emergency tech was just a kid, early twenties maybe, but he seemed efficient and kind. A thin, elongated cooling pad was draped over her neck. She answered the questions in a gravelly whisper, and tried not to be embarrassed for her lack of diligence.

She tried to remember the time, when Roy surprised her from behind. Four? Five o'clock? Unconscious for at least two hours then, a little more.

The blinking lights reminded her of Christmas trees and decked out houses in December. Pretty. So pretty. What was she thinking? Oh, right. What time Roy ... why was she thinking about Roy? Wait. A knife, the hiss of the blade exiting the sheath. She should work on a few knives. It had been a while since she forged a blade. Uncle Charlie probably had an order or two she could fill for him.

She blinked, slow and lazy. Why was she thinking of Uncle Charlie? He died five years ago. A thought straggled wearily across her brain.

"What … give me?" Her lips moved sluggishly, fat and uncooperatively.

The tech's head wavered above her. Was she under water? Why was his face swimming?

"Just something to help you relax, Miss Camden. Don't worry, we'll be at the hospital soon."

The kid smiled, and it melted, teeth and lips sliding over his chin. A Dalí painting come to life. Another heavy blink, and her eyes closed.

Jostling, shaking. Easing out of a box with a starry lid. Cullen's worried face, his lips moving and muffled nonsense filtering into her ears. A staccato of overhead lights: blink, blink, blink. A sensation of flying and rolling through the air. Too much. She squeezed her eyes, shutting out the bewildering images.

Darkness and silence.

"Jo? Jo, honey, open those beautiful blue eyes for me."

Cullen beckoned her from the depthless abyss, begging her to surface. She ached to stay, to simply *be*, but his voice was a magnet. Once, twice, her eyelids twitched.

"That's good. Come on, girl." Duke, too?

A slice of light appeared, widening. Bit by bit, her mind caught up to her surroundings. She was in the hospital.

"Hey, honey," Cullen said, leaning in. Her hand was enveloped in his. "Welcome back."

She swallowed, noticed her throat didn't ache as badly as before. Cullen handed her the cup of water before she asked for it. Smiling her thanks, she snagged the straw. The water was ice cold, blissfully so.

The marks around her wrists were noticeable, but fading. Raw, sore, almost like rug burns. Her fingers palpated her throat.

"How bad is it?"

"Bad enough that I'm not taking a day off until that man is found and back behind bars," Duke growled. "This is going too far. We don't even know if this is revenge or some wild goose chase treasure hunt."

"Actually," Jo said, around the straw between her lips. "We do. He talked a lot while he had a knife to my throat."

Cullen hissed, and Duke paced, muttering to himself.

"Kept talking about 'him'. Whoever that is. Roy claimed this other guy is the one running the show."

"The cousin?" Cullen asked. He still held her hand. His thumb drew tiny circles near the webbing of her thumb and forefinger. Even through the haze and trauma, he sent shivers cascading from her hand to her middle.

"He wouldn't say. Clammed up every time I asked. But I think so, yeah. Makes sense, both of them ditching the work farm within a few days of each other."

"And the cousin was first," the deputy provided. "Maybe they split up to divert resources from the prison?"

Jo shrugged. "Not sure. But it was weird. He kept saying he was changed, not the same guy I knew before. And right before he wrapped his arm around my throat, he asked me to forgive him for it."

Ropy tendons in Cullen's jaws flexed and throbbed. "Let me get this straight. He held a knife to your throat, strangled you, and left you; and he asked for forgiveness before he did it?"

"Weird, I know. But yeah. Also claimed he was looking out for me, protecting me."

Duke snorted. "What a crock. When I get my hands on him, he'll wish he never conceived the thought of stepping out of that prison."

A nurse pushed aside the curtain, entering the room with a cheery smile. "It's good to see you awake, Miss Camden. Just going to check your vitals, and then I'll let the deputy here continue taking your statement." The petite woman chattered more than a magpie while she went about the business of probing, squeezing, and poking. "One last thing. Were you assaulted in … um, any other areas?" She blushed, swept her gaze over the men.

"No," Jo answered quickly. "Nothing like that."

"Good. The doctor will be in shortly to go over your scan results."

"What scan?"

Cullen glanced at Duke, nodded in Jo's direction. The older man leaned on one hip, hooked his hands in his jeans' pockets. "They ran the test while you were in la-la land. I knew you'd never go for it awake."

"*You're* the one who told them to give me those goofy meds? Duke!"

"I am your next of kin, darlin'. You needed the rest anyway."

Probably. And yes, he was right. She wouldn't have had any fancy test on her own.

"We didn't know how long you were unconscious," Duke explained. "Had to know if any loss of oxygen had damaged the brain. A precaution."

If Jo had exercised more caution a few hours ago, she wouldn't be laid out on a gurney.

As if he read her mind, Cullen said, "We're done being lax about this whole thing. I have stitches and an aching head; you have bruising around your neck from a botched strangulation—"

"It wasn't botched," she interrupted. "At least, I don't think so."

"Explain," Duke said.

"The way he was talking, going on and on about how sorry he was, asking for forgiveness. I don't think he meant to kill me. It's like he wanted me out of his hair for a little while. Maybe to escape and not have me following him."

"That's crazy, Jo," the deputy growled. "He's a murderer three times over, at least that we know of. I doubt he'd think twice about vengeance on the one who put him away."

Maybe. Maybe not. But Jo had a feeling there was more to the story than X marks the spot.

Chapter 26

Friday, May 11, 2096

Two days later, temperatures soared, morale plummeted, and attitudes verged on implosion.

Roy and his accomplice appeared to have vanished from the area. They were ghosts; the only indications of their sudden and brief appearance were a healing temple gash and fading ligature bruises. A trap of sorts laid in wait near the old homestead. Ben and Duke swapped duty on surveillance, but to no avail. No one bit. Not even a nibble.

In the close quarters of the smithy, Cullen and Jo clashed; like a hammer pounding red-hot steel, sparks flew at the slightest provocation. Each eventually retreated to their comfortable areas of operation, calling a stalemate. He insisted she take it easy, and take time to heal. She pointed out that he had neglected to do the same. She wasn't blown glass. Hurt, anger, embarrassment, and indignant frustration warred within her. Therefore, Jo sweated out her temper near the forge, while Cullen resumed his farrier duties in the area surrounding Coleville. Rather than feel relieved, guilt prevailed.

Upon Jo's midnight release from the hospital, Duke had insisted that she take a room at the Silver Street Inn. The lawman claimed her creek-side cabin wasn't safe, because of the distance from town. At the inn, Jo would be near Cullen and Ben. While, truthfully, Ben stayed out on the trail longer than he did in town. The restrictions chafed.

She thought the only one happy with the current arrangement was whichever junior deputy pulled security detail. Shelley kept those guys in khaki and black well-fed. Tonight, Logan Strake enjoyed Shelley's vittles, keeping watch over the entrances to the inn.

Jo, however, was doing a whole lot of nothing. Sitting on the plush sofa with her feet tucked up beneath her thighs, she scrolled through the television channels with a bored finger. Each downward swipe in the air showed more of the same on the guide. Exasperated, she drew an angry X in the air. The unit powered off.

Night clung to the sky. Clouds covered the waning moon, and the wind howled indignant against the windows. Nothing to watch, no books to read, and too early yet for sleeping.

She paced, wandered, and found herself in front of the bathroom mirror. Tipping her chin toward the overhead light, she angled it left and right, scrutinizing the remains of Roy's visit. Greenish brown splotches dotted her neck in a roughly circular pattern. Thankfully, the swelling had diminished. The medicated cream provided by the hospital pharmacy worked to nearly erase the rubbed irritation around her wrists. Purple smudged half circles hung from her bloodshot eyes. She looked tired, wasted. Her wounds were healing, but her spirit spiraled downward.

Why had he left her alive? After the destruction of her home and business, and with the opportunity literally at his hands, he chose to choke her out instead of slicing her throat. Not that she wasn't grateful to still be breathing. But the whole thing puzzled her to no end.

Grunting at her pitiful reflection, she switched off the light, padded into the bedroom. Beside the queen-sized bed, the palm reader resting on the side table blinked to life. The image of an unopened envelope glowed on the screen. Curious, Jo shuffled over.

The message was from Ruth at the sheriff's station. Her heart thumped wildly in her throat. A copy of her mother's diary, scanned as an electronic version, was attached to the message.

Outside the second story window lightning flickered in the distance, throwing wild shadows around the room. She cast a hasty glance at the window, waited for thunder. Twenty seconds later, it lazily rumbled through Coleville. The tormented animal trapped in her chest clawed, desperate for release. Jo tapped the download icon, squeezed tight her eyelids and swallowed the fear gripping her esophagus.

April 27, 2064

Happy 6th birthday, my sweet Joleigh-girl! Each year of your life has been a blessing to your father and me. Oh, how I wish you could have seen your eyes light up when Daddy gave you that hammer! You glowed, my darling.

I decided today that you were growing too quickly. Ginny's toddling around getting into everything, and my brain feels like it's leaking out of my ears. So I got this journal and started writing, so that I could remember more than bits and pieces of your childhood.

One day it will pass to both of you. Try not to think too harshly of my ramblings. For better or worse, the thoughts on these pages will be written in love. Until tomorrow ...
Mama.

Outside, the heavens flashed and flared, illuminating clouds from within. Thunder rolled closer, more intense. As Jo devoured the words written in her mother's hand, the tears sliding over her cheeks mirrored the rain pelting and slipping down the window panes of the dimly lit borrowed bedroom. Page after page, entry after entry. There were bright shiny moments captured in time, and the ordinary scattered throughout. The storm pounded against the wall.

Then she realized someone was pounding on the door.

Reluctantly, she placed the reader on the bedside table.

Cullen's hand was raised to knock again when she swung open the door. His mouth opened to speak, but it clacked closed and open again.

"Hey, what's wrong? You've been crying."

Jo pushed open the door, motioned for him to come in.

She waved him off as she sat on the sofa. "Nothing, really. Ruth sent the e-copy of my mom's journal. I've been reading it for the last hour."

"Ah."

"It's hard, you know. Reading something she intended to give me when she was old and gray. I'm only about a quarter of the way through. Every day, Cullen. Even if it was just one line, she wrote something every day."

"Sounds like you're getting a chance to know your mom, even though she's gone."

The tears poured as she nodded her head. "Ugh. I've cried more in the last week and a half than I have in ten years."

He plopped down next to her on the squishy couch, wrapped a muscled arm around her back, squeezed her bicep. "You're so strong," he said. When she snorted, he added, "I mean it. Really. One of the strongest women I know. Even my father would think twice of crossing you."

She laughed through a nose-sniffle. "Maybe I should be the one to go to Austin. I could put him in his place." Chuckling, she grabbed a tissue and wiped her nose.

He rubbed his chin. "You may be onto something there."

She expected a laugh, a guffaw, something. "You're serious?"

Cullen shrugged. "Well, why not? You're a citizen business owner with a very real concern. And you don't take flak from anyone. Plus," he added with a wicked grin, "I'd love to see you take on the old man."

"I know you didn't come over here to recruit me as a lobbyist."

He smiled. "Nope. I came over here because I found our treasure."

Jo hopped up, slapping him on the arm. "You *what?* Why didn't you say something before?"

"Because you needed someone to listen more than I needed to tell you," he said simply, standing.

Grabbing him by the shirt, she pulled him to the door. "Let's go, bub."

The door of her room and those of Ben and Cullen made an elongated triangle. It occurred to her that her bedroom and Cullen's shared a wall. He pulled up SatNet, and initiated the holographic geography program … the same one used by the military. A blinking red light pulsed slowly north of Austin.

Jo pointed to the dot. "That's in the middle of a national reserve. We used to go hiking up there for mando-fun."

"Mando-fun?"

"Yeah, you know. Mandatory fun? It's a favorite Marine Corps pastime."

Shaking his head, he muttered under his breath. She laughed.

"So, anyway, I was reading that blasted riddle on a loop, and started doodling. I drew a head and two shoulders, put a wide open mouth in the middle of the 'head'," he explained. "Remember that part? *'A head between two shoulders, The mouth gapes wide.'*"

She nodded, a slow bob of the head. "And?"

"Well, it looked like a cave to me."

"Hmm. Yeah, I can see that."

"Best place to find a cave is the Hill Country surrounding Austin, right?"

"Yeah …"

"I pulled up the map, just planning to pour through the topography from ground view to see if I could spot a cave surrounded by a hill with two 'shoulders'. When I did, one word stood out. Balcones."

Jo sucked in a breath. "Balcony. *'The balcony holds the secret.'* Balcones Wildlife Refuge."

Cullen jabbed a finger at the full color three dimensional map floating above the desk. "Exactly. Makes sense. Your ancestor, or whoever it was, had his fortune stolen near Round Rock. Back then, the hike to the Balcones area would have been a nasty one, even on horseback. The trails are rugged, steep switchbacks, you name it. What was the guy's name anyway?"

Jo mumbled the answer.

"Say again?"

"Shifty Jake Sackwell."

"Shifty Jake? Really?"

"That's what he went by anyway, according to what was passed down."

"You're not making that up?"

"Sadly," she laughed. "No."

"He sounds more like the outlaw than the gold miner," Cullen laughed.

The red beacon blinked lazily.

"*What once was lost is now found inside. Below, the colored snake slithers south to the star,*'" Cullen quoted. "The first part is self-explanatory, if you know you're looking for buried gold. The colored snake part—"

"The Colorado River," Jo stated.

Cullen nodded. "Watch this."

He used his hands to manipulate the image so that it appeared one viewed the terrain from the ground. "If I put myself here," he said, dragging a little man to a point halfway between the squiggly Colorado and the winking beacon, "and select this view ..."

Amazing. Green grass interspersed with withered brown grew around Virtual Man's feet. Cacti grew spiky in abundance, scattered about amidst stones and boulders. Cullen tilted the view upward. A crooked hump of hill was flanked by two smaller ones, jagged and stone-covered. On the lower right side of the center hill gaped a black maw.   A cave.   Spinning the view so that Virtual Man faced southward, the curling Colorado River snaked toward Austin.

"Austin," she mumbled. Then louder, "The star! The Capitol."

Cullen nodded. "That's what I think, too."

Excitement quivered, tingling her hands. "When can we leave?"

"Tomorrow morning," he grinned.

"I'll be packed within the hour."

She walked toward the door, then turned and groaned.

"What?" Cullen asked, concerned interest playing across his face. "Are you nervous about being alone with me?"

She laughed, shaking her head. "Actually, no. It just occurred to me there is one obstacle keeping us from going."

"What?"

She sighed, blowing wispy strands of blonde hair from her face. "Duke."

Chapter 27

They topped off the charge of Cullen's truck at an electrifill station in Hearne, a flyspeck of a town dangling by a hope, a prayer, and the intestinal fortitude of a few hardy old timers. It was one of the towns abandoned during the Collapse, with a majority of the inhabitants either fleeing to Bryan-College Station or Franklin for employment or to join up with other family members. Most never returned.

Grime coated the filling station's plate glass window. Jo's reflection gazed back at her, muted and sepia-toned. Pinned advertisements flapped like clipped-wing birds on a bulletin board screwed into the exterior wall of the store. Across the road, the forsaken husk of a McDonald's restaurant loomed, vacant and forgotten. The yellow arches were pockmarked; and the midmorning sun threw lights through beams in the plastic, casting a dappled light show on the puddles in the pot-holed parking lot.

"Just about done," Cullen said. "Need anything from inside?"

Jo shook her head. "It's sad, isn't it?"

He cocked his head to the side. "What?"

"This town. Others like it."

"I suppose that's just the way it goes. Towns live and die all over."

"I studied the rise and fall of the United States in college history, how towns like this succumbed to the Collapse. Then after, with the secession, people scuttling out of high-risk cities into the surrounding towns, reviving some on the brink of dying. I guess Hearne didn't make the cut."

"It is what it is, darlin'," he drawled.

She rolled her eyes, grinned, and hiked a hip onto the seat of the truck. "Let's roll, Boss."

They shot southwest on Highway 79, the sun chasing the newer truck along a two-lane road. Homesteads dotted the way. Cattle munched along barbed-wire fences, chickens scratched and pecked in the yards of modest homes. The truck's windows were down, letting in the cool air the rain brought last night. Jo stuck her arm out the window, letting her hand ride the currents the way she did as a child on the rare occasion she rode in a vehicle.

"You know," she said, raising her voice to be heard over the drafting wind, "I didn't expect Duke to say yes so easily."

Cullen glanced over. "Me either. But what he said made sense."

"You really think the threat goes away just because we do?"

"No, but it can't hurt to be out of the area. They'll keep watching the old homestead, your cabin, and our shop. Ben had some motion-sensor wireless feed cameras he's loaning Duke. If something man-sized is around there, they'll know about it."

Jo pulled her arm inside the truck, rolled up the window until the glass was two inches from the top. Looking ahead at the road, she said, "Our shop?"

He flicked another peek at her, grinning. The white scar on his upper cheek folded into the laugh lines ringing his eyes. "Well, it's pretty hard to think of a smithy without the blacksmith. Especially," he laughed, "one as headstrong as mine."

Mine. Did he mean as an employee or something else? The tummy flutter hoped he meant more, as frightening as the prospect was.

"But I was thinking. How would you feel about a partnership?"

Stunned, Jo faced him. "If this is a joke, it's a really bad one, Cullen."

"Come on. You know I wouldn't joke about that. I know how much the Ironworks means to you. So?"

"Well, gee. Let me think. Uh, yeah! What are we talking?"

"Fifty-fifty."

Could have been worse. "Equal say?"

He nodded. "I would leave the blacksmithing to you; orders, repairs, supplies. Things like that. You'd have to handle my farrier needs, too. But you maintain creative control on the everyday stuff."

"What's the catch?"

"No catch, I promise. Look, when I bought the place, it was business. Grabbing a smithy at a rock bottom price to merge with my farrier business. And now that I've gotten to know the previous owner rather well, it makes sense to take you on as a partner rather than an employee."

Jo gazed out the window, wisps of escaped hair flying in her face in the breezy truck cab. They blew past a horse and carriage traveling along the horse path parallel to the highway. The buggy driver raised a hand in greeting, briefly seen and then gone. In the distance, over a rise to the north, buzzards cycloned above the tree line. She pondered his proposal, her lower lip snagged with her teeth.

"All right. I'm in," she said with a smile. "I don't see how I could say no."

Cullen pulled his right hand from the wheel, extended it across the center console to her. "Shake on it to make it official?"

She clasped his hand tightly, gave it a slight pump of affirmation. But he held hers hostage, took a second to lock eyes with her. Jo attempted to ignore the sparks tingling in her palm and failed. "I look forward to it," he said.

Good golly, she needed to get a grip.

Stunted, crooked trees blurred alongside them as they drove toward Austin. White cotton balls dotted the sky ahead of them, marching off across the wide Texas sky. Here and there they passed riders on the horse path, met oncoming vehicles. They spoke of their favorite music, of comfort food and hobbies. She was completely blown away when he stated that he was the one who did the leather tooling on his saddle. He seemed just as surprised that she owned a sewing machine and knew how to use it. An hour into the trip, he rolled up the windows and turned on the air conditioning, tuned to a classical station and set the volume low. They talked, warming to each other, testing the waters. She wasn't sure when it happened, their hands interlocking across the center console. Her belly warmed and she felt sixteen again.

For a brief moment in time, the reason for the trek from Coleville to Austin slipped from her mind; a tumbleweed there and gone. But when they reached the outskirts of Round Rock, where traffic increased and the number of horses thinned, she remembered. Round

215

Rock, the place where her ancestor was set upon by thieves and robbed of his hard-earned gold.

"I think it's grown since the last time I was through here," Jo commented.

"Yeah? When was that?"

"Hmmm. Sixteen years?"

He laughed. "That all?" Cullen turned his head and winked, squeezed her hand. She really hoped her hand wasn't as clammy as she thought it was.

Through congested city streets, he navigated, steering the truck skillfully among the other worker ants filing toward the intrastate.

"This traffic makes me twitchy," she said, sour.

"Really? It's pretty light so far."

"Hmph. City Boy." But she grinned to take away the sting.

A handful of nerve-wracking minutes later, the major artery leading north to south across the country came into view. It wasn't until she noticed the navigation system flashing that she realized Cullen missed the exit.

"Hey, you just passed the northbound ramp, oh wise one."

He steered with one hand, ran the other through his mop of hair. "Yeah, about that ..."

She narrowed her eyes at him, that itchy feeling settling between her shoulder blades. "Hmmm?"

"Well, since we're so close to Austin, I thought –"

"No. No, Cullen, you didn't –"

"It's only for a little while. He's really not that bad. Well, maybe he is. But Mom is super nice. You'll like her. And she, um, really wants to meet you."

"Cullen Miles, I am going to kill you."

"Think of this as a golden opportunity to present your case to an exclusive audience with the Secretary of State of Texas."

"That's exactly what I don't like about it," she complained. She tried to extricate her hand from his – when did he grab it again? – but he held fast. "I have no data, no preparation. I'm in climbing gear, for Pete's sake."

"I have no doubt you'll make your case. Besides, you're a partner, remember?"

She snorted. "I'm the help. At least, that's what he thinks."

He glanced at her briefly. "I will abash him of such thoughts."

"Abash?"

Grinning, he said, "It was my word of the day. Been waiting for a chance to use it."

In spite of herself, she chuckled. "You're such a goob. I'm never forgiving you for this."

They journeyed south, with thousands of others making their way toward the Capitol. Bracing her elbow on the window ledge, she cupped her chin.

Strategizing her case against the Secretary of State.

And biting her nails to the quick.

Chapter 28

The Capitol dome and the bustling downtown business district slid by, a conglomeration of government and industry buildings squashed into a packed handful of city blocks blurring through the side window. Unseen, to the north of the Capitol, was the nondescript edifice of the Department of Defense. Deep within that building, in the bowels hidden away and protected from prying eyes and itching ears, was the secured intelligence facility in which she spent three out of four years of her enlistment in the Marines.

For the most part, she had pleasant memories of her military service. Her entrance test results primed her for a position in intel; and though it wasn't a "boots on the ground" specialty, she preferred it to border rangers or Gulf protection. She was a network ghost, tasked with insuring the stability and defense of the Texas SatNet and web infrastructure. Jo remembered the first week on the job, shadowing a corporal, learning the ropes. The sheer number of attempted network incursions boggled her motivated boot mind. The next few years imposed a sincere appreciation for "ghosts" and their unseen efforts.

Now, driving along the intrastate, taking in the blur of life, she realized just how little she ventured out of The Hole.

Silence made itself comfortable in the truck, snuggled in and hunkered down. Every once in a while, Cullen peeked at her. Each time she caught his worried frown out of the corner of her eye, her inner self grinned. The mad had passed. He was right, but she wasn't about to let him in on it. This was a once in her life opportunity to take on one of the powerhouses in government. So she mentally plotted and schemed, planned and discarded arguments; formed her case around current legislation, tariffs, and production costs. It wouldn't be the first time she had taken on a powerful individual, but the Secretary of State was definitely the highest ranking thus far.

The sun shone down from a hair past its zenith, and as they turned northwest on Highway 71 its glare blinded them. Cullen activated the solar filter, cutting the edge off the blazing rays. Her curiosity got the better of her, and she broke the silence.

"I figured your folks lived in Austin proper."

"Nope, to the northwest."

"The uppity side?" she joked.

He glanced over with a grin. "You nailed it. Actually, as the crow flies, we won't be too far from the Balcones Refuge. Since we're not crows, we'll still have a bit of a drive to get there. Listen, I was thinking. If you aren't up to talking with my father about the steel taxation issue, you don't have to come in. You can take the truck and —"

"It's okay," she interrupted. "You were right."

Cullen gasped, clutching his throat, making moaning dying noises. She slapped him on the arm.

"Very funny, drama king."

"Hey, it's not every day those words come out of your mouth." He paused. "Say it again."

She laughed. "You. Were. Right. Happy?"

"Immensely."

"Anyway, smarty-pants. I'll likely never have the chance again in my life to go toe-to-toe with the guy. I'd be a fool to pass it up."

Cullen shifted in his seat, ran a hand through his hair. "Maybe we should think of it as a diplomatic discussion, rather than an out and out debate."

"Hmm. And you really think he'll sit stoically behind his desk, fingers crossed in front of him, and listen to my demands. In his house. From the mouth of 'the help'?"

A pensive hush settled between them. "Yeah. Maybe not."

Twenty minutes later, after rising and falling with the rock-strewn knolls of the Hill Country, Cullen signaled and turned left down a curving road paved with loose white gravel. After a mile of weaving through stands of stunted mesquite and a few oaks, a guardhouse rose from the ground. Stretching in each direction, like long and winding arms, was a tall security fence.

The guard's eyebrows nicked his hairline before Cullen managed to roll down the window.

"Hey, Shane. The old man home?"

Shane swiveled a nervous look between Cullen and the long drive extending into the distance. "He's home. But he wasn't in the best of moods when he came through an hour ago. I think he and the president had it out again."

The expansive iron gate, two car-widths across, swung open on well-oiled hinges. "Wonderful," Cullen replied. "How's Jill?"

A wide smile replaced the worried look on the guard's face. "She's great. Due in July. Another boy."

"Hey, man! That's great news! Congratulations."

Shane's cheeks colored as the two shook hands through the open window. "Is Mr. Miles expecting you?" He cocked his head sideways, pinning Jo with a questioning expression. "And a guest?"

Cullen winced. "Shane, this is Jo, my business partner. And no, he's not."

The guard nodded, reaching a hand to the combination earpiece and microphone he wore. "I'll just radio ahead, and –"

"No!" Cullen blurted. "I mean, let's make it a surprise. I'm sure Mom will get a kick out of it."

Lowering his finger, Shane nodded hesitantly. "If you're sure?"

"Yeah, it'll be fun." Jo snorted, and Cullen grinned. "He's been nagging me to come home for a visit anyway."

"Sounds like a plan. I'll see ya on the way out, then." Shane tipped an imaginary hat at Jo. "Ma'am. Welcome to Colorado Hills."

The white gravel drive led them another mile, maybe more, through hills and valleys of stony terrain with a smattering of cacti of various species. A few pecan trees peeked through the twisted screen of mesquite. Then the drive led them down more than up, descending at a considerable grade. Near the bottom of their descent, the land flattened and opened wide. Situated on an improbable sea of green grass, standing in stark contrast to the predominantly brown landscape around them, rose one of the grandest homes Jo had seen.

She swallowed a knot in her throat. "Um, Cullen. This is more than wealthy."

"You're telling me. Now you know why I live in Coleville."

221

The mansion – for there was no other word for the structure – had the feel of Old West and southwest tradition merged into one. Stucco coated the soaring exterior walls, a creamy gold. A wide hickory door, naturally stained, guarded entry at the front of the house. At three stories high, the house had an expansive center section, flanked by two-story wings on either side. Traditional clay tiles made overlapping waves on the roofs. A tennis court sprawled in the midday sun, heat shimmering off the green surface. So much green here. The water bill alone would bankrupt Jo within a month.

Cullen's truck halted in the side parking area. Jo hopped out, sucked the dry, hot air into her lungs. A cloud of fine, white sandy particles followed them, settling slowly to the ground.

She spun in a lazy circle, taking it all in.

"It *is* beautiful," Cullen admitted, standing shoulder to shoulder with her."

"And so green. Everything out here is brown, except for the cacti and the lawn."

"The river provides most of the irrigation."

"River?"

He nodded, pointing off into the distance. "Just over that cliff. The Colorado runs through, and it's one of the deeper parts. Wait until you see that view."

"Your family is fond of gates," she joked. "I suppose I can see why." A black iron fence and gate surrounded the home. She narrowed her eyes, studying the gate. Something tugged at her memory.

"The guard shack was added after Dad got into politics. When he was still in the private sector, we didn't have to worry about security as much."

They crossed the parking area, walked toward Cullen's home. He reached to open the gate, but Jo placed a hand on his arm.

"What?"

"Hold on." She traced the filigrees and swirls. Black wrought iron twisted and turned to simulate an intricate ivy-covered trellis. Grinning, she traced two vines. "What do you see?"

"It's really nice. Very detailed."

She held his hand, extended his pointer finger out.

"Watch."

With his hand cupped in hers, she ran his finger along the swirls of two iron vines.

Squinting, he said, "Looks like a J and a C." His head spun to nail her with a look. "No way."

Nodding, she grinned. "Yep. It's mine. Eight years ago, or so. But it wasn't ordered under your father's name. I would have remembered that."

"Probably the landscaper. Unbelievable. It's beautiful."

She leveled an unamused look at him.

"What? Oh! Not unbelievable, as in I didn't think you were capable of creating something like this. Sheesh, Jo. Relax. I was just thinking that of all the smithies in the country that I could have bought, it was yours. And your work is here, at my parent's place. Doesn't it seem ... well, providential?"

"Definitely a strange coincidence."

He opened the latch, swung open the gate on rust-free hinges, motioned for her to precede him. She dipped a mocking curtsy and sashayed through to his laughter.

"Surely you don't believe in coincidence?" he asked, her elbow in his hand.

"Why wouldn't I?"

"I believe all things work out the way God orders them, is all. He has a great sense of humor."

"And I'm the butt of His joke?" she snorted, shaking her head.

He took her by the shoulders, spun her to face him. "Don't you see, Jo? God sent me to you. Who else would have made you partner after buying you out?"

Chapter 29

Cullen jabbed the doorbell. Ten seconds later, a petite woman in jeans and a plaid button down shirt, with a steel-gray bun and a sun-dried face, opened the wide hickory door, squealing loudly enough to wake the dead. She bounced on her tennis-shoed feet, clapping her hands.

Once the ringing in her ears ceased, Jo opened her eyes to find the little woman wrapped around Cullen's waist, squeezing him for all she was worth. He was grunting and grinning, hugging her back.

"I've missed you, too, Rose," he laughed.

"Mr. Cullen, it makes my heart smile to see you, it sure does," Rose said, beaming. She gave him one last embrace, and stepped back, her neck craned to see his face. Then she slapped him on the arm.

"Ow! What was that for?"

Both hands on her hips, she chided, "For not telling me you were coming. I would have had your bed made up and steaks on the grill."

Cullen chuckled, put an arm around the diminutive woman. "It's not an overnight stay, I'm afraid. We were out this way on business, and thought we'd drop in."

"We?" She spun a puzzled glance until her eyes landed on Jo. She whistled, leaned into him and whispered conspiratorially. "Ah, now. She's a looker. You better keep your hooks in that one. This the new receptionist?"

Cullen must have caught the fire lurking in Jo's eyes and quickly said, "No! No, Jo's my business partner. Definitely *not* the receptionist."

Rose scuttled over to Jo, wrapped her wizened hands around Jo's calloused ones. "It's good to meet you, Miss Jo. Is this rascal good to you?"

Jo raised an eyebrow, and Cullen narrowed his eyes, and I-dare-you-look on his face. "Yes, ma'am. He sure is."

With a pat and a squeeze, Rose nodded. "He better. I raised him right. Mr. Cullen," she said, turning in his direction, "I'll go get your mama. She'll be right pleased to see you."

She now knew what it meant to be weighed and measured.

Betsy Miles clicked in on four-inch heels. Her gaze swept across the room, taking everything in. She clearly dismissed Jo, and focused on her son.

Jo both admired and feared any woman who wore a smart business blazer and knee-length skirt in her own home, especially a lady whose ankles never once wobbled on those sky-high sticks. The only skirts Jo had ever worn were those of the dress uniform issued to the women Marines. They were currently boxed up and shoved as far away from daylight as she could manage. But a woman caught unaware in her own home, mid-afternoon, in a pewter silver power suit? Tread lightly. Think landmines.

Betsy gripped Cullen by the shoulders, pecked a kiss on both cheeks, and showed her perfect teeth in a smile that didn't quite reach her eyes. Shoulders squared and spine straight, she had leaned in for a light hug.

"Cullen, dear. I'm so happy you're home." Betsy swiveled her chignon-styled head toward Jo. "And who is this?"

"This is –" Cullen began, but Jo interrupted.

"Joleigh Camden, ma'am. It's nice meeting you." Jo extended her hand, accepted his mother's light grip.

"Charmed." She turned her attention to her son. "Y'all come on into the parlor, and Rose will bring us some refreshments. I'll let your daddy know you're home, dear. He'll be pleased you're home."

Once they were seated, Mrs. Miles excused herself with a half-smile. The clack of high heels trailed off into the distance at a rapid click. She rivaled a metronome.

Jo slumped in her carved chair. "That. Was. Exhausting."

He threw his head back, hilarity erupting from his mouth. "You haven't even made it to good old Dad yet, honey."

Cullen stood, pacing the room. He thumbed through antique books meant to be seen and not handled, picked up framed photographs of his parents together with important individuals. Stared out tall leaded windows at the green lawn surrounding the massive home of his childhood. Jo wondered what he was thinking.

She fidgeted at the tea table, fingered the polished silverware place setting. Unable to stand the silence any longer, she rose and joined him at the window.

"Nervous?" she asked.

"Me? No. A little sad, I guess. Mom's giving me the cold shoulder because I haven't been home in a while."

Jo cocked her head. "How long?"

"Two years."

Her brows scaled her forehead. "Why so long?"

He shrugged. "I don't know. We don't see eye-to-eye; and every time I'm here, they remind me how I'm shaming them with my lifestyle."

"What lifestyle? Being a farrier?" She was incredulous when he nodded. "They're upset with you for eeking out an honest living amongst the general populace, you mean?"

"Basically, yeah."

She put a hand on his shoulder, squeezed. Cullen turned to face her, swept away a stray hair from her face and tucked it behind her ear.

"You really get it, don't you?" he whispered. "Why I left all this?" He gestured to the parlor, the tennis court through the window, the carpet of vivid green amidst an arid desert.

Jo nodded slowly. "I do. When we first drove up, I thought you were crazy to ever leave resources like this. But now … yeah, I understand. You want your work to mean something. To have earned your way in the world, rather than having it deposited into your accounts for simply existing."

He reached up, ran a familiar thumb along her jawline. "We never did get that date, you know."

Gulping, flushed, she whispered, "I know. We should do something about that."

His hand moved to the bruised shadows around her neck, and she glanced at his healing laceration. Such trouble in so short a time. Feeling reckless, she pulled his head down, stared into his eyes. Then she planted a chaste kiss on the wound he received because of her.

Jo smiled at him. "I hear that is the cure-all magic. Kiss it to make it better."

When he glanced to her neck and the bruises ringing it, she began to tingle. Especially when that cocky grin pulled the side of his mouth towards the thin white scar on the other cheek. "I could return the favor," he said quietly.

"Hmm. I'll think about it."

A bass voice boomed from the open parlor doorway. "Cullen! Boy, I can't believe you're here. You wouldn't believe the day I've had."

Jo's back remained facing the Secretary as he entered the room, his footsteps muffled on the plush carpet behind her. With one last desperate glance at Cullen, she turned, putting a bit of distance between them.

It was as if Sterling Miles hadn't seen her until she turned. He stopped, hooked his thumbs on the front pockets of his starched dress denim jeans. A silver buckle gleamed just below a bulging belly.

"Ah, you brought your secretary. How quaint. She will be more comfortable in the kitchen helping Rose sort out the refreshments." He waved a hand in a general backward direction.

Jo blinked, stared at him. The man did *not* just try to send her off to fetch food and serve him, did he? Cullen's palm gripped her waist, his arm wrapped around her.

"Dad, I'd like you to meet Joleigh Camden."

"Nice to meet you, young lady. The kitchen is through those doors, down the hall to the right. You can't miss it."

She narrowed her eyes, squared her shoulders.

"She's not my receptionist, Dad. She's my business partner, and the reason we're here. We have a few things to discuss."

Jo cracked her knuckles. Time to play with the big boys.

Chapter 30

The Secretary swapped stares between Jo and Cullen, his lips flattened in a slash across his face. A couple of times he opened his mouth to speak, but no words formed. He gaped like a koi in a fish pond. Turning on his heel, he paced out of the parlor and into the slate entry way, the cadence echoing off the soaring walls. He mumbled to himself as he disappeared down a hallway.

"Are we supposed to follow?" Jo asked.

Shrugging, Cullen took her hand. "He didn't kick us out."

After a few tense minutes, Cullen pulled Jo through the parlor doors. She soon lost herself in the warren of hallways and doors, following Cullen's lead, their palms tingling against one another. His feet never hesitated, even though his father was out of sight. Down one last corridor, to the last room on the right. The door stood ajar.

Sterling Miles towered over his massive walnut desk. Sky shone blue through the tall casement windows, reflected in the high gloss of the shellacked finish. An old fashioned calendar pad and blotter set adorned the top. No messy stacks or loose papers floating aimlessly. Cullen's father braced himself over the desk top with arms spread wide, and glared.

"What is the meaning of this ... this ... disrespect, son? I thought you were here to accept my offer."

Cullen sighed, ran a hand through his hair. "I said when you called I wasn't interested in running a campaign."

"Campaign?" Jo nearly flinched when the politician leveled a scowl at her question.

"And you? Did you use my son to get close to me?"

Fire raged beneath the surface of her skin. She swallowed the retort clawing its way out of her throat. Years of respecting the rank and not the person came in handy.

"Sir, until this moment, I have said a handful of polite words to you. And yet, each time you have spoken to me it was demeaning and insulting. Is this how you treat the normal people of this country? We," she said, nodding to Cullen, "came here today to calmly and rationally discuss the tariffs on imported American steel, and to discuss your plan to curb the out of control taxes being levied by Socialist America on imports to the Republic. I have no idea what campaign you speak of, and I honestly don't care."

Well, as far as diplomatic openings go, maybe not the most tactful.

Looking at Cullen, Secretary Miles sneered. "Who *is* this woman?"

Cullen tried to answer, but Jo beat him to it. "You can speak directly to me, Mr. Secretary. I am a blacksmith and your son's business partner. Our interests coincide."

"I have no interest in his or your interest, young lady. My son left a prominent career as an engineer in a high profile firm, which I arranged, and embarked on a ridiculous life in the country. Been listening to that good-for-nothing uncle Jules of his, if you ask me. And you, young lady. I do not know you, and I owe you nothing.

Cullen," he pleaded, as much as a chisel pleads with stone, "come home. I need your head to run things. I can't make a play for president without you."

President? Of the Republic?

Cullen sighed, replied to his father with a more substantial amount of patience than Jo could ever have done. "I am a farrier, Dad. It's what I love. I have no desire to head up a presidential bid. Ask Katie to do it." He turned to Jo, "My sister."

Sterling flapped a dismissal. "She's wrapped up in a case against human trafficking. Doesn't have time for it. But you. Come on, Cullen. You're forty years old, too old to keep dragging out this tantrum. Move back to Austin, set up a horseshoeing business here, for crying out loud. If it's that important to you. But take a break, get me elected, and then go back to it."

"Sir, your son's profession is crucial to the economy. Surely you see that."

"I know one thing for sure. I don't have to listen to *you* at all, not in my house. You can —"

Fire exploded. "But you *will* listen, *Mister* Secretary," she roared, silencing the old man. "I may not belong in your world. But I am a constituent in this country. A voter." She let that sink in. "Yeah, that's right. A voter. And you may have noticed that I can be quite vocal, too. We came here to talk steel and iron. Now, are you going to deal or do I start consulting with your opponent and the media?"

Father and son looked at her as though she had two heads.

"What?" she demanded.

Cullen surrendered his hands in the air.

A grin reminiscent of his son's started in the corner of the Secretary's mouth and grew exponentially. His eyes glittered, and his face transformed from haughty condescension to mirth. He roared with laughter, and Cullen followed suit.

Jo crossed her arms in front, angled her chin just so, and sniffed. "Men."

Another rumbling round of amusement ended with Cullen wiping a couple of stray tears from his eyes, and his father slapping the desk top.

"Oh! Oh! You have to keep her, son."

"Everyone keeps saying that," Jo mumbled.

"Young lady," Sterling began.

"Jo. My name is Jo, or Miss Camden if you prefer."

"Feel free to compare me to the derriere of a donkey, dear. I certainly deserve it. Please. I beg your forgiveness."

Steaming, feeling like the brunt of joke, she nodded nonetheless.

He motioned Jo and Cullen to the two high-backed chairs facing the desk, and sat across from them. Steepling his fingers under his chin, he said, "Now what do you want me to do about this import tax mess?"

***

The sun drooped fat and low, hovering over the silhouetted tree line, when Cullen waved to his parents through the kicked-up dust cloud. Truck tires gnawed the gravel with loud crunches. He waved to Shane on the way through the gate. Beside him, Jo slumped in her seat, deflated.

"You were brilliant."

Her head barely shifted his direction. "This is what it feels like to go through the wringer. Remind me to never do that again. Okay?" She groaned, seeming to melt into the warmed leather seats.

"But we have progress. That's something."

"Hmph."

"And he promised to look into South American steel, too, like you, um, suggested."

With one hand on the wheel, he snagged hers with his free one.

"We could always go back, take them up on the offer to stay overnight instead of camping like we planned."

Jo bolted upright. "No! Uh, I mean, there's no reason to inconvenience them."

Cullen activated the windshield's sunset filter. The west sun was blinding, molten. Sneaking a peek at the woman beside him, he grinned. He ran his thumb in circles near the webbing of hers, thrilled with the physical contact. Even more riveted because her hand remained snug in his.

One of the first horses he worked solo was a beautiful palomino Andalusian. The mare had roamed a thousand-acre pasture alone, for months after her owner's death. When the probate dust settled, and the horse passed to her new owner, Cullen's services were requested. Lucy was wild; skittish and beautiful. It took hours and bribery to win her trust; tiny steps forward and gallops back, but eventually he rubbed a rough palm along a shoulder and over an elbow; down the forearm and knee, until he cupped the hoof. After trust was established, the shoeing progressed without incident.

He hoped and prayed the blonde next to him proved the same. And he nearly sniggered thinking what Jo's reaction would be if she heard him comparing her to a horse in his head.

"Something funny?" she asked. Impeccable timing.

He couldn't keep the smile from his face. "Not especially."

"Gonna be like that, huh?" But she squeezed his outstretched hand all the same, sending electric shivers to his boots.

She cranked up the bluegrass. The twang of the banjo serenaded the hills and dells; and as they rode the paved ridges up, down, and around, he marveled at the emotion rising like tidewaters in a cave.

Contentment. Happiness, and surprise. Joy and relief.

A reconciled truce of sorts with his parents, a day spent with Jo. No head wounds, or breaking and entering messes. He could get used to days like today.

As the wide Texas sky blurred to either side, Cullen pondered normalcy. What would typical be with Jo in his life? An ordinary day, spent in and out of her company as he tidied horse feet and she banged away with that massive hammer of hers. They were flint and steel, fire and ice, light and shadow. Glancing over at the blonde firecracker next to him, he thought normal might very well be extraordinary.

Before he knew it, the road sloped to a bridge spanning the wide Colorado River, with the town of Marble Falls on the other side. The water sparkled in the dying orange glow, sparks dancing below and trailing into the distance. Boats skittered like water bugs, pulling inner tubes and skiers alike.

"Gorgeous," Jo whispered.

He agreed.

They stopped into the Bluebonnet Café, and pigged out on world famous chicken fried steaks. Greyscale and color autographed photos lined the walls, an imprint left by notable names since the restaurant's opening in the early 1900s. The pancakes were served on platters with nuggets of creamy butter; the golden crispy-fried steaks melted in their mouths nearly as quickly as the vanilla ice cream on top of warm apple pie.

An hour later, they waddled to the truck, each five pounds heavier than upon arrival. Leaving Marble Falls, they wound their way along snake-like Ranch Road 1431 to the east. A smudge of sun colored the sky in the rearview mirror. He rolled the windows down to let in the crisp evening breeze.

Next to him, Jo untied her hair, letting the blonde waves dance in the air. Fiddles and banjos dueled as they both put an arm out their respective windows and surfed the turbulence with bobbing hands. A single star shone overhead, leading them toward the cave that he prayed held answers. But until they arrived, he breathed in air kissed by rocky sand, and the soft hint of Jo's perfume; and everything was sweeter.

Chapter 31

The blue-white light bobbed and weaved, punching photons into the inky blackness. Jo's painful cries echoed across the hills, the various elevations playing tag with the sound waves.

"Ugh! Woman, will you just hold still?"

Cullen gripped the ends of her fingers with one hand and the wrist with his other.

"Ow!"

"Stop being a baby!"

"It hurts!"

Through gritted teeth, he enunciated, "I cannot help you if you don't stay still."

Moonlight painted the rocky hillside in washed out muted tones, halfway between grayscale and sepia. Color jumped out of the dark when the nodding beam highlighted their surroundings.

Cullen released her wrist, fumbled in his pocket for the tweezers. "I told you to watch out for them."

"They're everywhere. And for the record, this only happened because I tripped over *you* when you stumbled on that dumb rock."

He clamped the tweezers between his lips; and then one-handed, adjusted the headlamp so that it illuminated Jo's palm. He made a mental note to pick up some reading glasses when they made it home.

Near the base of her thumb, a cluster of miniature spikes erupted. There had to be at least a dozen of them, most sunk so deep that only a sliver of the thorns showed above the skin. Cullen pulled the tweezers from his lips, and targeted a subject.

"Ow! Sweet Pete, that *hurts*! Why are there so many cactus plants around here, anyway?"

He held the spine aloft, pinched between the tweezers ends. "See? Just a little bitty ole thorn." It gleamed in the light of his lamp, shiny and tan, with a slight sheen of blood on the end.

Jo swatted him with the other palm. "One down, a lot more to go. Just get it over with."

He felt sorry for her. Really. But he also admired the creative responses spilling from her lips. Some words he had never heard used in such a manner. It was everything he could do to keep from laughing at the tirade.

Aim, pinch, and pull. Listen to the grumbling, steady the offended hand. Repeat.

When the last thorn flew on the currents of the temperate breeze, he applied the numbing antibiotic balm from the first aid kit. Cullen wrapped her calloused hand with gauze. Holding it tight, he brought it to his lips and kissed it gently.

"Should make it all better, hmm?"

Was it his imagination, or did she shiver? Cullen raised his head. He ached to see her smile. Instead, she squinted against a thousand lumens. Wincing, he switched to the red filter.

Jo grinned, opened one eye. "A little." She faced uphill, shined her own torchlight across the stone and cactus-riddled ground. "How much farther?"

He glanced at the GPS on his wristcom. "A hundred yards, maybe. Nearly there. Hey?"

"Hmm?"

"Watch out for cacti."

"Funny," she said, rolling her eyes. "Watch out for rocks."

He snorted.

The rugged terrain was better suited to daytime admiration. Craggy hills, dusted with a thin layer of gritty soil, supported stunted and twisted trees. Limestone and granite lay sleeping beneath the rock-strewn earthen floor. Prickly pear cacti and yucca plants dotted the landscape, flashes of green amidst a sea of khaki and brown.

They climbed and slid in turns as the incline steepened, the last exhausting leg until the summit of the head-and-shoulders hill. Cullen's pack threatened to yank him backward. Ahead of him, Jo's foot slid, showering him with pebbles and grit; but he planted a hand on her pack and steadied her. She turned and smiled her thanks, her smile white in the narrow cone of light.

At last they reached the hilltop peak. It flattened out in a jagged semicircle around the left bump of what the riddle named a shoulder, extended to the right just past the dark cave entrance. The shoulder-ish hill on the right slumped, like the hill had broken a collarbone.

Jo arced her light in broad swaths across the wide shelf. "See any tracks?"

Cullen shook his head, the lamp strapped to his forehead strobing the answer. "Nothing big."

Near the dark cavity, Jo gasped and jumped, clutching her chest. "Ugh. Lizard. About gave me a heart attack." She waved him over. "Age before beauty, Boss."

The contents of his pack rustled and rattled as he lowered it to the ground outside the black hole in the rock. Switching the headlamp to high beam, he ducked beneath the slight overhang, scanned the interior from a distance. Long, squat, and narrow, the cave extended into the hilltop about fifty, maybe sixty feet. Rocky ledges jutted out from the walls, creating murky shadows the lamp couldn't penetrate. Cullen shouted into the cave, hoping to scare up any critters in residence. Nothing moved.

The highest point of the coarse interior stood a foot over his six foot frame. He used his steel-toed boot to search for snakes, swiping quick and hotstepping a retreat from the obscured shadowy parts. He turned, found Jo squatting in the entrance.

"All clear."

Fifteen minutes later, sleeping bags and gear sprawled fanlike in the center of the cave. A neat pile of deadfall gathered from the side of the hill waited near the cave entrance. Two propane lanterns hissed wavering light against the bumpy walls.

"We'll have to build the fire near the door, so the smoke will vent," he observed.

"Not too cold in here anyway. Too bad we didn't bring stuff for s'mores."

He grinned, squatted by his pack. With a flourish, Cullen presented a bag of graham crackers, chocolate, and fat marshmallows.

Jo stared at him, a silly smile on her face. He could look at it for days. "No way."

He shrugged. "Be prepared, I always say. But after supper at the Bluebonnet, I'm kind of surprised you're hungry."

"That climb burned off the apple pie. Maybe the steak, too. Go on," she shooed, "get that fire going. We've got a couple hours digging time left. Gotta fuel up for it."

The dry wood caught with the smallest flame, golden and orange tongues whooshing to life. He kept the fire conservative, not wanting to fill the cave with smoke. Gray wisps eased through the makeshift door, joining the inky night sky. He turned to find Jo exploring the cave with the portable shovel opened and resting on her shoulder. She knelt, probing the dirt floor with her shovel; then shook her head and moved onto another spot.

"Hang on," he called. "I've got a secret weapon."

"I hope it's explosives. So far, I hit rock after a few inches."

Cullen pulled a cloth carrying case from his pack. A round bulge filled out the bottom, with a long neck extending up.

With a curious look, she asked, "A banjo?"

"Nope. Creative guess, though."

He pulled the collapsed handle from the sack, opened it lengthwise, and screwed one end into the other. Then he extracted the round plate and affixed it to the end of the shaft, connecting the wires into the base.

"What in the world?"

"Be prepared," he repeated with a smile. He flourished a hand down the length of the tool. "This, dear one, is a metal detector."

"Sort of figured that out. What I meant to say was, why did you bring an antique, oh possessor of uber-modern technology?"

"Marshall loaned it to us. Turns out he's a bit of a treasure hunter himself, on his days off." Jo's brows rose. "He retrofitted it for rechargeable solar power, and it has an infrared feature."

"Nice. Well let's do this, hotshot."

They settled into a routine. Cullen manned the beeping wand, and Jo attacked any suspicious lumps shown on the screen with her shovel. When he wasn't looking, she added a pickaxe to her arsenal. They had divided up the nearly circular cave into clock-like increments. Side by side, they worked their way around the natural room. The space between them crackled with tension, fueled by stolen glances and flirtatious grins. Cullen expected to see lightning flashing between them.

It was going to be a long night.

Taking a breather a quarter of the way around, Jo walked over with a chunky, goopy s'more. They crunched and made sticky slobs of themselves, smiling like kids at summer camp.

"Hang on," he said. "You've got a little something here."

Softly, he smudged away a dollop of chocolate on her chin. The cave sighed, and the fire popped, cascading sparks into the air. They barely registered. He felt an inferno beneath his fingers, sparks in her eyes as they met his. Electricity sizzled as her hand gripped his, held at her chin.

"Cullen," she whispered.

A bonfire raged in his stomach, flared from the center to the ends of fingers and toes. Even his ears burned.

She bit her lower lip, said his name again.

"Hmm?"

Jo glanced at his lips, then back to his eyes, and murmured, "You're standing on my toe."

Those blazing blue eyes pinned him. He stood in the middle of a bonfire.

"Cullen? My toe?"

Another log popped behind him, loud enough to break the spell. Then what she said registered in his mind.

"Oh! Uh, sorry about that."

"It's okay," she said quietly. "You've got marshmallow on the end of your nose."

The tension exploded, and they both burst, laughing hysterically.

He wiped happy tears from his eyes, chuckling under his breath.

"Want to keep going, or give up for the night?"

She cocked her head to the side, and surveyed the room. "Let's keep going. It's not like we have to be up early.

Minutes turned into an hour, then a little more. In the rear of the cave, where a jumble of boulders made up the far wall and the ceiling only rose four feet from the floor, the metal detector screamed.

"Behind a wall of solid granite?" Jo groaned. "Really?"

The display screen glowed red, an irregular blob at the base of the wall. "Look. Does it seem like it goes down into the ground, too?"

Jo squinted, wavering back and forth between the rock wall and the screen. She sighed. "Yes. How are we ever going to dig through it though?"

It was a valid question, and one he didn't have the answer to.

"Why don't you grab a lantern, bring it over here."

She complied, grumbling the whole time about hardheaded male ancestors. Even covered in rock dust and dirt, her hair tousled, and clothes worse for wear, she still made his innards quiver.

Jo held the lantern aloft near the rocks. Cullen put aside the metal detector, examined the stone. He fingered a crack. "See this?"

She nodded, scooted closer to it. "Hang on. I've got a chisel in my pack."

Not only a chisel, but a solid hammer as well.

"You make those?" Cullen jutted a chin the direction of the tools.

With a twist of her mouth, she replied, "Do you really have to ask?"

Of course she did. The hammer pinged against the end of the chisel, the clang echoing in circles in the rear of the cavern. As the chisel wedged into the fissure, another opened two feet away, parallel to the first.

Cullen jabbed a pointer finger at the second break in the wall. "That's not natural."

Time crept and flew, seeming to take forever but flashing by in a blink. Two more gaps were revealed, along the top and bottom, forming a rough rectangle. Finally, coughing amidst a cloud of dust, Jo dropped the tools. Cullen inserted the end of the pickaxe into one side opening, and she did the same on the opposite side with the chisel. Applying pressure, they wiggled the block. A stone plug, carefully hidden in plain sight. They heaved and tugged and wriggled, until finally the wedge pulled free. It thudded to the dirt floor at their feet. With a stupid grin plastered on his face, Cullen aimed his headlamp into the black recess.

Through a wispy haze of dust, he saw a wooden crate. Small, about ten inches wide, six high. A rope handle faced him. He reached in, tugged. He felt the weight of its cargo shift as he withdrew the box. Jo reached up to support its weight, a grin just as silly as his stretching her mouth from ear to ear.

Thin gold bars the size of his hand gleamed in the lantern's light.

"I can't believe it," Jo whispered.

They placed the crate on the stone block that had previously protected it. After they unpacked it, a dozen rough-shaped bars of pure gold winked playfully.

Shifty Jake's recovered treasure glimmered in the artificial light of day for the first time in two hundred years.

Chapter 32

Stars in the night sky sparkled silver on black velvet. In the early morning hours, Jo stood outside the cave. Eyes upward, palms held to her sides reverently and spinning in a slow circle, she stared in wonder. So many stars, billions of miles away. And yet they shone on her, in Texas.

"Beautiful, isn't it?" a gravelly voice asked.

Startled, she spun.

Dressed in black, blending in with the night, the aged crone from Coleville waited expectantly. Only her silver hair glimmered in the wan moonlight.

Jo opened her mouth to speak, to ask how the woman knew where to find her. No sound emerged. It was if she *couldn't* speak. Her hands flew to her throat, eyes widened in fear.

The little old woman patted her arm. "Don't worry, dear. You're fine. I want you to think instead of speak. Nod if you understand." Jo bobbed her head, and swallowed the fear wedged in her throat.

"You're a mess, girl. Look." Her finger circled in the air and Jo's eyes were drawn to a circle of flames, ringing her inside. The heat kissed her cheeks, her bare arms.

"I know you have been through more hurt in this lifetime than many people know."

Roy. The name flooded her mind, and the ring of fire flared higher. He was responsible; and one day, she would know revenge.

Around her, the flames transformed into a roaring conflagration. They inched inward, tightening, threatening. She tried to scream but only managed a barely audible whimper. The flames crackled and expanded, devouring the air around her. Jo squeezed shut her eyes.

When she opened them, the wizened woman stood at her side.

"Do you know what is happening?" she asked.

Jo frantically shook her head, begging with pleading eyes in the place of her missing voice.

"You are consuming yourself, dear one. Hatred, anger, fear, resentment."

With each word, the smokeless fire climbed; until finally, even the stars directly above disappeared.

Tears streamed in rivulets down Jo's cheeks. Where was Cullen? How could he sleep through this?

At her side, the woman peered at her with a kindness louder than the snapping tongues of fire around them.

"Let it go, Joleigh."

"How?" Her voice! The stream of tears transformed into a flood.

"Return to the One who loved you first, child. He will show you the way."

"I don't –"

Woman and fiery circle disappeared, leaving no sign of their existence. Jo found herself on the far side of the clearing, teetering on the edge of the steeply sloped drop which led down the hill face. Below her, the tough, sunbaked land glowed a pale black and white, bleeding into distant murky obscurity. Vertigo set in, and the world tilted. She windmilled her arms for balance. With her breath held hostage in her chest, she fought the gravity pulling at her. She leapt back with a gasp.

Her feet slid on a circle of ice. She scrambled to gain a handhold, foothold, anything. Jo sensed rather than saw the basketball-sized boulder and latched on. The stone held, and her arms trembled, while her legs dangled over what was now a cliff. She fought, pumping her shaking legs, seeking another rock to steady herself. There! Her left big toe snagged stone, and she realized she was barefoot.

Cold penetrated her jeans and t-shirt. Breathing heavily, her weight balanced between one toe and a handhold, she trembled. The ice made no sense. It was May, for Pete's sake. In the feeble moonlight she could see the ice sheet stretching across the entire clearing. She scanned from left to right, seeking another rock or bush to use to get out of this mess. Goosebumps rose as sweat froze near the frigid ice below her. She made the mistake of looking down. Gulping, she squeezed shut her eyelids.

When Jo opened them, the steady glow of a well-heated forge appeared beside the entrance to the cave. The inky silhouette of a man shone in front of the fire.

She rubbed her eyes, confused, and then realized she was no longer in danger of falling off the cliff.

Jo blinked, and found herself standing a few feet away from the blacksmith. She knew it was her father.

"Ah, there's my girl. Where have you been?"

Where *had* she been? Something about a cave, a treasure. Maybe a bonfire? And Cullen, but where was he?

He waved his tongs in the air. "Never mind. Grab that hammer for me?"

She did, as natural as breathing. Daddy pulled the red-hot iron from the forge, transferring it quickly to the anvil. He pounded the metal. Sparks cascaded and flew, tiny orange fireflies freed from their iron captivity. She expected the pinging clang of hammer meeting iron, but it never came. Impact after impact, complete silence.

"Daddy, I think something's wrong."

But still he hammered, heated, and hammered again. Puzzled, Jo continued to watch as silent sparks danced around the forge. He grunted, nodded his head. Holding the work aloft with his tongs, her father twisted his mouth, squinted at his creation.

He held a perfect horseshoe, but it wasn't the dull gray of worked steel. Gold glimmered in the firelight, created its own flame in the reflections she saw in her father's eyes. And huge! The horse that would wear this shoe had to be monstrous. Neal Camden examined the shoe, sadly shaking his head.

"It's just not right, Joleigh-girl."

"But Daddy, it's beautiful!"

Unconvinced, he lowered it to the anvil's surface, then removed his leather apron.

"Guess I'll start over on it later."

He gripped the horseshoe at the left lower edge, swung it behind him. When she realized what he intended, she yelled, "No!" just as he flung it over the side of the cliff on the edge of the clearing.

Breathless, she waited.

A rumbling in the earth shook the ground at her feet. She stood alone outside the cave mouth. At the peak of the tremor, a gong sounded. Louder and higher-pitched, like the clang of hammer on steel magnified a hundred-fold. She rocked and pitched with the earthquake, eyes closed, begging her father to give it one more chance. The golden horseshoe bounced and tumbled, tolling each landfall with a clashing knell that brought her to her knees, whimpering.

Jo bolted awake, shivering in sweaty terror. Her heart galloped, raced, pounded a frantic beat in her chest. By the glow of embers and the dying firelight, Cullen's face rested serenely in sleep.

A dream. It had all been a dream. Gradually, the virulence subsided, and she eased her eyes closed. Not to sleep. No, she doubted she and sleep would hang out for the duration of the night. But she longed for another glimpse of her father's fire-silhouetted face in the moonlight.

Fire.

A log popped and crackled. Charred logs settled and crumbled.

The crone and the fiery ring! She had nearly forgotten that part. What was it she had said? *Return to the one who first loved you.*

With measured breaths, she calmed her racing heart and pondered the words repeated in her dream. Who loved her first? Obviously, her parents. But they were dead. Frustrated, confused, she shook her head, rolled onto her back. The cave ceiling hovered, black and ominous. One crate of gold, and what looked like another couple of crates buried farther in. She and Cullen would tackle that today. And then what? Waltz into Coleville with a fortune in gold? Hardly.

She turned her head to the right, watched Cullen's eyelids flicker under the weight of dreams. His mouth turned up on one corner, and laugh lines deepened around his eyes. So peaceful.

A dull clunk thudded into the silence. Adrenaline shot through her veins, her throat swollen in apprehension.

They were not alone.

Jo bolted, shedding the sleeping bag, and she yelled Cullen's name. At the mouth of the cave, where the firelight was brightest, Jo caught the shape of a hunched man, running.

Cullen awoke, groggy. "Wha?"

"Someone is here! Wake UP!"

He stumbled to standing. Jo struggled to get her feet in her boots, cursed the slow-motion with which they moved. She did a quick survey of the cave and found the crate of gold gone.

"Cullen!" she yelled, frantic. "Someone took the gold!"

The last remnants of slumber fell away from his face, and he scanned the area with narrowed eyes. He stomped his boots on, and they lunged toward the cavern's entrance.

Before they covered two paces, an explosion rocked the hill. She and Cullen pulled up, sliding and skidding, as stone tumbled in on itself. A cloud of rock dust and gritty soil clouded the air, sending them both into a fit of coughing.

Cullen held her arm in the dark, shaking as he expelled the debris from his lungs. In utter darkness, they stumbled, stunned, retreating to their sleeping area near the rear of the cave. Her ears rang from the blast, and her chest felt full of sand. Cullen pulled her to the ground. She felt the slick satiny material of her sleeping bag half beneath her. Jo rustled around, seeking the flashlight. She could hear Cullen doing the same. Finding hers first, she flicked it on.

Murky dust floated everywhere in waves. By shining the light on Cullen, she helped him locate his headlamp. With both beams sweeping the area, they discovered the awful truth. The mouth of the cave was completely sealed.

They were trapped.

Chapter 33

Cullen grunted under the weight of a larger granite chunk, hobbling it to the side wall of the cave. The pile of excavated rock seemed pathetically insignificant when measured against the hours they had spent picking at the newly fallen wall. Jo dropped her pickaxe and helped him haul it, groaning under the heft. On a mumbled count of three, they heaved it, careful to avoid dropping it on their toes.

Jo's big toe already throbbed with the memory of her earlier klutziness.

Shoulders burning and back knotted, she rolled her head and said, "I need a break."

He nodded his assent in the dim light of the single, rationed lantern. Cullen knelt beside the growing mound, balancing on the haft of the pickaxe. Around them, dust sparkled in the light, forming a nebula in the dark. Her initial panic of being walled in had ebbed to a mild irritation, replaced with a keen determination to see the morning sunlight on the other side. And once she escaped, she was going after Roy. She fiddled with her wristcom for the thousandth time, the muted green glow showing the time and no signal.

"Nothing changed in the last minute and a half?" Cullen joked.

Jo shrugged. "Didn't expect it to, really. But I had to check."

"We'll get out of here. The rock wall is pretty thick, looks like; but they're coming loose easily. It'll take a few more hours."

She glanced around the interior, but most of the cave crouched in shadows. "But how many hours of oxygen do we have left?"

"Plenty. Want to split up? Take a lantern to the hidey hole and I'll keep plugging away at this mess?" He nodded his head to where the entrance once gaped.

She thought about it, making her decision. "Let me take over there. You go on back and dig. I need to vent some frustrations and craft a plan for bringing Roy in."

Cullen cracked his neck to the side, the vertebrae popping hollowly as he sighed. "Leave that to Duke. It all needs to be done by the book, so the new charges will stick. I bet Ben Tucker is on his scent. Heck, he could even be in custody now for all we know."

"Do you believe his story? Roy's, I mean? About the accomplice?"

He twisted his mouth to the side. "Yeah, I do. There were the other prints Duke found. Plus the timing of the break-in at your cabin and Roy's escape from the prison farm. I don't know if his story is legit, but I definitely think he's not alone."

Jo nodded, his opinion reflecting her own. "I guess the big question is who collapsed the cave door."

"Hey."

She looked up from her study of the dirt floor. He stood before her, arms out in invitation. Well, what could it hurt?

His arms felt nice, cocooned around hers, snug but not suffocating. He smelled of sweat and earth, raw man. She shivered, tingling all over.

"Cold?"

She shook her head as best as she could, with it wedged into his chest.

"We're going to get out of here. You know that, right?"

She muffled, "Yeah." It felt so right, sheltered in his arms. Why had she fought against him for so long? This was natural, easy. Shoulders relaxing, she melted into him, laying her head against his chest. His heart beat steadily, thumping against his rib cage. He rubbed slow circles on her sweat-dampened back. Oddly, the butterflies in her chest beat their wings in time with one another, rather than the hickledy-pickledy nerve-wracking jumble to which they once danced.

Jo tilted her head, found him staring down at her. One last mad cry of warning sounded in her rational mind, a clanging cymbal crying caution.

She ignored it.

Standing on her toes, she rose, leveling her eyes with his. That rakish grin she had once hated swept up the corner of his mouth. With a quick inhale, the butterflies rushed to her throat and she leaned in. Her chest beat wildly as her lips met his. Warmth flooded her body as his arms abandoned the hug, and his hands cupped her face. Her eyes slid closed as he deepened the kiss. Jolts of electricity shot to her hands and feet as he nipped her bottom lip. He slid a palm, cupped the back of her neck, arching and steadying her as she lost herself in him.

Sometime later, she pulled away, trembling. It amazed her that the cave wasn't glowing. She drew deep breaths, suddenly nervous and shy. *She* kissed *him*!

Cullen lifted her chin with a thumb, captured her with a stare. His eyes twinkled like amber in firelight.

"About dang time," he whispered.

She laughed out loud, slapping his bicep. Her cheeks colored even more. To cover her embarrassment, she unwrapped her messy topknot and flung her head upside down to redo it. With that situated, she retrieved her tools.

"Don't get used to it, Boss." A flirty grin flashed across her face, and he shook his head, laughing.

"Yes, ma'am."

Time inched forward, creeping along with each swing of the pickaxe, every ping of hammer against chisel. They worked at opposite ends of the cave, but found themselves shooting furtive glances across the dark cavern. On Jo's end, the mass of rock shifted bit by heavy-laden bit, one mound shrinking as another multiplied.

Behind her, Cullen hooted. Jo jumped, spinning around.

"What?"

"Come here. Bring your flashlight."

She joined him, noting the enlarged opening of the once hidden hole in the wall. "You've made some progress."

"Wait until you peek inside," he replied with a smile.

Bluish-white light illuminated the depths. She leaned in to get a better angle. When she saw what was hidden in the recess, her eyes widened in surprise. Cullen gripped her shoulder.

"I can't believe it," she said, stunned.

Five wooden crates, identical to the stolen one, were haphazardly stacked inside. Jo had to crawl through the widened cavity to reach them. Cullen anchored her at the knees when she tipped in, losing her balance.

"Thanks," she threw over her shoulder.

"No problem. I like the view."

Jo snorted. "Behave, mister."

With a heave, she plucked the top crate off the stack, muscling it and herself into the cave proper. She pried the top off with the end of the pickaxe while Cullen watched, his hand resting lightly on her shoulder blade.

By the glow of the lantern, they counted twelve gold bars, the yellow gleam of the metal seeming to ingest the light and magnify it. Jo gripped Cullen's hand.

"I never really believed the treasure existed," she admitted. "Thought it was just a story passed down for fun. But this," she said, pointing to the gold bars, "is real."

"You're a wealthy woman, Miss Camden."

Her head swiveled side to side in slow motion. "What do I do with a bunch of gold bars?"

"I know a buyer in Austin. He can be discreet."

Her world would be turned upside down if the press discovered the story. Combined with the assaults, property crimes, and escaped felons? Forget about privacy if that happened.

She brushed a few stray hairs from her face. "First thing we have to do is make it out of this place." Considering the remaining wooden boxes, she said, "Let's leave the others in place until then."

Cullen nodded his agreement; and shouldering his pickaxe, sauntered to the remainder of the collapsed stone. They chipped and chiseled, lifted and carted rock after rock. Some small enough to lob onto the growing pile near the side wall, others requiring both of them to move.

Weary from the lack of sleep, exhausted from hours of excavating, Jo meandered to her sleeping bag and slunk down. She grabbed a meal bar from her pack, ate it numbly. So much to process. Her brain felt overloaded, clogged. She nibbled the bar, and chewed through problems in her head. Somehow, beyond reason, she was now rich. A crazy part of her wished this had happened *before* she lost the smithy. But then, Cullen wouldn't be in the picture. And that was another morsel to digest. Somehow, the man had wormed his way into her life, into her heart. She cared for him.

All these emotions warred in her mind. Regret, anger, caring, frustration, shock. A thirst for vengeance and justice ripped through the jumbled mass, leaving exasperated resolve in its wake. She would see Roy behind bars, hopefully with a death sentence trailing him to a maximum security facility. For her mother. For Ginny.

Jo was holding an empty wrapper, sipping from a canteen, when Cullen dropped to the ground beside her, huffing from exertion.

"I think I've figured how to carve out a tunnel of sorts, instead of moving all the rock."

"Hmm."

"Hey?" he asked. Concern painted his face. "What's wrong? I thought you'd be over here tallying the riches."

Her smile didn't reach her eyes. "I'm okay. Just thinking."

"About what you're going to buy me first?"

She nudged him, leaning in to give him a gentle shove. "Funny."

"Hey, I'm only interested in you because of your money."

"Hmph. Okay, this may sound weird. But can I run something by you?"

Cullen nodded. The air around his headlamp shimmered with a glittering dust halo. "Shoot."

"I have these … dreams," she began.

Jo told him of the old woman in her dreams, and her message that happened in real life as well. How her father and the crone seemed to be warning her of something. She spoke of the fiery circle and the terrific fear she felt inside it. When she drew to a close, Cullen remained silent, his stare focused on something far away. He chewed his lip, seeming to mull it over.

"Forgiveness."

"Forgiveness?"

Nodding, he continued, "Who loved you first?"

"My parents, I guess. But they're both gone."

Cullen was shaking his head. "No, honey. I have no doubt they loved and adored you more than any other person on this earth. But the One who loved you first was God."

She groaned. "Look, Cullen. I believe in God. I do. It's just – how do I put this? He doesn't seem all that interested in *me*. Where has He been? I was saved when I was a kid. It was easy, then. Believing, trusting. It feels like He abandoned me along the way. And it's hard to put my trust in that. How is faith supposed to help me now? With all this upheaval in my life?"

"You accepted salvation when you were young? Trusted that Jesus died so that you can live with Him for eternity?"

"Yeah. I did. But after Ginny died, and then mom … I guess I went my own way, fended for myself."

"But you understand that Jesus forgave you for all the wrong you had done and would do in your life?"

She hesitated. "It made sense when I was a girl."

"Forgiveness, Jo. It's about the sinless Son of Man dying for a world wrecked by sin. No, hear me out," he said when she opened her mouth. "You have to get this notion of revenge out of your heart, honey. Roy Milligan committed atrocities. He took your sister and mother from you. I know that. But Jesus died for Roy, too. For the murderers, the liars, the gluttons, every flawed one of us. He paid the price on that cross. He even forgave the man hanging on the cross next to him, while He gasped for air on His own. That kind of forgiveness is what you need to hold onto. It's what God can provide."

Tears leaked down her cheeks as she quietly sobbed, convicted.

"Baby, I know this is hard to hear. You're one of the strongest women I've ever met. But if you don't let this go, if you don't release this hatred from your heart, you will never truly be free."

She turned to him, tucked her head onto his chest. Comforted by his strong and steady heartbeat, she cried quietly. Never in her life had she felt so confused, so guilty. All these years of hating. A few words uttered in the dark had the power to cleave her heart's stalwart wall.

She cried, and Cullen held her close, whispering words she couldn't distinguish. Then she realized the words weren't for her.

He was praying over her.

A rattling rumble resounded, echoing around the cave. Startled, they both turned to the collapsed entrance. Again, the sound repeated, and then a narrow beam of sunlight stabbed the darkness. They scrambled to their feet, ran to the source.

"Hello!"

"Hey! Can you hear us?"

Their cries came simultaneously.

"Jo? Cullen? Can you hear me?" a familiar voice yelled through the tiny opening.

"We're here!" Cullen shouted. "Is that you Ben?"

"Yes! Don't worry! I'll have you out soon."

With renewed purpose, they attacked the stone barrier. Ben chiseled away with what sounded like a jackhammer from the other side. After a while, a head-sized hole appeared near the top of the former entrance.

Ben Tucker grinned from the other side. "Y'all sure know how to get yourselves in trouble."

Cullen wrapped his arm around her shoulders, squeezed. "It's good to see your face, man." In the light of day, Cullen's face appeared sun-bronzed from all the dirt and dust floating in the air. She could only imagine the tear tracks and smudges on her own. Nonetheless, she grinned along with him, nodding to Ben.

And just as the rock wall crumbled beneath their continuous chipping, the wall around her heart began to disintegrate. Fissures let in an alien warmth, a light that bolstered and comforted.

This was love.

Chapter 34

Jo gulped icy water from a steel canteen, the metallic aftertaste ghosting across the back of her tongue. Her feet dangled a couple of inches from the ground as she perched on the tailgate of Cullen's truck. Clouds blocked the noonday sun, gracing the hillside with intermittent shade. A few yards away, the men leaned against the side of the tracker's truck, wrapped up in conversation. Ben gestured with his hands, animated, while Cullen nodded intermittently.

Up the hill, just out of sight over the crest, the cave crouched, a hull empty of its wealth and in much worse shape than when they arrived. Ben's borrowed jackhammer had made quick work of the fallen stone, chewing through the obstruction like a hot knife through butter. They had worked to enlarge a tunnel wide enough for them, their gear, and the buried crates. Once the contents of the cave laid scattered in the open, and Jo and Cullen breathed fresh, warm Balcones air, an invisible weight lifted from her chest. They rested, and then began the long, heavy haul to the trucks waiting by the road below. She was thankful for the additional, and enormous, hands of their rescuer.

Now, by the side of the winding ranch road, she sipped water and studied the clouds in the sky. She clutched a coin-shaped disc in her left hand. Jo eased back, lying on the sun-soaked metal, the warmth working to ease knotted muscles. Holding the thin circle a foot above her face, she examined the smooth metallic surface. It was a tracking device, Ben had said. Not the most modern or technologically advanced, but it had accomplished its purpose. She and Cullen never thought to be concerned about the possibility of being followed, trailed. Ben discovered the homing beacon stuck to the underbelly of Cullen's truck. They had been careless. Again.

Supine in the truck bed, Jo absorbed the heat and pondered the tale Ben had recounted during the treks up and down the hillside.

After Jo and Cullen departed for Austin, Ben returned from his trip to Bastrop empty-handed. With that lead a dead end, he checked in with Duke at the sheriff's office. While he was regrouping with the deputy, the call came in. A Coleville resident's vehicle was missing and believed stolen. Automobiles were few and far between in the bucolic town; and the citizen, a prosperous builder, had invested geolocation services at the time of purchase. With a click, Duke pinpointed the four-wheel drive truck on Highway 79, headed toward Austin. The coincidence spurred the lawman to action. This could be the break they needed in arresting Roy, and an accomplice if he had one.

Duke had instructed him to pursue the thief; and once located, to follow and observe. Ben's legal jurisdictions allowed him to apprehend and retrieve suspects and wanted criminals, and the deputy intended to utilize him to the fullest. Duke remained behind to monitor the homestead surveillance cameras.

Ben easily traced the suspect, coming to within two miles and holding steady, out of sight. His prey was a blinking blue dot on the map of his onboard navigation system.

Jo figures she and Cullen were extracting the first crate of gold around the time the tire blew out on Ben's truck, sidelining him in the middle of nowhereland between Rockdale and Taylor. Ben admitted to punching the side of the truck a half dozen times, and his knuckles corroborated his confession. Once the tire was changed, traffic slowed him further. He lost nearly an hour after all was said and done.

The silver circle pinched between her dirty fingers allowed someone – it had to be Roy – to follow them to the cave. Her skin crawled imagining that man stalking them, watching them work and sleep. By the time Ben picked out his tracks amid the rock, sand, and cacti, and discovered the cave, the truck thief was a hasty shadow darting down the hill. Then the explosion rocked the hilltop, and the concussion knocked Ben to his knees. The fleeing silhouette no longer mattered.

While Cullen and Jo picked, hacked, and coaxed rock inside the cave, Ben was waking several neighboring families in the hopes they would have a jackhammer. Hours later, successful in his search, he returned and assaulted the barrier. Fortunately for them, Ben began hammering in the area Jo and Cullen had concentrated their efforts.

Should she be thankful for the insidious tracking device? If not for Roy or whoever's bad intentions, Ben never would have found them. The sun peeked its golden head around the pewter-lined clouds, and the silver disc in her hand reflected the light; like a child, she followed the white circle of light bobbing on the wall of the truck bed.

Cullen's smile appeared above the dancing white circle. "I can see you're deep in thought."

"Hmm. Sort of. What's the word?"

"We'll follow Ben to Coleville and go from there."

"Any news about Roy?"

He scratched the top of his head, running five grimy fingers through tousled hair. "May not have been him, you know. But yeah, the truck was found abandoned in Marble Falls."

She sighed, then sat up with a grunt. "Took the gold and ran, probably."

"Maybe this will all be over."

Jo left the wishful statement hanging in the heated air. "Listen, about the gold. I think we should —"

Ben shouted her name, his alarmed tone bouncing her out of the truck. Dust eddies spun from their boots as they bolted over. The tracker held a hand aloft in a halt pattern, and cocked his head as he listened to the voice coming through the ear bud. His eyes grew saucer-like.

"Okay, yeah. We'll be there as fast as we can, Duke." He paused, casting a glance at her and Cullen. "Got it. Thanks."

"Saddle up, kids. We have to get back to Coleville."

"What's the rush?" Jo asked. Anxiety crept up her spine and crouched on her neck.

"Duke has Roy in custody."

"How did he capture him? The trail cams?"

Ben shook his head. "He surrendered. Walked right into the sheriff's office, and turned himself in."

It couldn't be Roy.

The shattered, hunched husk of a man slumped on the bench behind the clear walls of the holding cell scarcely resembled the cruel and cunning stepfather haunting her memories. His hair was the same. Bedraggled, oily ropes grasping for his shoulders, but not quite reaching. But he was thinner, emaciated; his shoulders stretched wide, but the muscles were longer and leaner. They mocked his previous bulk.

Either Roy hadn't seen her come in, or he was ignoring her. He stared at the floor, his head cradled in his hands, braced by elbows on his knees. If she didn't know the man, Jo would say he seemed defeated, despondent. But then again, he turned himself into the law. It's possible he *had* admitted his failure, and saw no other option than to give up. Somehow, she doubted it.

Duke stood at her side, his sandpapery hand gripping her shoulder. Neither said a word. As the observation drew uncomfortable, she sighed.

"Go ahead," she instructed. "Let's get this over with."

The deputy keyed the locking panel so that audio became available. Roy's head snapped up.

"Oh, God, Jo! You're safe!"

"No thanks to you. Where's the gold you took?"

Confusion fluttered his eyes, and he shot a questioning glance at Duke. "What gold?"

Her jaw clenched, and shoulders tightened. "The gold you took just before blowing up the entrance to the cave."

"He did what?" Roy rushed to his feet, approaching the transparent cell wall. His palms flattened, white, against the panel. "Were you hurt?"

Rather than answer the question, she decided to study him. He seemed genuinely concerned for her safety. This didn't fit, didn't mesh with his pattern.

Roy turned to face Duke. "I told you, Mr. Massey. I was trying to help Jo. That's why I turned myself in. He's insane. There's no telling what he'll do. But," he said, mumbling, "I guess you kind of found that out."

"What are you rambling about, Roy?"

"My cousin, Jerry."

"Jeremiah Franks? The one who escaped before you?"

Roy nodded, frantic. "Yes. I'm telling you. He's crazy. Wait. You said gold? Did you find it?"

Jo narrowed her eyes at him. "You have no idea, do you?"

"That's what I've been trying to tell you!"

Cullen spoke, and Jo flinched. She hadn't heard him come in. "I believe him, honey."

The strange thing was, she did too. Despite their history, and even though he had strangled her a few days ago, she knew he told the truth. Cullen's hand found hers, and she squeezed her thanks for the encouragement.

"Why don't you tell me what you're rambling about?"

The man paced the narrow confines of the holding cell. He chewed his lip, taking turns shooting looks at Jo and studying his hands. Finally, the pacing ceased and he sat on the built-in bench.

"I need you to hear something else first."

When Jo opened her mouth to protest, he overrode her.

"This has to happen the right way. Will you listen?"

Finally, she nodded assent. She grabbed a chair from the corner, and perched in front of the door. "Go ahead."

"I … I killed Laura. Your mother."

Jo's fingers dug into the wooden seat beneath her. She spun to Duke with a question on her face. He nodded.

"Everything is being recorded."

Roy acknowledged this with a roll of the eyes, but he continued nonetheless. "Poisoned her. I'm not proud of it. I live every day with the evils I've done."

His tale was nothing short of shattering.

One day he had been in a bar, tossing back a few and shooting pool with the guys, when a man across the room started running his mouth about buried treasure.

"Wasn't long before people were shouting for him to shut up. But for some reason, I couldn't get it out of my head," Roy admitted.

He bought three more rounds for the stranger before he had the information he needed. A friend of a friend of a friend said the heir lived in a flyspeck town outside of Bryan. Roy packed up his meager belongings and moved to Coleville.

"Mama said she met you at the feed store. You helped her carry out some horse feed," Jo said softly.

Roy nodded, a sad look on his face. "Got hired on two days after moving here."

He found reasons to run into Laura Camden around town, and soon he began courting her. One day over lunch, while both Jo and Ginny were in school, he casually brought up the legend of the stolen and recovered gold. Laura had laughed herself to tears, Roy relayed. She asked if he thought she'd be living in a run-down homestead in the country if she had tons of gold at the ready. Undaunted, he pursued her, eventually asking her to marry him in the off-chance there was something around the old house that would give him clues about the gold.

Roy looked deep into Jo's eyes. "Wasn't no love involved. We both knew it. But she needed a man around the house, and she thought I needed the companionship. Your mama was a kind woman. I know that now." His voice broke at the end of the quiet statement.

Jo studied the scuffed toes of her work boots, closed her eyes to ward away the tears. She would not cry in front of this man.

She listened, numb, as he confessed his rage and frustration for the lack of wealth; ignored his excuses for killing her sister out of hatred and jealousy. Jo found herself shivering in the corner of her mind used for stowing away the uncomfortable and hurtful memories of her childhood. She barely heard him justify poisoning her mother in the hopes Laura would leave him riches in her will; or at the very least, having her out of the way so he could tear down the home looking for it. In that obscured corner of her psyche, Jo rocked to and fro, wailing at the injustice, at the lengths a man would go out of greed. So lost in Roy's wrenching tale was she that she nearly missed his quiet confession.

"After my incarceration in Huntsville, a chaplain approached me one Sunday. He held a book in one hand, looked me straight in the eye, and asked me if I knew Jesus."

The statement yanked Jo from her own inner prison. She rose abruptly, the chair clattering to the floor behind her. But Roy continued, and her denial increased tenfold.

"Didn't happen then, or even in a few weeks. That chaplain hounded me for months, every other Sunday. One day, he passed me a Bible. Told me to read it. I tossed it in the corner under my rack after he left."

Jo didn't like where this was headed, refused to believe his unfolding fiction.

"But I'm telling you, that Book was like a fire under my bed. It burned. In here," the inmate said, pointing to his chest. "Until one day I fished it out of there."

Cullen's calm voice from within the dark, dank cave returned to her mind. *Jesus died for Roy, too.* She shook her head, trying to cast it out.

"The next Sunday the chaplain came, and asked me the same question he always asked. 'Son, do you know Jesus?' That day I told him I didn't yet, but I had questions. Not long after, in the middle of my cell floor, I gave up wrestling with God. I confessed all my sins to the quiet around me, and asked Jesus for His salvation. And it was the most beautiful experience I have known in my life."

Unable to contain her rage, Jo bellowed, "You ruined my life! You killed my baby sister, poisoned my mother! How dare you sit there and tell me about Jesus!"

She blinked and found herself on the sidewalk outside the sheriff's office. Jo had no memory of rushing out. Cullen embraced her, a muscled protective shell against the ugliness of the world.

He made shushing sounds in her ear, rocked her gently. "It's okay, honey. He won't hurt you again. Shhh."

How long they stood under a baking sun, she had no idea. She sobbed, and he comforted. Her heart rate slowed and steadied, her shoulders relaxed. To be held, to rest in silence and understanding. It gave her the strength to dry the tears and face the criminal inside. Jo fortified the wall around her heart, and willed herself through the glass-paned door.

Roy slouched on the bench. When she returned, he swiped tears from his face with the sleeve of his shirt.

"Please," he begged.

She held up a hand.

"How does Jeremiah Franks play into this?" she asked.

Roy sighed. "Jerry was at the work farm doing his time when I got there. Breaking and entering." He paused, as if seeking permission to continue. Jo nodded. "I tried to tell him about how my life was changed by believing in Jesus. I confessed the wrongs of my past, in the hopes it would help him see how much God can change a man. Instead, he became fixated on the one part that reeled me in."

"The treasure."

Nodding, he said, "Yeah. But he played along, led me to believe that I was making headway with him. That his heart was softened like mine was. When he ran, I knew he had conned me. Sort of ironic, that. Anyway, the only thing I could do was go after him, try to protect you from him."

"You escaped from prison to keep him from hurting me?"

Disbelief dripped from the question. It wasn't possible. She had *lived* with this man, and she knew his true nature. But Jo would play along.

"So where is he now, after the stunt at the cave?"

"I don't know. But I can get him to come here."

Chapter 35

Cullen studied Jo through the glass-paned door. She observed the inner happenings with eyes deadened by shock and disbelief. Bitterness swept across the contours of her face. It jutted her chin, and pulled the corners of her mouth into a frown. Accusation blazed from stormy blue eyes. The dying sun cast a halo around her, highlighting her yellow-gold locks and the wispy strands caught by the wind. With arms locked across her chest, ropy forearms taut and feet planted in a wide stance, it was as if she dared the criminal behind Cullen to make a break for it. She shredded his heart and left it in shambles on the scuffed wooden planks of the sheriff's station.

Would he ever tire of studying her? He hoped not. Jo was fire and ice, a raging whirlwind and a gentle breeze. She could erupt like a dormant volcano, abrupt and devastating; but her smile took him to a gurgling brook through the woods, peaceful and happy.

Cullen hated the despondency he and Duke agreed to foster, but it was necessary.

Duke crouched at Roy's feet, securing a tracking and immobilization band around the felon's ankle. Cullen waved a soothing hand at Jo, and studied the device.

"What's the range on it?" he asked.

"It's variable. The base unit has an alternate band as well." Duke paused, his faced scrunched up. "I think a quarter mile will work for the operation."

Cullen ground his teeth, and Duke seemed to sense his reservations.

"If we're too close, Franks will know we're there. If Roy ventures a step past the set radius, the band will send a shock like a stunner, and he'll go down."

So far, Milligan had been the epitome of cooperation and subdued respect. Cullen hoped the attitude reflected a true change of heart, for the sake of the sting operation, and for Jo. A glimpse out front found her pacing the sidewalk, her eyes averted.

Beside him, Duke calibrated Milligan's electronic leash, setting distances and stun levels. Satisfied with the progress, the deputy nodded.

"We're all set. Let's make the call."

Cullen turned to Roy. "You sure he'll bite?"

Nodding, the man replied, "Yeah. He's a greedy son of a gun. If he thinks we missed some gold here, he'll be back as soon as he can."

The grizzled deputy returned Roy's confiscated wristcom with a warning. "Audio only. No video."

"Yes, sir."

Duke asked Cullen, "Do you think she'll want to be in for this?" He jutted a chin toward the front of the office.

Outside the window, Jo's pacing had ceased. Her back pressed upon the wide glass window, the wrinkles of her shirt flattened against the pane, her head hung low. He imagined her boots were crossed at the ankles, but he couldn't see them. Her arms remained locked in a protective X over her midsection.

"No. She still needs some time, I think," he replied.

Duke gave the go-ahead nod, and Roy dialed his cousin's number. As the call connected, the deputy quietly reminded him, "Speaker on, please."

"Well, well, cousin," a scratchy voice answered. "You still in that Podunk town?"

"You better start thanking for me staying," Roy replied.

"Yeah? Why's that?"

"Because I found a couple crates of shiny silvery stuff, that's why."

"Silver, eh?"

"Looks hand-smelted, but there's a lot of it. What'd you find?"

"Aw, nothing. Dead end. Lost 'em outside of Austin," Jerry grumbled, coughing. "How much, you reckon?"

"You're not holding out on me, are ya, Jerry? Because that wouldn't be a good thing to do."

"Naw, naw. Like I said, zip. Nada. I'm just holed up, looking for an opportunity to slip on down to Mexico and find me a pretty little señorita."

"Well, that suits me just fine, cousin. I've got plans for all this silver." Roy laughed, egging on the conversation. "Hope your señorita treats ya right, man."

There was a pause on the line. "Guess I could mosey over that way, for old times' sake. You owe me a cut, the way I see it."

"Now, listen here, I –"

"Don't you try to wiggle out of the agreement, man. Yeah, Mexico can wait. I could use some travel funds."

"I did all the work, all the digging around. You was off gallivanting across the country, playing hide and seek with the mark. Deal was you got a cut if *we* found the treasure. Well, Jerry, way I see it is *I* found these crates. I'll dig up the rest myself, without your help."

"What do ya mean, the rest? There's more?"

Roy chuckled. "Mm-hmm. I found his little hidey hole."

"What'd you do about those trail cams the lawman done put up?"

"Shoot," Roy bragged, "just snuck up on 'em and turned 'em off from behind. Anyway, the dig is out near the tree line, not near the old house. Look, you comin' out or what?"

The air hummed, silent. Finally, "Yeah. Where ya at?"

Roy flicked his eyes to the deputy, and Duke nodded. "Got me a campsite set up in the thicket east of the old place. I checked for tracks. Ain't no one been out here, 'cept me."

"I gotta find a ride. Had to ditch the truck I borrowed. I'll be there tomorrow sometime. Just stay low. I'll find you."

"Bring a shovel," Roy joked.

"Whatever. Just be there."

Cullen held his breath, waiting to make sure the call disconnected before speaking. Duke snagged the communicator, lifting Roy's wrist, and verified the end of the call, saying, "Step one is done."

His gaze floated to the front window once more, only to find Jo no longer stood outside. "You're sure about letting him wander?" he asked the deputy, with a jut of the chin at the felon.

"Can't see a way around it. We don't know where Franks is. He could be here in town, but I doubt it. They knew we were onto them. Right?"

"Yeah," Roy said. "We knew. I ain't going nowhere. Told you, I'm trying to right my wrongs, and keeping my cousin away from Jo is important."

Trust a convicted murderer? That is what it came down to?

"I see your gears turning, Cullen," Duke said quietly, grabbing him by the elbow and ushering him across the room. Behind them, the placid escaped convict reclined with this fingers interlocked and resting on his stomach. "I don't like it either, to be honest. Don't see as we have much choice. I've got Logan hidden in the brush on the west side of the OSR. He'll radio any vehicles coming into town, and we'll check the plates for each one. Ben's already in place out by the old homestead. He knows how to stay hidden. If Franks shows up out there tonight, we'll know about it." The deputy gripped Cullen's shoulder. "It's almost over."

"But is it? For Jo, it's starting all over again. With Milligan's confession and the diary as evidence, there will be another murder trial. She'll have to testify again, and you know the attorney will dredge up Ginny's death, too."

"Getting these two behind bars is my priority. We'll deal with the rest as it comes."

Cullen lifted his shoulders a hair, worked out the kink that had taken up residence behind his right ear. Jo was nowhere in sight. Unable to wait any longer, he shook the lawman's hand, saying, "I have to find her."

"I know you do. Go. I'll deal with Roy."

***

Her fork chased the last bite of pecan pie around the white dessert plate. A tall glass of sweet tea, half empty and dripping with condensation, sat ignored beside it. Idly, she watched a water bead turn loose and slide downward, gravity pulling it to the damp napkin acting as a coaster. The drop melted into the paper, quickly absorbed, disappearing.

Laughter rang out from the booth in the corner. A toddler cried at the one behind her. Kevin, the cook, bustled in and out of view of the pass-through window.

She chased the last bite of pie, wondering what happened next. Better yet, what was going on at the sheriff's office? A tension headache flirted with the base of her neck, creeping long fingers up and over her skull. Across the diner, at the opposite end of the countertop, Ruby watched protectively. Jo saw the dark woman out of the corner of her eye, polishing the same spot on the counter with her sparkling white towel. Behind her, the door jangled its welcome, and Ruby's towel halted mid-swirl. The jagged tendrils gripping her head tightened, and her fork froze. In her periphery, she caught Ruby's nod at the newcomer, and the woman resumed her imaginary cleaning.

"What's the special?" Cora asked, slapping her hands on the counter and plopping down on the red vinyl-topped stool.

"Frustration. Betrayal. Greed."

"Hmm. Sounds less than appealing."

Jo half-turned her head toward the feisty doctor. "I'm sorry. I should go."

Cora laid her hand atop Jo's. "Stay. Please. I don't get a break from Miss Kate very often, and we need to talk."

"Is Shelley watching her?"

"Yep."

"And you're on Jo Duty?"

"Figured that out, did you?"

She shrugged, attempting to coax relation into her shoulders and failing miserably. "The menfolk want me surrounded 24/7. It's sweet, but impractical."

"The let's just look at it as a heart-to-heart between friends."

"Ah," Jo mumbled, bitter. "One of *those* talks."

Ruby appeared in front of them. Jo caught sight of her crisp, white apron; but her eyes remained focused on the mostly eaten pie.

"I'll have a slice of that delicious looking pie, Miss Ruby," Cora ordered.

The doc thanked Ruby as the pie plate clinked in front of her. Jo had to smile at the purr coming from the red-head's throat. She stabbed the last piece of her own pecan heaven. In companionable silence, they ate their pie while Miss Ruby cleaned the sparkling not-dirty-at-all countertop.

Cora wiped her mouth, and laid the napkin on the empty white plate. "Remember when I said I had a story to tell? The reason I'm licensed to carry a weapon?"

"Vaguely, yeah."

"A couple of years ago, I was abducted from my home by a man bent on vengeance," she began. She inhaled deeply. "He thought I killed his wife through witchcraft, of all things."

Stunned, Jo latched onto the word that stood out. "Witchcraft?"

Cora nodded. "Strange, I know. Of course, he couldn't have been further from the truth. I found Christ while in college, in Socialist America."

Whistling, Jo reevaluated her image of Cora. "That must have been quite a challenge."

"It was. My best friend, Missy, became a believer as well. She had years of infertility, and I couldn't help but share my hope with her. The hope I found in knowing Jesus. Missy died in childbirth. I delivered a healthy baby boy, and then an embolism stole her from all of us.

"It took a long time to realize how grateful I was for having the courage to witness to her, despite the laws. But her husband – Gordon – he thought I had corrupted his wife by witnessing to her. He was a law enforcement officer, and as hard as nails. No wife of his would believe in one faith. When things started to go wrong after William was born, Gordon saw me praying over Missy. In his rage, and jealousy, he accused me of casting spells that led to Missy's death."

"Cora, I had no idea. How awful."

"Not only did he toss accusations at me, but he persecuted me in the courts and through the medical board. When I was found not liable in Missy's death, he started coming after my family."

Jo found herself digging stubby fingernails into her legs, the denim rough under her fingertips. Indignant anger surfaced, knowing the sweet and sassy doctor had suffered for her faith.

"He sounds completely insane."

Cora nodded in agreement. "Soon after he targeted my parents and brother, I made the decision to seek asylum in Texas. My application was approved, and a few weeks later I moved to Cotton Springs. Gordon showed up on my doorstep one night. I thought it was the local deputy, Jimmy. Instead, I opened the door and Gordon pistol whipped me. We ended up hours away, somewhere in the Big Thicket. He beat me repeatedly. When Ben and Jimmy – the deputy – caught up to us, tracked us down, Gordon had me tied to a tree. He was going to burn me alive. Just like a witch, he said."

She gulped some cold iced tea. Miss Ruby had given up the pretense of cleaning, and stood gaping at Cora.

"Well, I'll be, sugar. You've been through so much," Ruby said, wide-eyed. "Now that I think about it, seems like I heard it on the news. And that was you, sweet girl. Mm, mm, hmmm. There's evil walking this world." Ruby swept her gaze to Jo. "You know a bit about evil, too, honey. The only thing that'll get us through it is the Good Lord."

"Why is everyone preaching to me lately?" Jo flung her hands in the air. "I *do* believe in God, you know."

Cora reached out, squeezed Jo's hand. "I haven't know you long. But I feel a connection to you. I have no doubt God sent Ben and I here for a reason."

"Are you going to give a sermon on forgiveness as well? Because I can tell you, I've already had a few."

Ruby popped her towel at her. "You hush your mouth, girl. Miss Cora's trying to help you."

The doc flicked a smile across the counter. To Jo, she said, "No. I won't tell you what to do. I forgave Gordon, with God's help. And don't get me wrong. Forgiveness means healing. It doesn't mean forgetting. Forgiving someone gives you the chance to be free of the burden of hate."

"I thought you weren't lecturing me," Jo complained.

"Ha! I'm not. Not really. The reason I told you my story was so you could hear Gordon's."

"What do I have in common with a crazy man?"

Two patrons on stools at the opposite end of the diner looked up from their dinner, staring at Jo. Maybe the outburst was louder than she intended.

"Gordon acted out of hate. Anger, vengeance, jealousy. All those things tumbled around inside until it ate away at his soul. He didn't know God, and I promise you the devil made use of him. But you say you do believe, right?"

"Yes," Jo hissed, exasperated. "He's just never been there for me!"

"Hmm. I think if you really concentrate and reflect, you'll see just how often He has been there for you. And when you return to His love, He can help you battle the need for vengeance. He can free you from the hate. And I promise you this."

Cora paused.

"He's the only one who can."

Chapter 36

Cullen found Jo slumped on a red vinyl-upholstered stool at Ruby's Plate, with Cora Tucker at her side. The fiery doctor had an arm draped across Jo's shoulders, and it seemed to be the only thing holding his woman upright.

His woman.

Tall, bold and golden, with ropy muscles and a courageous broken heart. Whether she felt the same tug, the same possessiveness, he didn't know. He rather hoped she did.

The bell above the diner's door announced his arrival, but only Cora's head swung to investigate the intrusion. Her smile was worried and sad. She whispered, and Jo swiveled in slow motion. Cora's arm slid from her shoulders, surrendering Jo into his care.

He didn't know what to do with his hands. Go to her, envelop her in his arms and not let go? He ached to do so. Instead, his thumbs tucked themselves into worn and dirty pockets.

Jo slid a few coppers beside her empty plate and glass. She rose, her mouth slashed with firm resignation. He could tell by the set of her shoulders that she had her emotions locked down. Though he understood, he wished she would turn to him for comfort.

Time. What they didn't have was what was most needed. Simply an unattainable luxury at this point. By this time tomorrow, two criminals would no longer threaten them, and they could start over.

Jo grabbed Cora, and hugged her, fierce and swift. Cullen held out his hand in invitation. Hand in hand, they exited the cozy diner.

Normalcy interrupted their walk to the inn. Young parents swinging a toddler between them, accompanied by innocent giggles. Streetlamps flickered to life, their solar cells charged and ready to shine throughout the night. Shod horses clopped along the street, either with riders or pulling wagons and buggies. Businesses extinguished lights, and owners locked doors after a long day of work. How quickly this town had become home to him, how easily and seamless. If not for the woman gripping his hand, Cullen wasn't sure he would feel the same. They were content in their silence, letting the evening bustle provide the conversation between them.

He opened the door of the Silver Street Inn. Jo walked through before him with a quiet word of thanks. The glorious scent of Shelley's cooking invaded his nostrils, and he saw Jo's nose edge up slightly, like she was searching for the source of the smell. And if he wasn't mistaken …

"There you two are," Shelley bubbled, a towel slung over her shoulder. "You hungry?"

Jo opened her mouth, but Cullen cut her off. "Starving."

"Seems like you missed a date a few days ago. Care for another try?" The innkeeper's grin threatened to overtake her ears.

"That would be lovely, Shelley," Jo said, smiling. "Thank you."

Their hostess beamed, waving them toward a candlelit table set for two. "Sit, sit. I'll get the salads."

As the tiny woman disappeared through the door leading to the kitchen, Jo raised a curious eyebrow. Cullen shrugged.

"Just go with it," he advised. "And I really am starving."

She mumbled something about men and their stomachs as he pulled her chair out from the table. He grinned as she sat in front of him, and he kept his hands on the chair as she scooted forward. Cullen leaned down, and from behind, kissed her cheek.

"Rogue," she chided. "Sit down before you get yourself in trouble."

"I will, but only because I get to look at you."

"And because it will be easier to eat."

"That too."

Shelley went with a more traditional choice this time around. After their salads, she presented the main course. Golden fried chicken, still hot from the fryer, rested alongside green beans dotted with bits of bacon. Loaded mashed potatoes completed the trio. Even though he nearly excused himself to loosen his belt, he managed to kill a slice of turtle cheesecake after the entrée. Across the table, Jo groaned.

She pointed to her dessert plate. "Seems a shame to waste half the slice, but I can't eat another bite. I won't have to for a week."

They cleared the table themselves, not wanting to bother Shelley with the menial task. In the kitchen, they found a note instructing them to leave the dishes in the sink. Jo snorted and rolled her eyes, then proceeded to rinse and load them into the dishwasher. On the way through the dining room, Cullen blew out the candles.

Upstairs, the couple stood outside her door. Jo keyed it open.

"I can't wait until I get back in my own house," she noted with a sigh. "Or for all of this to be over."

"Soon."

Cullen pushed open the door for her. A few steps in, she turned to him. "Coming in?"

He feigned surprise, a hand splayed dramatically over his heart. "And besmirch your honor?"

She laughed, a quick bark. "Besmirch?"

"My vocabulary is endless," he replied simply.

"Just get in here. I'll take my chances with a sullied reputation. We need to discuss the plan anyway."

Ah, yes. That ugly bit of business. Sinking into her sofa, identical in style, but not in color, to the one in his quarters, he purred softly at the pleasure of putting his feet up on the coffee table. At the opposite end, Jo sat in the corner with her feet tucked under her backside and looked at him expectantly. Then a yawn attacked her, and she covered her mouth. Unable to fight it, he succumbed to the yawn as well.

"Dawn's going to come quickly," he noted.

"I feel like I haven't slept in a week."

"It's almost over."

"I know. At least, I hope so. Is he out there," she asked, pointing a finger toward the window, "walking around free?"

There was no need for her to specify who.

"Duke thought it best, on the off-chance Jeremiah Franks was hiding out somewhere nearby."

"Who'd he put on overnight surveillance?"

"Ben agreed to do it. Logan's on the west end of the road."

"When do we go out?"

Cullen ran calloused fingers through his hair. "Look, Jo, I don't think –"

"I won't be cut out of this, and you know it."

"But I don't see the point of putting you in danger."

"And I refuse to sit by and let others take risks. This is my fight, Cullen. Let me fight it. When do we go out?"

Stubborn, hard-headed, frustrating woman. He loved her like mad.

The admission sent a jolt of adrenaline coursing from center mass to the ends of his extremities.

"What?" she asked.

"Hmm?" How had love happened?

"You're staring at me like I grew a second head."

His mouth was a parched desert. Swallowing was painful. He mentally whispered a desperate prayer, asking God to calm his racing heart. Okay, so it was more a frantic, wordless utterance than a prayer. Yet, peace flooded in its wake, and the beats slowed their spastic staccato. Everything was as it should be.

Still, his palms sweated like crazy.

"Cullen?"

He blinked, and patted the cushion next to him. "Don't worry, I'll be a good boy."

Still, she hesitated, skittish and wary.

"Please?"

"You'll behave?"

"Scout's honor."

Jo pursed her lips, squinted her eyes. "You were never a scout."

"Busted. Get over here anyway."

A RECKONING OF FIRE | Jennifer Osufsen

"I'm too tired to argue."

She scooted over; but when she got within reach, he pulled her close, her back angled into his chest.

"Relax," he chided. "Let me hold you. That's all. I promise. No hanky panky."

Jo's shoulders vibrated with muffled laughter.

"We're supposed to meet in that little stand of trees just past the footbridge at dawn. You, me, and Duke. From there I'll circle northwest around the old homestead, and Duke will go the opposite. If the homestead is the center of the circle, Roy will be at three o'clock to the east. Duke will set up just south of him, and I'll be north. You can join Ben in his position.

"I don't need a babysitter," she complained.

"He's not a babysitter. There's just not another good vantage point. Beyond the tree line is the clearing, wide open space. Nowhere to hide."

She yawned again, raising a hand to cover her mouth. "Then we wait?"

"Pretty much. Honestly, Duke doesn't need me or you. Ben's legally covered because of his bounty hunter license, with escaped felons involved. But I think Duke knew we wouldn't sit around here playing checkers or twiddling our thumbs."

"Yeah," she replied, lethargically. "I suppose."

Moments passed in the quiet, dim living room. Their chests rose and fell in time, easy and calm. His arms framed hers, the warmth of her skin a balm to his heart.

"Cullen?"

288

"Hmm?" His eyelids sluggishly blinked, a yawn temporarily closing them.

"Do you truly believe Jesus would save a murderer?"

"My brain has a hard time rationalizing it, but my soul knows the answer is yes."

"And Roy? Should I believe him when he says he's a changed man?"

Rather than answering her question, he eased her forward. His hands unraveled the messy topknot, and he draped her long, blonde hair down her back and shoulders.

"I think," he began, as his fingers worked out the tangles, "God lives in the believer."

"The Holy Spirit."

"Yes. And while we are still human and sinful, and always will be, God counsels us and gives us strength to do the impossible. Even a murderer."

"I don't want to believe him," she whispered.

He pulled her to him in a tight embrace. "I know, honey. That's the hurt, the anger talking."

Warm drops pelted his forearms. He kissed the crown of her head as she cried. Each teardrop deflated her, until she melted into him. She rested her head halfway between his chest and the sofa, and he let her cry. Anger welled inside him, as if she transferred the pain of injustice from her soul to his with her tears. What a hypocritical heart he had!

Through the second story window, the last remnants of the sunset cried their last. Pewter clouds dipped in coal drifted across a slate blue, star-dotted sky. The silhouette of a bat swooped across the darkened pane. Light from the single illuminated lamp reflected in the glass, a subdued amber glow warring with the night outside.

The slow-blink of impending slumber pulled at his eyes. Against his chest, Jo rested warm and heavy, sleeping. As much as he wanted to savor the feeling, his body had other ideas.

Seconds turned to minutes, and minutes swept the stalwart hour hand clockwise. A lazy rain crept from clouds to the earth while Cullen and Jo slumbered, nestled on the plump sofa.

In his dreams, they danced beneath the century oak, wild and carefree.

***

Jo watched the departing shapes of Cullen and Duke meld into the hazy mist clinging to the dawn. She snugged goose-pimpled arms to her midsection, and wished for Cullen's warmth; the same way it enfolded her this morning when she awoke to his wristcom alarm. No one was around to witness the rosy blush on her cheeks. With one last departing glance, she stepped from the footbridge to the horse path at its base. Her route varied from that of the men, but only slightly. She ambled through the drizzle to give them time to get into position. This weather could be a blessing and a curse. Easy for them to disappear; just as simple for a wanted criminal to do the same.

Coleville dozed, ignorant of the wandering of its blacksmith or the veiled danger skirting the area. She was a gray shade floating through a wet, steel curtain. Her boots slogged through clay, her soles lifting with a popping suck, and landing with a wet slap. By the time she veered from the horse path, a couple dozen yards before the Y-split to the old homestead, her feet resembled the lumpy mud cakes she made as a girl. What she needed was a —

There! A sharp, flat rock caught her eye. She knelt down, palmed the rock. Angling her knee to the side, Jo scraped the stone first along the inside of her boot, then the outside, repeating the action on the other. She swiped muddy fingers across the thighs of her jeans, and rolled an achy neck inflamed by the rain and a night spent sleeping crooked between Cullen's chest and the couch.

She spun at the sound of a twig snapping behind her. But her momentum carried her too far, and her feet planed across the slick surface of the wet clay. The fall knocked Jo onto her back, forcing the air in her lungs out with a *whoosh*. Flecks of light winked in and out, and it was a full count of ten before the first coughing inhale filled her lungs.

Stupid! She was so on edge that even normal woodsy sounds had her spooked. Now she was soaked, caked in sticky, clay mud from head to toe. From *bruised* head to toe, she clarified with a wince. She must have hit a rock.

Jo grumbled her way to standing, then leaned over with hands on knees to catch her breath.

"Well, good morning, cupcake," a gravelly voice crooned behind her.

Oh, no. This time, she pivoted slowly, dread creeping in waves as steadily as the rain had begun to fall.

Jeremiah Franks grinned from three feet away. "That was quite a show, sweetheart. Now, what's a pretty little girl like you doing out here all alone at the break of day?"

His wet hair drooped in dirt-caked ropes around an evil smile. He had lost an eye tooth since his last mugshot. Jo looked past him, surveyed the terrain behind. But all she saw was a screen of steadily falling rain, and fuzzy vague shapes in the distance.

"Don't even think about it," he warned in a growl.

She refused to be a lamb led to slaughter. Her training kicked in, and Jo lunged at him, felt his nose snap as the heel of her hand connected with his face. He collapsed with a gurgling yell. She darted past him into the murky woods. Rain pelted and stung her face as she ran into the gray oblivion. She skittered and slid, her arms windmilling to find balance, then launched herself forward once more.

Trees sprung to life in front of and beside her in the blink of a waterlogged eye, ashen specters interfering with her escape.

A vicious howl erupted behind her, and she knew then that the chase was on. She ran, ducking and dodging until she found herself in a narrow clearing. Jo turned to see how closely Franks followed, saw only the faintest shadow of a man in the distance. Her heart galloped with joy, knowing she would be near the old homestead soon. She whipped her head around once more.

Jo never saw the limb, never heard the crack that was the sound of her head colliding with the twisted arm of a docile mesquite tree.

Chapter 37

Confused images stitched themselves together, a maddening quilt of disorienting blocks. Bewildering impressions of scissoring legs churning up mud, and trees swinging like stunted pendulums from the sky melted together with pulsing throbs of agonizing pain. Full consciousness emerged in searing sparks of misery. Hammers pounded in her forehead, and with the jolt of every step he made, she resisted a groan.

She was slung over Jeremiah Franks', his shoulder the fulcrum in her midsection. Sparkles danced and winked; her eyes rolled in their sockets. Jo resisted the urge to grab her head. Some primeval instinct screamed for her to remain lifeless, keep him thinking she was still knocked out. Her skin crawled at the touch of his anchoring hold on her legs.

Out of the corner of her eye, Jo noticed the rain had slowed to a misty drizzle. A wave of nausea clawed its way from stomach to throat. Concussion, then, most likely. She shoved the sensation deep into her digestive tract, refusing to succumb to it.

Were Cullen and Duke in place? Jo needed some way of letting them know to hold their positions, not to be chivalrous heroes. She spent the next few minutes thinking and wincing and fighting the urge to vomit. Desperate, she turned to prayer.

Lord, if you still hear me, please let me live. And help me warn the men to stay back. She hesitated, unsure. *Uh, amen.*

She had no sooner prayed the last two words than Franks' boots halted. By the way her body pivoted along with his upper torso, she assumed he was scoping the area near Roy's improvised campsite. The felon then continued his trek at a slower pace.

"Over here!" Roy called.

"Keep your voice down, you idiot," Franks hissed.

Jo smelled wood smoke the closer they got. She continued the inert ruse, praying it would be enough.

It didn't prepare her for being tossed to the ground like a sack of potatoes.

Blemished sky blurred with green foliage in a sickening arc. The ground slammed into her, knocking the wind from her lungs for the second time in day. A snap exploded in white-hot pain. All pretense of unconsciousness jetted out across the rock-strewn muddy earth. Jo's eyes flew open, and she tried to gasp; but no air remained in her lungs. Wide eyes teared at the searing pain in her side. A broken rib, her logical inner voice informed her. Maybe two.

"Want to tell me why I found her snooping around?" Jeremiah demanded in a growl.

"How should I know?" Roy replied. "I just got up. Stupid birds goin' on and on. Where was she?"

"Near the split."

Shuddering breaths haltingly refilled her lungs. Jo groaned and turned toward the warmth of the fire. Her eyes met Roy's briefly before she squeezed them shut. Salty tears traced her cheek, landed in the corner of her mouth. She drew her legs into the fetal position.

"What'd you do to her?"

Jeremiah spat on the ground, barely missing her face. He barked a harsh laugh. "She did that to herself. Ran smack into a tree, and did all the hard work for me." He doubled over at his own joke. "All I had to do was haul her over."

"Did a tree do that to your nose?" Roy chuckled at his joke.

"Funny." Franks drug a hand under his nose, swiping at the dried blood.

Concentrating harder than she had in her entire life, she funneled every excruciating pain signal into her mind's lockbox. Despite the exercise, agony threatened to overwhelm her. The pulsating throb in her forehead beat in time with her pounding heart, and even the smallest of inhalations stabbed her side.

"She ain't goin' nowhere from the looks of her," Roy commented. "Leave her be. You bring a shovel?"

"Figured you would have one if we needed to dig more. Where's the silver, cousin?"

Beyond the smoldering fire, Roy stood, arching and twisting the kinks out of his back. At the moment, Jo held little sympathy for the man. She knew for a fact how hard the ground was. As far as she knew, he hadn't been abused by it like she had.

The man she had hated since the age of ten held a silver bar aloft, grinning wickedly. Her silver, but Franks' didn't know it.

"That's it?"

Roy chuckled. "Naw, the rest is in the tent."

Jo struggled to sit up, first resting on her forearms and then hands pushing into the wet clay, shoving her torso upward. She tucked her knees to the side, supporting herself with one arm.

"You won't get away with this, Roy."

"I already have."

"Shut up!" Jeremiah yelled at her. His leg poised to strike, but Roy stopped him before he could kick.

"We'll deal with her later, Jer," Roy stated, appearing unworried. "Look at her. She couldn't run if she wanted to."

Jo swiveled her head between the two convicts, swallowing the hurt, a bitter pill. She narrowed her eyes, tried to fortify her voice. "You *stay away* from me, the both of you," she warned. It came out as a hoarse whisper. *Lord*, she prayed, *let the men hear the warning.*

Jeremiah's muddy steel-toed boot slammed into the side of her thigh. "I told you to shut up!"

She grunted under the assault. Just bruises, she reminded herself. Bruises heal. It was almost over, almost over. Jo shot a watery glare at Franks, who ignored her. He shuffled over to Roy, and snatched the rough bar of silver from his cousin's hand.

"Easy man," Roy drawled. "Plenty to go around."

Jeremiah pressed a blackened thumbnail into the metal, grunted. "More, huh? Show me."

Roy jutted a thumb in the tent's direction. "In there."

Franks swept open the canvas door flap, ducking his head to peer inside. The tent floor crinkled as he jerked the crate into the daylight. While his attention was elsewhere, Jo swept a probing gaze into the surrounding trees. Roy warned her with a faint shake of the head, and then leaned over to pick up another silver bar.

He tossed it lightly, smacking it against his palm. "And I think there's more."

"Yeah?" Jeremiah's head remained down as he shuffled the bars in the wooden crate. A warning sounded in Jo's head at the nonchalant tone.

Roy lifted his chin to the left of the campsite. "The dig spot over's there."

"And this crate came from there?"

Alarm bells clanged, and Jo tried to stand. Something wasn't right.

"That's what I said, man. Look, you going to help me get it out of the ground, or what?"

"Tell me something, Roy," Jeremiah said quietly.

"What?"

"Where's the dirt?"

A confused look scurried across Roy's face. "Dirt? All around man. You're covered in it." Roy laughed, unease creeping in.

"And yet the crate isn't."

The words hung heavy in the air.

"Aw, man. You think I'd put it in the tent all covered in muck? I cleaned it up first."

"It's too clean, cousin." Franks regarded Roy and Jo in turn, then the silver pile at his feet. A stun pistol appeared in his hand. He swung it to chest level and aimed it at Roy. "Who got to you?"

Nervously, Roy scoffed at the accusation. "What are you talking about, man?"

Franks whirled the pistol, targeting Jo's center mass. "Was it you?" he spat.

Jo remained silent, glaring. She kept her attention on the two felons, steadying her eyes away from the men hidden in the brush.

"I'll be happy when you both are dead."

He trained the pistol on her, his grip never wavering, but his head swiveled from her to Roy and back again. Roy plastered a smile on his face, and put both hands up, palms forward.

"Hey, man. Would I have called you out here if anyone was on to me? Let's get the rest of the goods and get out of here. Go down to Mexico and find us a couple of pretty señoritas and sip some margaritas. Put the stunner down, cousin."

Franks lowered the weapon, albeit warily, and pulled it toward his chest. He peered at the weapon, his lips pursed. He cocked his head to the side, and flicked a switch on the side of the pistol.

"All right, cousin. I'll take your word for it, for now. But her?" he said, flicking a glance in Jo's direction. "She's a liability we don't need."

In slow motion, the stunner raised. His arm straightened, taking aim, but it happened sluggishly. In crisp detail, the end happened in increments. Jeremiah Franks' lips turned up in an evil grin, his yellowed and broken teeth shining from beneath the grime of his face. His mouth pulled up bit by bit, like a strobed image in the dark. At least she would die on her feet. The calm she felt belied the danger.

His forefinger hooked, millimeter by millimeter, as the verdant leaves of the live oak beside him slow-danced in the breeze. She inhaled, tasted the rain and wet clay, the earth and the sky.

His finger crept to the trigger, and the world stood still.

Jo closed her eyes, and waited for death.

***

Cullen watched, helpless, as Jeremiah trained the pistol on the woman he loved. Jo stood hunched, brave and hurting. But she held her ground and didn't flinch when the stunner landed on her. Unable to stop himself, he low-crawled toward her. He hoped Ben and Duke were doing the same.

As he drew nearer, he heard Roy arguing with his insane cousin. One look at the man told Cullen that Franks was cunning and evil. Milligan waved his arms, pointing and gesturing at the crate of silver, and then in the direction of the false dig spot they had faked the day before. Roy was supposed to have led Franks to the dig, where the men were to surround him and take him down.

Now only a few yards away, Cullen heard Roy trying to convince Jeremiah to stop worrying about Jo and just come with him to excavate the rest of the treasure. When Franks lowered the pistol, Cullen was sure that his own exhaled relief was loud enough to compromise his position. He slithered forward, the soggy ground under him absorbing the sound. His shirt scraped against the rocky earth. A button snagged on a stone as he crawled.

Cullen was two yards from the clearing when Jeremiah leveled the pistol at Jo's chest for the second time. Both of the bad guys faced away from him. Roy's shoulders stiffened.

The look on Jo's face broke his heart. Sad surrender and resignation melted her visage into an image of stone. The light fled her eyes.

Roy shouted, "NO!"

From the tree line, three men sprung forward as if shot from a cannon. Roy lunged at an angle, using himself as a shield. There was no sound from the stun pistol. Milligan's body knocked Jo's to the ground. He landed with a thud, rolling to a stop beside her.

Ben crashed into Jeremiah Franks, the mountain-sized man lifting the escaped felon three feet into the air before slamming him to the earth. Cullen and Duke descended on Jo at the same time.

"Jo! Honey! Oh, God, please!" he pleaded.

Her eyes wobbled, blue orbs shaking and twitching. Then she gasped, and crumpled onto her side, coughing and shaking.

"Oh, thank you, Lord," Cullen praised. "Jo, baby. Can you hear me?"

She groaned, tears leaking from her eyes. "Nnhh."

He cupped her face, kissed her forehead. "You're going to be okay, sweetie. I promise. Duke?"

Cullen looked up and found the deputy examining Roy. Blood pulsed from under his head, and the lawman leaned over with an ear to Roy's nose. With one hand, Duke searched for a carotid pulse. He exhaled and nodded, with a grim slash of smile.

"He's alive. Barely."

He angled his head to see behind him. Ben had Jeremiah Franks prone on the damp ground, his arms laced and secured behind him. The giant bounty hunter pinned the con with a hefty knee, his full weight behind it. Ben nodded sharply.

"Cullen?" Jo's voice whispered, halting at the end of his name. It was the most beautiful sound.

"I'm here."

"Roy?"

He leaned closer to hear her. "He's beside you, baby."

"Alive?" Her eyes fluttered open and closed.

"Barely."

"Help … me up. Please."

Duke heard, and lent a strong hand. They raised Jo into a seated position near Roy's head. Cullen supported her as she leaned over.

"Roy? Can you … hear me?" Her own voice wavered, weak. To Duke, she asked, "Was he hit?"

The deputy shook his head. "No. His head smashed against a rock on the way down. It's bad, Jo."

Roy's eyelids flickered, opened to slits. "Unnggh."

"Roy, it's Jo. Can you hear me?"

His eyes remained slitted open, and he grunted, faint.

"Thank you," she whispered.

She sank into Cullen's arms, and said, "I forgive you."

They sat in the silent woods, soaking in the wet mud of a rainy morning. The man she hated for most of a lifetime laid dying beside them, his lifeblood making a puddle on the rain-sodden ground.

With a shuddering rattle, Roy breathed his last and left to be with the Father.

Chapter 38

On the outskirts of town, behind a tiny church covered in peeling white paint, they said farewell to a despised man. The headstone, simple carved gray granite, proclaimed Roy Milligan's name and dates of life. How many of those years were spent being the object of someone's hatred? Jo fixed her eyes on the mounded dirt and clay mix covering the last remains of the stepfather she loathed. She was a fake, a fraud standing in a stiff new dress the color of fresh butter. Bitter shame hunched her shoulders.

The last three days of numb existence had taken their toll on Jo. A day of resting in bed under the watchful, no-nonsense eye of Doc Cora; another of police reports and endless official statements. The Texas Rangers came to Coleville to collect Jeremiah Franks, who would now face kidnapping, breaking and entering, assault, and attempted murder charges on top of those for his prison break.

"He's going away for a very long time," the Ranger assured her.

Yesterday, she and Cullen arranged for the confidential conversion of her gold and silver bullion to coin. His contact in Austin, Mr. Yates, possessed a reputation for discretion and integrity, and Jo trusted Cullen. The agent was scheduled to arrive later in the afternoon.

Throughout it all, Jo wrestled with forgiveness. The pardon she extended to Roy when he was dying in the clearing was right and true, given freely because she no longer had the drive to withhold it. Those words had erupted from the core of her soul, the place she knew the Holy Spirit occupied. Her logical brain struggled to justify it, while her heart knew it was impossible.

And so, she found herself staring at her long shadow laid across a mound of dirt, gripping Cullen's hand, afraid to let go. Not of his hand, but of the anger. It had been her constant companion, fueled by injustice, bitterness, and loathing. Self-righteous hatred drove her nearly every day of her life, on a subconscious level; pushed her like the whip smites the slave. For she was a slave. Jo had buried the love known as a child, and embraced the bitterness instead. Bitterness shackled her to hatred. After so many years, how could she change?

Cullen squeezed her hand, and she nodded, silently telling him to proceed.

He looked to those gathered around the grave. Ben held baby Kate in one arm, and encircled Cora with the other. Cora dabbed her eyes, and encouraged Jo with a smile. Duke stood at the foot of Roy's grave, somber in his dress uniform. He, too, nodded in encouragement.

Cullen walked to the head of the grave, behind the tombstone. He held a worn Bible in his hands, and bowed his head.

"Father, we ask for your comfort and peace as we say goodbye to Roy," he prayed. "He became one of your children, and for that, we rejoice. Through Jesus we pray, amen."

He drew in a deep breath, and met Jo's tearful stare. "This is a hard thing to do. I know, in here," he said, tapping his chest, "that Roy accepted salvation. That he was forgiven and redeemed, the same as I was at the age of fourteen. But I seem to have taken on the hurt of the woman I love, and forgiveness is incredibly hard."

Her eyes blinked in rapid succession. He loved her?

Cullen ran fingers through his shortened hair. Just yesterday, she complimented him on it and pushed her own long fingers through it. Her fingertips remembered the texture, and tingled. He loved her.

"The man who took so much from her saved her life. He put himself in the line of fire, and lost his life, to preserve hers. So while forgiveness is hard, gratefulness is not. Without him, Jo wouldn't be here. The Bible reminds us in 2 Corinthians 5:17, 'Therefore, if anyone is in Christ, he is a new creation; the old has gone, the new has come!' We know that Roy was a new creation because of the evidence of his actions." He grinned at Jo, a tiny tug of the lips toward his ears. Then he placed his hand atop the tombstone. "Thank you, Roy."

When he rejoined her, Jo sank into him. Cullen enfolded her in strong arms. She allowed herself to be held, to be comforted. To be loved. And in so doing, she surrendered.

Utterly, completely surrendered. Not just to Cullen's love, but to God's. She opened herself to His care, and asked Him with half-formed words and burdened impressions to forgive her; to remove the hate from her heart, and teach her to love the way He wanted.

Like a tender morning glory, she bloomed, basking in the love of God. The warmth seared, banishing darkness and enveloping her in light. In the midst of the glow, she heard, "*I will never forsake you.*" Truth branded itself on her soul.

She wiped away the wetness on her cheeks, and discovered the others waiting under a gnarly oak. The baby crawled at her parents' feet, tugging at Ben's slacks. Jo would miss the tracker and the doctor. Maybe she and Cullen could visit Cotton Springs sometime.

She and Cullen. Jo thought of them in the same sentence more often than not. For the first time, she felt at ease with the phenomenon. Happy.

Jo led him to the others, with one last glance over her shoulder at the newly dug grave. Under the tree, Duke pulled Jo to his chest, rubbing rough circles between her shoulder blades. He smelled of spicy cologne and a hint of sweat. She imagined his stiff-collared uniform was stifling. He released her with one last, gentle squeeze.

She linked her arm through Cullen's under the shade tree. "What's next?"

"I don't know about you," Duke said, "but I could use a glass of Miss Ruby's sweet tea."

Ben grumbled his agreement. "You don't have to ask me twice."

Cora shot a wry grin at Jo, and swooped her chubby daughter up and onto her hip in one smooth, practiced motion. She angled her head with a questioning expression, and began walking toward the footpath that bisected the cemetery.

Cullen leaned down and whispered, "Go ahead. I'll meet you there." He pressed a kiss on her forehead.

She grabbed his head by both sides, and pulled it down to hers, foreheads touching. "I'll be counting the minutes, City Boy."

"Remember the truce, Miss Priss."

Rolling her eyes in true drama queen fashion, she punched him on the arm. The jab jolted her broken ribs, made her grimace in momentary pain. But the way he rubbed his bicep made the ache worth it. With a grin, she lengthened her stride, catching up to Cora. Kate babbled, holding a conversation chocked full of gibberish with her mother.

"Looks like I was right," Cora gloated, straight to the point.

Jo laughed, glancing at Cullen. He and the men hung back a dozen paces, ambling along and speaking in quiet voices. Jo's cheeks colored when she realized she was laughing in such a somber place. Cora noticed, and waved it off.

"Life should be celebrated and joyful."

Cora's short heels clicked when they hit the church's parking lot; the flats on Jo's feet absorbed the noonday heat.

"How's the head?"

Jo held a hand in the air, rocked it back and forth. "Eh. It's been better."

"The last couple of weeks have been pretty trying for you."

"Understatement of the year."

"Bah buh bah ba," Kate interjected.

"You said it kid," Jo laughed. "Listen, since I have your mostly undivided attention—"

"And I'm not patching one of you up …"

With a snort, Jo said, "That, too. I have something for you at the inn."

"You've already given me one of the most eventful vacations ever."

"You must keep your husband on his toes."

"That I do," Cora chuckled. "He *did* marry a red-head. And we don't need a gift. The bounty pays for our services. I've enjoyed getting to know you and Cullen both."

"I have gold," Jo blurted. "And silver. Lots of it. I'm assuming Ben told you."

"He did. No."

"Yes. I'm not really giving it to *you*. I'd like to donate it to your clinic."

Cora stopped, narrowing her eyes at Jo. "You got to him, didn't you?"

The picture of innocence, Jo batted her eyes. "Whatever do you mean, Dr. Tucker?"

"Ben. He told you I wouldn't take it for myself; for us, I mean."

"I am not admitting to any such thing."

The doc sighed, and turned to confront Ben, who had caught up to the women. With a pointed finger, she jabbed the air between them. "This is your fault."

"What?" Ben's eyes were electric green saucers.

"The gold. You told her I wouldn't turn it down, if it was for the clinic."

"I remember no such conversation," he said robotically.

"Ugh! Fine. I'll take it. But only because it's for the clinic."

"Two," Jo said with a grin.

"Two? No. No way. I can't –"

"One for each hardhead you treated."

Cora's mouth opened and closed repeatedly. Then with a sharp nod, she stalked off, the baby on her hip chatting happily.

Cullen wrapped his arms around her from the back, nestling his cheek to hers. "You keep giving it away, and there won't be any left."

"I survived without it before. Plus, I have a lead on a man whose family is loaded and powerful. I'm not worried."

"Cheeky."

"Mm-hmm."

He smacked the side of her face with a loud kiss. "I like cheeky."

Later, with bulging bellies and loosened belts, Jo, Cullen, and Duke waved to the rear window of the Tuckers' truck as it drove away from Coleville. Ben, Cora, and Kate carried their gratitude, promises of a visit, and two bars of gold with them northeast to Cotton Springs. She owed the couple far more.

Exhaustion fell, nearly smothering her in its intensity. Jo wilted against Cullen, physically and emotionally spent. Her head throbbed, her ribs burned, and she wanted out of the dress as soon as humanly possible. Cullen seemed to sense her thoughts, because he gripped both her biceps, spun her gently in the direction of the Silver Street Inn, and nudged her forward.

"Go on. One more night at the inn won't kill you."

"It's midafternoon. The *you know who* will be here later for the *you know what.*"

"Fine, a nap then."

Too spent to argue, she settled for grunting assent. She was halfway down the block before it occurred to her that Cullen was not beside her.

She turned, cupped her hand, and yelled, "Are you coming?"

"In a few minutes," he answered. "I need to ask Duke something first."

Weary and worn, Jo's feet struck the pavement to the pounding beat of her head. Cullen could deal with business to his heart's content.

She was going to take a nap.

***

"What's so darn important that you won't let me change out of these confounded clothes?" Duke complained.

Cullen's gaze followed Jo until she rounded the corner.

"You're the closest thing she has to a father."

"Yeah. So?"

"So," he replied, "I'd like to ask permission to court your daughter."

The weathered deputy threw back his head and laughed at the sky. When he recovered, he wiped his eyes. "You sure about that?"

"Yes, sir," Cullen replied with a grin. "Very sure."

"Should have known you were a glutton for punishment. And, son?"

"Yeah?"

"She can dish it out."

Cullen shook the deputy's outstretched hand. "I look forward to the challenge."

The older man grinned and spun on his buffed black heel. Before he was ten feet away, he stopped and half-turned. "Oh, one other thing."

"What's that?"

"Hurt my girl, and I'll put you in a cell."

He tipped his hat, and moseyed toward the station, whistling a peppy tune.

Cullen took his time returning to the inn. He wandered the town, making small talk with new acquaintances. Then he stopped by the smithy to use Jo's hammer and chisel.

He paid a visit to Marshall at the post office, both to say hello and to pick up mail. Cullen was still laughing as the door jangled his departure. The look of complete befuddlement on the postmaster's face when Cullen dropped a two-inch square cube of solid gold onto his open palm would stay with him forever. Without Marshall, they would still be floundering.

His last destination was an office on the edge of town. An hour later, he left there with a sheaf of signed papers and a thoughtful look.

He begged a key to Jo's room from Shelley. Cullen could have knocked on the door, but he'd rather wake her gently. The lock snicked, and he pushed open the door, a quiet shooshing over plush carpet. His heart caught in his chest at the sight of her.

It appeared she had been too exhausted to make it to the bedroom. One leg hung over the side of the sofa seat, her foot shoeless. The other remained – just barely – on the couch, the shoe snug on her foot. She snored like a chainsaw, and her head had missed the pillow entirely. A thin line of drool silvered in the afternoon light.

She was the most beautiful thing he had seen in his life.

Cullen tried to awaken Sleeping Beauty with a chaste kiss on the lips, fully expecting her lids to flutter open gracefully.

He waited.

She snored.

This time he planted a row of kisses from the corner of her mouth, around her jawline, and up to her temple. Jo stirred, smacking her lips, and mumbled something unintelligible. Fighting a very real urge to laugh hysterically, he shook her shoulder gingerly.

"Jo, honey. Wake up. It's nearly time for Mr. Yates to be here."

"Ungh."

He brushed strands of spun gold away from her face, and out of the drool line. With a last kiss to the forehead, he had an idea. He walked to the refrigerator, and withdrew a cold bottle. Beside her, he cracked it open, and the sizzling bubbly hissed its hello.

Her eyes opened fully, then closed halfway again.

"Hello, you," he said.

"Gimme."

"Sit up, first. I don't want you to ruin your dress."

She complied, moaning all the while. She extended one hand for the Dr Pepper, and the other swiped away the drool on her chin.

"Ugh, gross. Sorry about that."

"I have something to show you."

She guzzled and nodded.

He placed the papers in a neat stack on the coffee table in front of him.

"What's that?"

"A real estate contract."

The sleep crease on the side of her face climbed along with her left eyebrow. "Yours?"

Nodding, he said, "There's a little house on Hickory that caught my eye when I first arrived."

"You're sure, then?"

He wanted to memorize her like this. Happy, exhausted, drool-faced, with disheveled hair. Because he had the sneaking suspicion she looked like this every morning.

"Positive."

She surprised him by bursting into laughter.

"What?"

"You," she said, catching her breath. "You give up city life in Austin to move to the sticks of Coleville. Only to settle for a house in town. You really are a city boy at heart."

Jo plunked the half-empty bottle of Dr Pepper onto the coffee table, rose, and settled herself on his lap all in one fluid motion.

"But you know what?" she said quietly, leaning in close.

"What?"

She kissed him long and slow, and a few stars dropped out of the heavens. Then she whispered in his ear.

"You're *my* City Boy."

Epilogue

The old place no longer haunted her dreams. Brown knee-high grass rustled in the late summer breeze, thirsty from a summer with less than average rainfall and the scorching Texas heat. Around them the clearing swayed with a hiss. Blown dust glittered in the late evening, the setting sun igniting billions of tiny floating particles. Grasshoppers whirred and buzzed, unperturbed by the shell of a home or the ancient memories ghosting around it. Kase and Jasper cropped and chewed a stone's throw from the singed and crumbling fireplace, the last remnant of her childhood home.

Blackened bricks brought flames to her eyes, memories of the fire she set at the age of twenty-one. Young, hasty, and so very angry, Jo had acted with vindicating self-righteousness. It was a way to sever herself from the unhappiness of her childhood, a desperate attempt at closure. Instead, in the same way a wildfire seeds life and new growth, arson had only fed the inferno of anger and hate.

It took a fire of a different kind to satiate her soul.

"Penny for your thoughts."

They were side-by-side on a faded quilt which had seen better days, lying on their backs and searching for shapes in the clouds.

"There it is again. The penny thing."

"Smart-aleck."

"Giraffe!" she said, pointing to a long-necked cloud. "I was thinking of the day I set this place on fire."

"Oh, good thoughts, then."

Her head flopped to the side to stare into his warm, tawny eyes. "They used to be. I mean, when all I could think about was killing Roy. But now? I don't know. Seems more like the actions of a frantic kid."

"How old were you?"

"Twenty-one. Old enough to know better, and young enough to still think I knew everything."

"Pig."

"What?"

"Pig. To the left of your giraffe."

"Dang, that puts you ahead."

"Do you concede defeat?"

"For today," she acquiesced. "It's getting late. We should get home."

"I wish you lived closer to town."

"And I wish you had built in the country closer to my place. But alas, you're a city-slicker."

"More like a one-horse-towner," he laughed.

She reached over to slap him on the chest. "No mocking my town."

"Our town," he said quietly.

Jo sat up, swiveled her torso around to offer Cullen a hand up. "Our town."

They stood, brushing themselves off, and she rolled up the blanket. With a whistle, she called Kase. Jasper wasn't far behind the mare. Jo tied the roll behind the gorgeous tooled saddle Cullen gave her a month ago. The man spoiled her rotten. Jasper lowered his head to munch on a rare patch of green grass. She turned to search for the gelding's owner.

He stood beneath the century oak at the foot of Ginny's grave. His head was bowed, either in prayer or contemplation. A gust of wind pushed the empty swing, looking for all the world like it was powered by a ghost. She shivered.

Cullen beckoned her with a hand and a grin, and she couldn't resist the latter. How had she ever despised his school-boy smile? It was precious; as precious as a man who paid his respects to her long-lost sister. The short trip through the tall grass made her grateful for the jeans and boots she wore. Chiggers would have ruined a great afternoon.

"What's up?" she asked as she reached his side.

He pointed to the shaded ground around the white cross grave marker. At its base jutted three volunteer daylilies, their orange petals only just beginning to open.

"Thought you'd like to see it."

Cullen swept her up, brought her in close. With one hand, he hugged one of hers to his chest; the other he held slightly to the side as he began to sway.

The wind kicked up, and the smell of dry earth and Cullen's cologne tickled her nose. Side to side they moved, dancing to the sounds of nature's symphony.

"I dreamt of this once," he noted, his voice warm in her ear.

"Self-fulfilling prophecy?" she teased.

"I can see I need to romance you more, oh cynical one."

She angled her head to plant a tender kiss on his cheek, and then laid her head on his shoulder. "I think you do just fine, Mr. Miles."

"Ah," he said, "but I think I have something else up my devious sleeve."

Jo chuckled, pulling him closer as they danced in a lazy circle.

He released the hand held tight against his chest, reaching behind him. The dancing ceased, and she looked at him with a quizzical expression. Cullen presented a folded sheet of paper to her, and retreated with a grin.

Curious, she unfolded the paper. The wind caught the corner and fluttered it. Then, when she read the contents, her widened eyes met his. Her mouth gaped.

"Is this what I think it is?"

"The deed to Camden Ironworks, yeah. It's yours honey," he said quietly. "It always was yours, you know. Not technically, but in spirit."

A fist wedged itself in her throat.

"You're giving the smithy to me?"

"Already done. It's yours, free and clear."

It was too much, and she said as such. He waved her off. "I have the farrier business to keep me busy. But I expect you'll supply my horseshoes and tools, right?"

"Come here," she demanded, her palms against both of his stubbly cheeks.

She kissed him thoroughly, drowning in her love for this man who was her lifeline. His mouth was warm beneath hers, and the bristled hairs above his lip grazed against hers. He nipped her lower lip, and she growled, deepening the kiss. A few minutes later, she left him gasping for breath.

"Wow. Wow, I should have done the whole give-you-a-business thing sooner."

She laughed, and said, "I love you."

"Love you back." He looked around the clearing, and she mimicked him, discovering the disappearance of the sun. Animal-shaped clouds burned red, like smoldering coals.

"It'll be dark soon," she noted.

"I hate to leave. Oh, I have one other thing to show you."

"Yeah? Are you deeding the farrier business to me, too?" Her smile stretched ear to ear.

"In a manner of speaking," he said. He walked to the white cross of Ginny's grave, and turned to her. Kneeling, he opened his hand, palm to the sky.

The diamond ring blazed with a light all its own. All rational thought fled her mind, leaving a bright blankness in its place. Cullen's lips moved, but white noise filled the space between her ears. Then it all disappeared in a fabulous explosion, and real life flooded her brain once more.

Worry flitted around his eyes. "Jo? Did you hear me?"

Her head shook side to side, her eyes transfixed by the simple yet elegant ring in his hand.

"Will you marry me, Joleigh Agnes Camden?"

It began with a nod.

Then it escalated to joyful tears.

And then a booming *WHOOP* erupted from her diaphragm, scattering a flock of crows from a neighboring mesquite tree. Jo jumped up and down in place, nodding like crazy.

"Yes!"

She skidded to the ground next to him. "Yes, yes, yes."

He slid the platinum circlet onto the ring finger of her left hand, and she held it aloft.

"Yes," she said again, "I'll marry you. On one condition."

His brows rose nearly to his hairline. "Duke wasn't kidding when he said you'd be difficult to court."

She'd deal with Duke later, then. The old bear.

"What's your condition, then?"

"I will marry you if …"

"Yes?"

"You tell me who divulged my middle name, so I can properly hurt them."

About The Author

 Jennifer grew up beneath the tall yellow pines of east Texas, but currently resides in the northwoods of Minnesota. Writing allows her to escape into a world devoid of dirty dishes, mounds of laundry, sticky floors, and piles of toys. Most of the time you'll find her spending time with her best friend and husband of sixteen years, or with the five hooligans she birthed.